I0551593

A Charlie Draper Thriller

Big Sky Dead

By

Dave Folsom

This one's for Sandy, my wife, best friend, editor, live-in critic, and our three daughters who made our life complete.

This book is a work of fiction. Names, places, or incidents are either products of the author's imagination or used fictionally. Any resemblance to actual events, localities, or persons, living or dead, is purely coincidental.

Scaling Tall Timber Press
Box 34
Roscoe, South Dakota 57471

All cover art and photography by the author.
Copyright 2013 All Rights Reserved

© Dave Folsom 2013 All Rights Reserved
This book may not be reproduced, copied, or used in any form without the expressed written permission of the author.
Paperback Edition

ISBN -13: 978-0615762234
(Scaling Tall Timber Press)
ISBN-10: 0615762239

Table of Contents

Chapter One	7
Chapter Two	19
Chapter Three	35
Chapter Four	47
Chapter Five	61
Chapter Six	75
Chapter Seven	89
Chapter Eight	107
Chapter Nine	121
Chapter Ten	133
Chapter Eleven	149
Chapter Twelve	167
Chapter Thirteen	183
Chapter Fourteen	197
Chapter Fifteen	213
Chapter Sixteen	223
Chapter Seventeen	237
Chapter Eighteen	251
Chapter Nineteen	269
Chapter Twenty	287
Chapter Twenty-one	305
Chapter Twenty-two	315
Other Books by Dave Folsom	321

Chapter One

Eastern Montana

T he man on the floor was dead. Very dead, if there were such a condition. Dead was dead; there was nothing he could do about it. Sheriff Roscoe Hornsby's twenty-year-long law enforcement career exposed him to a cornucopia of recently deceased individuals of all ages and sexes. It told him a medical degree and a flock of health professionals would not get this one up. Three large caliber wounds to the upper chest made that fact clear as spring fed water; a bit of overkill though, Hornsby thought, wasted ammunition for sure and suggesting an elevated level of anger on the part of the shooter.

"Is he dead, Ross?" The voice came from the front door and belonged to Randall Ruskin, owner of the house and several other rentals in town. "I told you something wasn't right."

"Randy, stay the hell outside like I told you," Hornsby said, stepping through the debris-covered floor while drawing his weapon. He had been Sheriff twelve years and he'd drawn his Glock not more than a dozen times. There had never been a need outside of sapping a belligerent drunk. Of those, he had plenty; cowboys, itinerant farm hands, and sheepherders all with a craving for the bottle during those rare winter times when there was little else to do. Sore-headed, hung-over, and sheepish, Hornsby crowded them into his single twelve by twelve drunk tank/jail cell and let them sleep. On a busy Saturday night and a full tank, he handcuffed the overflow to the oak railing across the front of the office and they had to sleep on the hardwood floor.

The man's body lay sprawled on his back, arms outstretched in a slowly expanding pool of dark blood in the middle of a furniture-void living room. The holes in his chest spoiled a much-washed red Carhartt t-shirt worn over faded tan Dickies. The Sheriff guessed the man's age at about forty to forty-five with light brown thinning hair and streaks of pre-mature gray; a stranger though, not a local. No hint of recognition rose in Hornsby's mind to block the vision of hours of paperwork.

The room was far from empty; it contained the makings of a sophisticated chemistry lab and dozens of plastic-wrapped and mailing tape secured packages. Hornsby guessed cocaine, which he knew cooked crack or was sold as an inhalable powder. Hornsby had seen a lot of coke and knew this pile represented over a million dollars in potential revenue; definitely enough to kill for. A nearby table sat covered with a variety of chemicals, most of which had potential to lift the roof off the house if miss-used. He recognized the ingredients for cooking meth. In Chicago, they were been as plentiful as household cooking oil. In Montana, anhydrous ammonia, used everywhere as a soil enhancement during farming, also provided a plentiful ingredient for meth manufacturing.

The house itself showed unremarkable, plain construction, ranch-style, three-bedroom rambler with the third bedroom the size of a large walk-in closet. Several years beyond needing a complete remodel, the dated structure classified as either a low-rent income

8

producer or a bargain-priced fixer-upper. Hornsby cleared the rest of the house following his Model 23 Glock .40 through each room. The two larger bedrooms contained expensive grow lights and a sophisticated watering system nurturing a robust crop of multi-aged marijuana. Behind the grow tables the sheetrock walls were water-stained and speckled with dark spots of black and green mold. Careful not to touch anything, Hornsby surveyed each room with a cop's eye without finding anything of interest. Back in the living room, Hornsby searched the man's pockets for identification and found zip. Unlike current television programs, he lacked a fully staffed forensics lab. Anything that was not obvious would require the Tri-county Medical Examiner's officer's special touch, a minimum of two hours away.

Sheriff Hornsby, an Undersheriff and three deputies, represented the law enforcement presence in one of Montana's larger counties area wise, but with the least amount of residents. The nearest city of any size sat sixty miles east in another county. Antelope County sat in the shadow of the Rocky Mountains, with the eastern half in the Great Plains and the western half dominated by the Crazy's, a heavily forested, steep-sided mountain range scraping tall into the state's famous Big Sky. Covering over five thousand square miles, the county could count a scattered population of twelve hundred, a quarter of which were over sixty-five. Primary income came from large ranches where cattle and sheep outnumbered the fiercely conservative inhabitants ten to one. In years past the crime rate hovered near zero, but recent statistics mirrored the largest population centers.

Hornsby surveyed the front room again and it reminded him of his long career as a Los Angeles police detective. Only the surrounding prairie and lack of water felt different. The home sat a half mile south of town on a wind-swept, ten-acre plot of scattered prairie grass, sagebrush, and barking prairie dogs. Over recent years, the renters had been mostly transient workers, single cowhands and an occasional older retired couple. The rent barely covered the upkeep, but Ruskin advertised it as valuable income property while looking for a cash-flush stranger seeking a bargain. So far, none had appeared. Hornsby stepped onto the porch, closed the door, sealed it with crime scene tape, and prodded Ruskin down the stairs onto the driveway.

"I need to get in there. It's my place," Ruskin complained.

"No, you don't, Randy, it's a goddamn crime scene. Nobody goes inside until the ME gets here from Lewistown."

A black Lincoln, raising clouds of prairie dust skidded to a stop in of front of the driveway. The car had tinted windows causing the Sheriff to draw again and put both hands on his county-issue Glock while he stepped behind his patrol car. He held the gun at his side waiting. When the Lincoln's door opened, he lifted it up and pointed it at the car. A black Lincoln and a dead body behind him in the house demanded caution and he growled, "Randy, step behind me, Goddamn it. Do it now." When Ruskin did not move, he shouted, "Now!" Ruskin moved.

The man in the Lincoln stepped out with raised hands, slow, as if he knew the Sheriff would shoot if he made a wrong move. "Sheriff Hornsby?" the man said, "your office said you'd be out here somewhere."

"And who the hell are you?" Hornsby said his Glock not wavering and still pointed at the stranger's chest.

"Appreciate it if you'd lower that cannon, Sheriff, I'm on your side. My name's Draper, Charlie Draper. I believe you were told I was coming."

"Got some ID, Mister? You'd better, because I've never heard of you. If you don't, I might be inclined to shoot your ass right here and now. So, reach for it nice and slow and if you get anywhere close to that piece under your left shoulder I will kill you where you stand."

The stranger stared at first and Hornsby tensed, ready to shoot. The man had hard eyes, dark, displaying no fear and appeared to be analyzing the situation. He stood tall; Hornsby guessed well over six feet, enough weight to make him difficult to handle when it came to a street fight and a sense about him that hinted at a good deal of hand-to-hand combat training. He had on faded jeans, black cowboy boots, and a dark blue sport coat that hung loose from wide shoulders. His face deeply tanned, the beginnings of age lines at his eyes indicated he would never see forty again. Hornsby decided he was not going to take any chances; a single false move and he would shoot. Any mess could be cleaned afterward.

"Sheriff, I'd really hate it if you shot me, so let me tell you I am armed; I'm Federal and here to help you. I'm going to pull back my coat and show you my gun. I will pull out my ID with two fingers of my left hand and lay it on the roof of your car where you can reach it. Okay with you?"

"Okay, but do it slowly. Just so you know, you won't be the first asshole I've shot, and I won't hesitate to shoot you," Hornsby said.

"I believe you, Sheriff. I was told you were a no nonsense son-of-a-bitch."

Hornsby watched close as the stranger pulled back his sport coat and exposed a leather shoulder rig with a quick-draw holster holding a black handled Glock. He could not be sure but guessed a .40 or .45 caliber. He looked like someone who would carry a dangerous weapon. With two fingers, the man picked a leather ID case out of his shirt pocket and laid it carefully on the roof of the Sheriff's car.

Hornsby reached for the case without taking his eyes off the stranger, opened it and glanced at it. It looked legit, with a federal seal, identifying a Charles Draper as a federal NSA agent (retired).

"Says here you are retired," Hornsby said.

"I still do occasional contract work," Draper said.

"So, what's so goddamn important in my little county that it brings a fancy federal spook clear out here in the boonies?"

"We have an undercover DEA agent that has been here a couple of months and hasn't reported in when he should have. My job is to find him and extract him."

"You got someone I can call to confirm what you say? This is rural Montana; we're particular about feds snooping around without letting us know what's up." Hornsby's Glock had not moved off the center of Draper's chest. With dead body only yards away, his cop's instinct would not allow him to lapse into carelessness.

"They were supposed to notify you that I was coming, but it appears somebody dropped the ball," Draper said, "so whom would you believe if they called you in the next few minutes?"

"Here's my problem, friend; I've got you armed to the teeth, a dead body behind me in a house full of drug manufacturing equipment and no backup within thirty miles, so I'm not sure I'd believe the fucking Governor if he called, which I doubt he would. So this is how this is going to go down; I'm going to come around the car with my .40 Glock pointed at your chest and I'm going to ask you nice and polite to put your hands behind your neck so I can handcuff you. You make even a twitch the wrong way and I will shoot you dead. Then we'll see if your story checks out and if..."

Hornsby had felt a searing pain through his chest in the instant before everything went dark. He did not feel the gun drop out of his hand nor the impact of the ground as it smacked him in the face.

Randall Ruskin who stood silent behind the Sheriff during the conversation with the stranger screamed when a second shot rang the prairie air and dropped him to the ground in the instant following the Sheriff's collapse.

***

Draper ducked behind the Sheriff's cruiser and pulled his Glock. He knew it would be useless against a long-distance shooter but until he was sure of the enemy, it gave him comfort. He had an M4 in the trunk of his own car, but getting to it was risky. Silence ensued. He pulled out his cell phone and called 911. After a minute, he crawled around the car following his Glock to where the Sheriff lay. The officer had a large exit wound high on his chest bleeding onto the ground, his breathing shallow, but alive. Draper opened the cruiser door and searched for a first aid kit, found it, opened it and grabbed a wad of compress bandages. Stripping the packages as fast as he could, he stuffed four into the wound and pressed hard on the officer's chest while scoping the landscape west of the house for movement or sun reflections. There were no more shots and about fifteen minutes later another Sheriff's Department car skidded to a stop with lights on and siren wailing.

Draper holstered his gun and added that hand to the Sheriff's chest. A deputy came around the car with his sidearm pointed at Draper. Draper ignored the weapon and barked, "The Sheriff's hit hard, how far is the ambulance behind you?"

"About ten minutes," the deputy said.

"Check the other guy, I've got this one at the moment," Draper ordered. "Stay low, there's a shooter out there to the west."

The deputy stepped over to the other man's body and knelt down. He turned to Draper and said, "He's dead."

"Both these men were shot from distance, so if I was you and you have a long gun in your trunk, I'd grab it and scope those woods out there for a shooter," Draper growled. "I'd do it myself but I'm a little occupied.

"On it," the deputy said and ran to his car. In a couple of minutes, he was back. Draper could hear the man's footfalls and the clunk of the weapon on the car's roof. He couldn't see the deputy, but he relaxed a bit knowing he had backup.

"How's the Sheriff?"

"Not good," Draper said, "he's shot through and he's lost a lot of blood. That ambulance had better get here quick."

"Worse yet it's near a hundred miles to the closest hospital."

"Shit!" was all Draper could say. He reached into the Sheriff's pockets with one hand searching for keys hoping that if the Sheriff had locked the house he'd be able to enter without having to break in. He found a ring of keys and slipped them into his pocket.

"Just who the hell are you?" the deputy said.

"Name's Draper."

The ambulance arrived and began work on the Sheriff. Two efficient EMT's had him strapped on a gurney and inside in short order.

'I'm going to follow the ambulance, but don't you go anywhere, Mr. Draper. I'm going to send out the Undersheriff. I'm sure he'll want to talk to you. I'll send the undertaker/coroner out to pickup Randy's body.

"I'll be here," Draper said.

Draper stood in the driveway and watched until the both emergency vehicles were out of site before he went to the Lincoln's trunk and lifted out a customized M4 with a high-power scope. He attached a thirty-round magazine, racked the bolt to load the first round and flipped on the safety. Locked and loaded, Draper went hunting. He concentrated on an Aspen copse atop a knoll about three hundred yards behind the house. He didn't attack it directly but instead took a circular route keeping him behind the uneven terrain and scattered pines. He maintained the same three hundred yard distance until he felt his position was approximately behind where he estimated the shooter's stand was located. In a flat draw he crossed fresh vehicle tracks, something light, only bending over the grass, but not leaving distinct marks in the soil. Something similar to a slow-moving four-wheeler he decided. Draper listened but heard only the gentle afternoon breeze and the sound of branches rubbing together. The four-wheeler tracks were singular, heading toward the copse, indicating he might still in the area. Draper waited. For ten minutes, nothing happened. He tensed when he heard a four-wheeler start. The man came fast, winding through the trees until he reached the one Draper hid behind. There his throat ran into the barrel of Draper's M4 at about fifteen miles an hour. Not fast enough to kill, but hard enough to dump him on the ground where Draper put his twelve-sized boot not gentle on the man's chest and pressed the barrel of the M4 into his left cheek.

"One move, asshole, and you die," Draper said.

The man on the ground choked coughing a little blood several times before he said, "Who the fuck are you?"

"I'm your worst nightmare, asshole. You have about twenty seconds to live unless you tell me why you shot the Sheriff. Be brief, I don't have a lot of patience or time."

"Go to hell!"

The barrel of the M4 bounced off the man's head leaving a satisfactory gash, which began to bleed in rivers. The man grunted with a gurgling sound and passed out. Draper figured he had at least a half hour before the Undersheriff arrived. Plenty of time to mess a little more with his captive.

He slapped the man's face and said, "Hey, asshole, no time for sleep. You keep playing around and I'll make you regret you were ever born. Tell me what I want to know now or in a few minutes you will be begging me to kill you."

"You have to help me," the man said, soft, between clenched teeth.

"No, I don't. I'm not a cop. In fact, I'm a worse asshole than you, my friend. I know how to kill very slowly, with you screaming for mercy."

"Fuck you," the man said.

"You know what kneecapping is?" Draper said his voice conversational and low.

His captive stared without responding.

"I can see you don't. Let me explain. Kneecapping is I destroy your knees one at a time. It can be done a number of ways, but I have this nice M4 carbine in .223 caliber that makes a hell of a mess of bone and flesh at close range. I just press the barrel against your knee and pull the trigger. The expanding gasses and the bullet pretty much

16

make mincemeat out of your joint. Do them both and you're a wheelchair case for life. That's assuming the shock, blood poisoning, gangrene or a host of other complications don't kill you first. In my experience, most men will give up their mother after the first knee. The second is rarely necessary. But, then maybe you're tougher than I think. What do you think? One or two; it doesn't matter to me."

"What do you want to know?"

"You kill the guy in the house?"

"Yeah, he was an undercover DEA agent."

"Who do you work for?"

The man fell silent, prompting Draper to press the M4 against his left knee.

"Don't, please, they'll kill me."

"I'll kill you if you don't.

"The *Luces del Norte* cartel. They run the drug trade out of Mexico.

"Who's the head honcho around here?"

"I've never seen him but I'm told his name is Joey Diez. That is all I know. I'm just muscle. They sent me out to take care of the DEA guy."

Draper used plastic zip ties to bind his hands and feet and a third one to tie him to the four-wheeler's trailer ball.

"I'll send someone out to pick you up. It might not be until morning seeing how the local authorities are busy cleaning up your mess, so if the coyotes visit tonight just holler at them. Maybe they'll go away. Wolves now, that's a different matter. They're bigger and more ferocious. Tear a man to pieces in minutes; but fortunately not too many around."

"You can't just leave me here."

"Yeah, I can," Draper said. He walked a hundred yards away thinking about the DEA agent. He had read in the man's folder that he had a wife somewhere and a couple of kids. Draper stopped, stared at the ground a moment, and turned around. The man tied to the four-wheeler looked smug thinking his captor had returned to take him back to the house. Draper had no such intention. Instead, he triggered a single .223 bullet into the man's left knee. "That's for the DEA agent's family and food for the coyotes," he said and turned away. He could hear the man's screams halfway back to the house. By the time he entered the yard the air was silent.

Chapter Two

Eastern Montana

D raper used the Sheriff's keys to open the front door of the house and stepped into a meth factory. The man lying on the floor of the living room had no identification, but the physical description in the report told him he had found the missing DEA agent a bit late. Draper spent a couple of minutes looking through the house, found nothing of interest, retreated to the front porch, and relocked the door. He took a moment to reflect on what the killer had told him. He found it hard to believe that this seemingly amateur cookhouse, albeit large, gained financing from a Mexican cartel organization. It appeared a little far afield for what he knew of cartel operations. It did not fit the usual mold he knew and the killer back in the trees was not Mexican. There were no signs of big city gang membership; no obvious criminal activity associated with drug smuggling. According to the briefing he received, there were no reports of active stash houses. He had seen a few Mexican's around, some maybe illegal, but all appeared hard working and law abiding trying to feed their families.

By the time Draper reached his car and restored the M4 to the Lincoln's trunk, he could hear a siren. A cloud of road dust followed blue and red flashing lights. Draper leaned against the Lincoln and waited. Lights and siren off, the Sheriff's Department cruiser slid in behind Draper's car and the abandoned County Sheriff's vehicle.

The plain-clothes officer who stepped out wore a white sweat-stained Stetson, a bright Brushpopper long-sleeved shirt, Wrangler jeans and rolled-over, dust-covered cowboy boots. He looked like a range cowboy, medium-height, an inch or two under six-foot. Lean, hard, and a tad bow-legged, his sun-wrinkled face appeared the color of aged copper. He wore a belt badge-holder that shone in the afternoon sun.

"Are you Draper?" the man said.

"Yeah," Draper said, not wanting to show much until he got a better read on the man.

"Got some ID?"

"Yeah."

"Gonna show it to me?"

"You askin'?" Draper said.

The officer stared hard at Draper until a careful smirk started at the corner of his mouth. "So what we do now, pissin' contest or what?"

"Horse turds at twenty paces or you can just ask nice. Besides how do I know you didn't steal that badge and cruiser?"

"Fair enough; sorry, it's been a rough afternoon. My name's Dean Sterling, I'm the county Undersheriff, which means I'm in charge now that the Sheriff's been shot. I learned you were going to be around just an hour ago, but given recent incidents, I would appreciate seeing some ID.

"Not a problem," Draper said and handed over his ID.

The officer glanced at it and handed it back.

20

"Okay, fill me in," Sterling said.

Draper told him everything he knew, minus a few details about the shooter in the trees. "I've got him tied to his four-wheeler but he might be a little worse for wear."

"How so?" Sterling asked.

"He resisted arrest so I had to shoot him a little."

"How much is a little?"

"In the knee."

"Hell, you're making my job easy. The undertaker will be by shortly to pick up the bodies. Let's go retrieve the asshole in the woods."

Draper led the Undersheriff to the copse where he had left the shooter. As they walked, Draper asked about the Sheriff.

"Nip and tuck so far; it's a long way to trauma care from here, so he's going to be some past the critical hour before they arrive. You know, I've been with the department nearly ten years, been to the FBI academy a couple of times, lot's of training classes in Billings, yet up to two years ago the most excitement we had was drunk cowboys and an occasional domestic dispute. But lately something has changed. All of a sudden we got drugs, shootings, and murder."

"Unfortunately, you're catching up with the rest of the country."

"Yeah, and we've got a budget that barely covers our salaries and the commissioners want to cut a deputy."

"Welcome to the real world," Draper said.

"So, what are you, ex-special forces, spook, CIA, FBI, or what?"

"Something like that," Draper mumbled.

"What's that mean, none of the above or all of them?"

"You don't want to know."

When they walked up to the four-wheeler, Sterling said, "Looks like the coroner will have three to retrieve. You usually kill your captives?"

"I do when they resist."

"Hog-tied zipped to the four-wheeler and he resisted?"

"He confessed to killing the DEA agent in the house and shooting the Sheriff."

"Whatever you say, it works for me, but remind me never to get on your bad side, though right now I'm considering buying you a couple of drinks when we get back to town. You do drink, don't you?"

"Only if I'm alone or with somebody," Draper said.

It was late evening before Draper drove into Highmore, the county seat, supporting a population of five hundred or so hardy souls, who made their living supporting the livestock and farming industries. He drove past huge fields of dryland winter wheat, irrigated alfalfa, and many square miles of native grass rangeland. Low lying pine covered hills surrounded the valley and the more rugged Crazy Mountains lay to the southwest in the distance. A mile out of town, a fork-horned buck antelope stood on a low hill guarding his group of does. Highmore consisted of a hardware store, Senior Citizens Center, a bar, brick facade bank and the local grain elevator surrounded by large new shiny grain bins. In the center of town, taking up an entire block sat a three-story granite courthouse. It did not look like a major crime city. Quiet and peaceful, Draper couldn't help imagining cowboys and farm hands playing cards and drinking beer at the local bar. The highway went through the middle of town and was its only paved street. The Sheriff's office sat on a gravel covered side street.

Draper parked the Lincoln and walked into the County Sheriff's office. Greeted by a pretty, a dark-haired woman in her mid

22

to late thirties, she sat outside a low oak guardrail. It separated her from three cluttered oak desks forming a tee and a single office in the back. Draper assumed the office belonged to the Sheriff. Sparse was the word that jumped into Draper's mind. The nameplate on her desk read Mindy Sterling.

Mindy Sterling smiled at Draper and said, "Can I help you, Sir."

"I'm going to take a wild guess here that you are either Dean's sister or his wife."

"Wife," she said, "nepotism runs rampant in small towns."

"Damn, I was hoping for sister."

"You try that line all the time?"

"Occasionally," Draper said.

"It ever work for you?"

"Not so far," Draper said.

"Well, keep trying, you might just get lucky," Mindy Sterling said giving Draper a hundred dollar smile. "You want to talk to Dean?"

"I do."

"He's in the Sheriff's office. It looks like a long night," Mindy Sterling said, turning serious. "Go on back."

Draper walked through a swinging gate in the wooden railing, walked past the three desks, and knocked on the wall of the office.

Dean Sterling looked up with tired eyes and pointed at an oak captain's chair. "Sit," he said.

Draper sat waiting while Sterling stared at the papers on his desk. "Sheriff didn't make it."

"Sorry," Draper said, "He seemed competent and a good guy."

"He was, and a friend. I've been with this department ten years and he taught me everything I know. Right now, it doesn't seem enough. It's a good thing you killed that son-of-a-bitch or I'd be tempted myself."

"Hard being a cop," Draper said, "there's nothing much good about what you have to do most days. The illegal drugs industry brings the worst out of both the suppliers and the users."

"So just who the hell are you? I tried to look you up, called a couple of guys I know and nobody's ever heard of you. Nothing on the internet and hell, everyone alive is on the internet."

"That's the way it is. I travel around some. I came here to find a missing DEA agent."

"And you found him dead?"

"I did."

"So what now; are you going to leave or what?" Sterling asked.

"I think I'll stick around a while, see what turns up." Draper did not intend to go anywhere. Finding the DEA agent was only part of his agenda.

"Thought you might," Sterling said.

"How about I buy dinner for you and your wife and we get to know each other. See if we can figure out just what the hell is going on here," Draper suggested. "Is there a restaurant in town?"

"Don't feel much like eating, but it'd be better than sitting around here," Sterling said. "Restaurant is part of the bar."

Draper followed the Sterling's down the street a block and off the main drag a half block to a small cafe attached to the bar fronting on Main Street Inside, an eclectic assortment of tables showing years of use sat pre-set with water glasses and silverware. The menu was limited to grease and gluten but wasn't bad taste-wise. The

24

conversation ran light at first, with little substance. Draper liked it that way since it gave him a chance to study the pair. He liked what he saw. The cowboy and the former prom queen were a mismatched pair, but they d been married for better than ten years so it seemed to work. The cowboy appeared tough, but it remained to be seen if he could handle cold-blooded killers. There was not any doubt in Draper's mind that there might be a few around.

They were midway through the meal of roast beef, fried potatoes, and a green vegetable mix when it started. A heavy-set older man walked in wearing a Brooks Brothers suit in a blue pinstripe. He looked twenty pounds overweight, soft and carried himself like a middle-aged Beau Brummell. His companion was muscle. Big, ugly, and a rock hard knuckle-dragger; his work was head breaking and he looked capable. Draper pushed his chair back away from the table but did not stand. Sterling was at a disadvantage because both men were behind him. He turned in his chair and said, "What's on your mind, Mr. Boulton?"

"We need to talk, Deputy," Boulton said.

"Come to my office in the morning and we'll talk. Right now I'm having dinner with my wife and a friend," Sterling said his voice firm, low and direct. "And, for your information, I'm not a deputy; I'm the Undersheriff, which means according to county regulations, I'm the acting Sheriff until the County Commissioners meet and determine otherwise."

"We'll see about that. This is my town and I make the rules," the fat man said.

Draper saw the swing coming, surprised by how fast Sterling moved. The head-breaker's fist missed by inches and Sterling's right fist hit the fat man just below his breastbone dropping the man on his ass with his eyes rolled back. The head-breaker, off balance when Draper hit him full force on the side of his neck with his right. He followed with his left, breaking the man's nose. The fight was over as fast as it started.

Sterling rolled the fat man over and cuffed him. "Damn it, only got one set of cuffs."

Draper reached in his coat pocket and pulled out a zip tie. "Be my guest," he said. "These things are easier to carry around."

It took an hour to move the two from the restaurant to the county jail, a single cell cage at the back of the Sheriff's office. They marched the two down the main street in full view of the locals. The fat man bitched all the way, until Draper threatened to break his nose also. Walking back to the restaurant Draper said, "Nice move back there, you've had a little training."

"Only a little in the army; mostly I learned in bars and getting beat up a lot. When you're five-ten and one seventy, technique becomes important." Sterling said.

"Tell me about the two we just put in jail," Draper said.

"The fat guy is named Andrew Boulton. He owns half the county split between a cattle operation and farming. The home place is about ten miles north of town and guarded like Fort Knox by armed staff. Sheriff Hornsby was convinced Boulton was a mobster and I half-way agreed, although we couldn't find anything to confirm it. Lots of money, spreads it around liberally to those that can help him and cries at the County Commissioners that the Sheriff's Department is overpaid and staff bloated. I'm probably going to get fired for arresting him."

"How long can you hold him?"

"Technically, seventy-two hours, but I'd bet there's a fleet of attorneys on the way as we speak."

They reentered the restaurant to find Mindy Sterling talking to the café staff. She grabbed her husband's hand and said, "You all right?"

"For the moment," the acting Sheriff said.

Mindy Sterling looked at Draper and said, "Thank you."

"Looked to me as if your husband was capable of handling it alone. I just made it easier," Draper said.

"I'm glad you were here anyway."

"How about the other deputies, can you trust them?" Draper asked Sterling.

"Yeah, Sheriff Hornsby picked them carefully and I approved. I'd be surprised if either one weren't okay."

"All right," Draper said, "let's try to stay ahead of Boulton and company.. While they're in lockup, let's go visit the home place, hit them before they have chance to prepare."

"Right now?"

"When better? They won't be expecting it while they're scrambling around trying to get the boss out of jail."

"Okay, sounds like a ballsy move, I like it," Sterling said.

"Please be careful," his wife said.

"Here's the deal," Draper said, "for the next few hours you are no longer Acting Sheriff. What we are going to do may creep into the illegal side of things. If that bothers you I'll go alone, but you know the place and I'd appreciate some backup."

"Hell, I have a feeling just talking to you is probably a crime, so count me in. Like I said, it's likely I'll be fired tomorrow anyway."

They used Draper's rented Lincoln for the trip to avoid any connection to the Sheriff's Department. They stopped at Sterling's house to drop off his wife. It stood alone on a large lot, with a two story Victorian-style home that Draper guessed would have Mindy Sterling's personality stamped all over it. Sterling went inside and returned a few minutes later carrying a new-looking AK-47 and a couple of thirty-round magazines.

"I bought this myself because the department didn't have the budget for it." Sterling said.

"Handy to have," Draper said.

"I haven't practiced much with it."

"No need, designed for fire-power, not accuracy."

Draper drove into a moonless night following Sterling's direction. At fifteen past ten pm, they turned into a gravel surfaced two-lane road guarded by a large sign that announced they were entering the *Andrew Boulton Land and Cattle Company. No Trespassing, No Admittance Without Authorization. Trespassers Will Be Prosecuted to the Full Extent of the Law.*

A couple hundred yards away Draper could see a lighted guard shack, outside of a ten-foot chain-link fence topped with razor wire. The main gate appeared to roll on tracks and the whole area was lit up like a secured military installation.

"Doesn't look like they want any casual company," Draper said. "Seems a little overkill just to keep cows from wondering."

"Ya think?" Sterling said. "I've never been inside, so I'm no help. I do know the main house and outbuildings set over there next to the foothills.

"Why don't you crawl into the back seat, down low where no one will see you without looking."

"Why?"

"Don't want anyone to see you. Let me deal with the gate guard."

When Sterling was hidden, Draper drove unhurried toward the gate, stopping when he was next to the guard shack. The guard was not friendly.

"Sir, do not get out of your car. You are trespassing on private property. Turn around and leave or risk arrest or bodily injury."

"Who the hell are you and what are you doing on my road?" Draper slurred his words just enough to imitate a lost drunk. His acting skill was lost on the guard.

"Turn your car around and go back the way you came in unless you want real trouble. Back up to the turnaround and I want to see taillights quick." The guard's voice left no room for argument which told Draper something beyond the gate needed a look-see, but through the guarded gate wasn't a viable option."

"Okay, okay, you don't have to be grumpy about it," Draper mumbled and shoved the Lincoln into reverse with a slight pressure on the gas so the car jumped back a few feet. He looked at the guard with a silly grin and said, "Opps!" before continuing to back very slowly. He backed into a wide turnaround, maneuvering clumsily before lining up with the road back to the highway.

"What the hell are you doing?" came from the back seat.

"All part of the act, I don't want them to think it was anything serious, just some drunk taking a wrong turn," Draper said.

"So, now what?" Sterling said.

"Not sure; is there any other way to get a look at the property without getting caught?"

"Doubt it. Ranch property extends many miles into those mountains. Some of them are damn rugged; you'd have to grow wings to see it all."

"Is there somewhere we can rent a small airplane?"

"Billings, probably."

"Nowhere closer?" Draper said.

Well, there's Chauncey Flynn, rancher east of town, he has two, I think. He flies all the time, but I don't know if he rents them out."

"I want to rent a plane. No pilot; I'll do the flying. The less anyone knows about what we are doing, the less likely there'll be questions.

"Chauncey flies mostly hunters looking for big game, but that doesn't happen until fall. I can call him in the morning and ask."

"Do that," Draper said.

Draper dropped the Acting Sheriff off at his house a little after eleven. He declined the offer of coffee and found the local motel, a six room establishment facing the highway. He paid for a week to the night to a clerk deep into a romance novel. She smiled, took his money, made him sign the register slip and was back at reading before Draper left to find his room. Number six was on the end and suited his needs. He parked the Lincoln, flopped on the bed and was quickly asleep.

Draper rose at five am, showered, dressed, and wishing for coffee when Sterling banged on his door at six. He opened it to the Acting Sheriff who said, "I called Chauncey this morning; he says he'll rent us the Piper Super Cub if you are a licensed pilot and checked out in that kind of plane.

"No problem. I can fly anything that has wings."

"I think he'll need a little proof of that. I believe you, but he may not want to take your word on it."

"Let's go talk to him," Draper said.

The Flynn ranch lay east of town requiring and eight mile trip east on the highway and a two mile cruise south toward the mountains. They pulled into a group of older but well-maintained buildings that that included the main house, a couple of smaller homes for permanent ranch hands, two big barns, loafing sheds, hay storage, equipment storage, maintenance shop, and several small outbuildings. Surrounded by tractors, balers, hay rakes and tilling equipment, all of which had age with signs of recent maintenance. Draper was impressed. If Flynn took care of his airplanes as well as the rest of his equipment looks, Draper would be comfortable flying them. The hanger, its windsock limp, sat behind the barns on the end of a well-packed and oiled runway.

Flynn stood inches short of Draper's height, with broad shoulders, barely contained in a faded Carhartt jacket. Close to sixty, Draper guessed, with a short white beard, white hair and friendly blue eyes. Draper liked him instantly.

"You the pilot?" he said, shaking Draper's hand.

"Yes, learned to fly in the military, I can fly most anything with a prop on it and some of the smaller commercial jets." Draper handed him his pilot's license card that included commercial, instructor, multi-engine and commercial jet certifications.

"Impressive. You don't mind if I take a short hop with you in the Cub before I turn it over. The rate is a hundred an hour, two hour minimum. Includes the first tank of gas; you buy the rest.

"Sounds fair, no problem with check ride."

"Well, she's out and ready, let's do it.

Flynn led Draper to a fully restored 1960 Piper Super Cub painted bright white with cherry red engine cowling and trim.

"Nice!" Draper said. "Love the color."

Flynn smiled and watched while Draper did a careful pre-flight, walking around, looking, moving the control surfaces and checking everything. "Looks good," Draper said, "let's take her up."

Draper sat forward with Flynn in back in the tandem-seat Piper although both seats had control sticks. After starting the engine, he glanced at the still quiet windsock, did his magneto check and taxied the short distance to the runway end.

"Ready?" Draper said turning back to the rear seat.

"The plane is yours," Flynn said.

Draper set the flaps on full, eased the throttle forward to maximum and the little plane jumped forward. At forty-five, he increased back pressure on the stick and let the Cub climb out until it reached cruising speed. When they reached one thousand feet, Draper flew a box pattern that took him back to the runway where began a left-hand landing approach shooting for a touchdown close to the spot where they started. In a show-off tactic, he dragged the tailwheel as far as he could before letting the Cub settle to the ground. When it slowed enough to turn around, he taxied back to the hanger. Draper braked and shut off the engine while Flynn maneuvered the bottom and top halves of the entry door.

"Neat trick with the tail wheel," Flynn said. "That takes a lot of practice. How many hours you have in a tail-dragger?"

"Wild guess would be sneaking up on ten thousand. Don't know for sure; stopped counting a long time ago."

"Well, I got this and an 180 Cessna, you are welcome to use either one anytime."

When Draper tried to pay the man, he declined. "We'll settle up when you get back. I trust any friend of Dean's."

"Thanks, Chauncey," Draper said.

Draper and Sterling climbed into the Super Cub and Draper made sure the Acting Sheriff was buckled in. "Flown much?"

"Actually, a bit; Chauncey always volunteers his planes when we have lost hunters and missing kids."

"Good. Help me out if there is anything you think we should look at that I miss," Draper said.

Draper took off and climbed to five thousand feet. He wanted to be high enough to scan a large area, plus have enough altitude that the little plane would be lost in the morning sky and there'd be little engine noise on the ground. If needed, they could always drop down for a closer look.

The air was cold and stable and the little Piper sailed smoothly on a northeast bearing toward distant low mountains that surrounded the central valley. The town of Highmore, not much more that a spot in prairie, slid by underneath and shortly they could see the outline of chain link fence surrounding the banker's property.

The ranch would have looked unremarkable had it not been for the fence. The usual outbuildings surrounded a modern-looking main house, large, two-story, with crisp landscaping and fresh paint. Large loafing sheds, long feeding areas with automatic feed distribution, auto-watering stations and covered hay storage dominated the flats beyond the house.

"I don't see anything out of the ordinary, what are we looking for?" Sterling shouted over the engine noise.

"Don't know; look for something that would account for a high security fence."

Beyond the grouped buildings around the main house, a gravel road led up into the foothills. Draper banked to follow it. Beyond the low hills, in a small valley Draper could see a new-looking metal building with high walls. He guessed the dimensions at a hundred by hundred-fifty, large enough for storing large equipment or hiding something illegal, the question was what? Parked alongside the building were three two-ton trucks with cargo van bodies on them. "What do you suppose they are using van trucks for?" Draper said. He had to repeat his rhetorical question when Sterling leaned forward and shouted "What?"

They flew around another half-hour without seeing anything unusual. There had to be a reason for all the security other than protecting the cattle from non-existent rustlers, Draper thought. Something illegal came to mind, but the choices seemed scarce. Drugs maybe, but the population of Montana, barely reaching one million, didn't classify as a large market.

Draper turned the Cub southeast and headed back to Flynn's ranch. He was not sure what he'd expected to find, but he had hoped for better than little or nothing.

Chapter Three

Eastern Montana

Draper slept during the afternoon heat. He had dropped Sterling off at the Sheriff's Office and returned to his motel room. He laid on the bed staring at the ceiling most of the first hour without coming to any conclusions. At a little after five pm, he rose, looked out the motel window onto lengthening shadows. His cell phone rang.

"Draper, you busy?" Dean Sterling's voice said.

"Not at the moment."

"Mindy wants you to come over for dinner, if, of course, you don't have plans."

"I was going to go shoot some bad guys, but it can wait."

"If you do, please go over into another county. I've got enough problems as it is."

"You still employed?"

"Temporarily. Boulton's high-priced counsel showed up at noon with a release-on-bail order from a judge in Billings. Boulton threatened to have me fired as soon as he can get the next commissioners meeting scheduled.

"How much pull does he have?" Draper asked.

"Looks about fifty-fifty from where I stand."

"When do you want me for dinner?"

"How about six?"

"Sounds good."

Draper walked to the Sterling house since the distance made driving seem silly. The people he met on the way looked at him curiously as small town folks tend to do when a stranger is about. Most were friendly; spoke without suspicion, while chatting about the weather in passing. When he knocked on the Sterling's door, Mindy answered.

"Hi, Charlie, come in," she said.

Draper followed her into the front room filled with tempting cooking odors. "Thanks for the invite; I always appreciate a home-cooked meal."

"I hope it isn't overdone. Dean had to run back to the Sheriff's Office. Couple of cowboys started drinking early and got into it at the bar. He should be back soon. Meanwhile, would you like beer or some wine?"

"I'll have whatever you're having," Draper said.

"I'm having White Zinfandel if that's okay. Grab a chair anywhere."

Draper picked one end of a well-worn couch that looked as if its only purpose was guests. The furniture looked early relative, dated but comfortable. The room felt warm and the decor fresh. The only newer fixture was a large flat-screen television hanging on one wall.

"Mindy returned with two glasses of wine and handed one to Draper. "I'm glad to get this chance to talk to you. Dean seems to think you are an okay guy."

"What do you think?" Draper said.

Mindy had sat in one of a pair of mismatched recliners before she answered. "I'm reserving judgment, for now, but what I've seen so far isn't bad, just a little mysterious."

"Hell, I'm an open book, ask me anything."

"Married?"

"No."

"Not ever?"

"No."

"You aren't going to tell me much, are you?" Mindy Sterling gave Draper the look some women use when men answer in monosyllables.

"I answered truthfully."

"Single word responses aren't what I was looking for."

"Not much to tell."

"Girl friend; or someone special?" Mindy Sterling was not about to give up.

"There was for a while, but she was shot by an assassin and nearly died. It changed her in ways both of us had trouble understanding. Nobody's fault, we just drifted apart."

"You still care about her though, right?"

"I do."

"I'm sorry, Charlie. Please forgive me, but I'm a little protective of Dean."

"Understandable; I have an adopted daughter, just recently made it legal. I'd gladly shoot anyone who tried to hurt her."

"Really, how did that happen?"

"I found her out in the desert in Arizona, dirty, half naked, and scared. She'd escaped from a Mexican whorehouse and was running from drug cartel killers. She's a senior at U of A now working on a degree in nursing." Draper waited to see if the Sheriff's wife would be shocked.

She didn't show any signs and said, "How old was she?"

"Sixteen. She'd been a captive for almost three years."

Mindy Sterling didn't say anything for a moment and only stared at Draper. He met her look and said, "What?"

"I can't imagine how horrible that must have been."

"She's a hell of a strong young lady."

"I guess," Mindy Sterling said. She continued to stare at Draper and he fidgeted wondering what was really on her mind. Finally, she said it.

"Dean thinks you killed the shooter out at Ruskin's place in cold blood."

Draper hesitated. He did not know Mindy Sterling well, but something told him she needed to know and the reason. "I'll admit to shooting him because he deserved it. He shot Sheriff Hornsby, the owner of the house and a DEA agent who had a wife and a couple of kids. It's likely they weren't the only ones. He tried to escape, not to mention he would have shot me in a heartbeat if given the chance."

"Did you have to shoot him?"

"How would you feel if someone killed Dean for no reason except he was in the way. Let's say the law caught the shooter and spent the next two or three years trying to put him away, while some bleeding heart liberal lawyer made a fortune defending him. And even if he was convicted, worst case scenario, he spends the next ten or fifteen years living in nice digs, with three squares a day, recreation time and lots of companionship while the victim's family suffers. That doesn't equate to fair in my book."

"I'm sorry, Charlie. I just had to understand."

"No problem, you deserved to know." Maybe I should go; it looks like Dean might be a while. I could come back another time."

They heard a car pulled up outside. Now dark, Draper looked and it was not Dean. "Are you expecting company?"

"No one but Dean; it isn't him?"

"Don't think so. Go into the kitchen and lock the back door. Then holler for them to come in but stay in the kitchen." Draper drew his Glock and waited. When the door opened, there were two of them. The first man through had a chrome-plated Smith and Wesson automatic leading. Draper double-tapped him in the chest, knocking him back into his partner. The second man tried to bring his weapon around too late and Draper's next two bullets slammed him against the doorjamb where he slid to the floor. He could hear Mindy Sterling crying his name behind him. Draper followed his Glock into the kitchen where a third shooter had a snub-nosed revolver pressed into the side of Mindy's neck. Her eyes wide with fear, she blinked tears rolling down her face.

The man holding the Acting Sheriff's wife in front of him left little for Draper to aim at that would not endanger the woman. "Seems we have a standoff," the man said. "I suggest you put your gun very carefully on the floor and kick it toward me otherwise I'll have to blow this pretty lady's head off."

Draper said nothing. His choices not first-rate, he wrestled with the fact his target was little more than a sliver of a man's head behind the woman's; a risky shot. He also knew her life was not worth a nickel unless he did something. The only bright light was the idiot had not cocked the revolver. That meant to fire it he would have to pull the trigger through its double-action. Possible, but time consuming and not likely if you are dead. Decision made, Draper applied steady pressure to the Glock's trigger and shot the man through his left cheek. The gun dropped with the man collapsing on the floor and Mindy Sterling screamed and fainted. To Draper it happened in slow motion as he followed the man down with the Glock in case the kill required a second shot. It did not.

Draper knelt down putting his arm behind Mindy Sterling's neck and lifted her up to a sitting position. She grasped his free arm and buried her face into his Brushpopper shirt dampening the cloth with tears. Suddenly, she leaned back, looking up and said, "Dean? What's happened to Dean?"

"Come on, I'll take you to the Sheriff's Office and we'll find him."

"My dinner, it's ruined." Mindy Sterling said, tears still flowing.

"It's okay. I'll shut everything off and we'll deal with it later. The cops are going to have to clean up the mess these boys made."

Draper helped her up. She was still shaking, so he held on to her. "We'll go out the back door, try not to look."

They walked the two blocks to the Sheriff's Office. Draper's arm stayed around her waist for the first block. Then she said, "I'm okay."

"You sure?" Draper said looking at the deep red mark on the side of her neck left by the intruder's gun barrel. The angry mark looked like a bruise in the making under a neon lit storefront.

"Yes," Mindy said, followed by a moment of silence. "Did you kill them all?"

"I did. There were two more at the front door."

"Good," she said, so soft that Draper had to strain to hear her.

The Sheriff's Office bustled with activity when Draper and Mindy Sterling stepped in. The Acting Sheriff appeared to be in an intense argument with two men Draper did not know and the rancher Boulton.

Draper walked up and touched Sterling's arm. "Need to talk to you, Dean, it's important."

Sterling looked at his wife's face and immediately said, "Let's go in my office."

"Wait a minute, Deputy, Goddamn it! We aren't done here," Boulton said.

Draper stepped up close to the man and said, "You take a good look at me, asshole, because I want you to remember me. Tonight someone tried to harm Mrs. Sterling and I'm wondering if you aren't behind it. If you were, and I'm convinced of it, I'll be coming after you and all the hard-cases and razor wire in the world won't save you. Consider yourself warned." Draper gave the man a little shove that sent him peddling back, sputtering.

"What happened, Charlie?" Draper was sure Sterling knew it was something bad from the look on his wife's face.

"Three assholes with guns tried to break into your house and it wasn't an invite to dinner. You have three bodies messing up your living room and kitchen. One of them was holding a gun at Mindy's neck," Draper said, never taking his eyes off Boulton.

"What?" Boulton said. "I don't know what you're talking about."

"So help me Boulton, if I find out you had something to do with threatening my wife, I'll come after you myself and this State won't be big enough for you to hide. Now get the hell out of my office and let me deal with something critical," Sterling said.

When they were alone, Sterling took his wife into his office and held her for a long time. Draper gave them space and sat in the main room with two deputies. The older of the two held out his hand and said, "Mr. Draper, my name's Mario Lopez; thank you for helping Mindy. She means a lot to all of us. The youngster over there is Deputy Valentine." Draper shook hands with both men.

"I suggest you show us the crime scene, so we can secure it and get old man Donovan busy cleaning up," Lopez said. "Since its Dean's house, I'm going to take lead and suggest he and Mindy find a motel room for the night."

"So how did you get into law enforcement, Deputy Lopez?" Draper asked.

"My parents came here after the war, illegally, paid for by a local rancher who needed workers. He furnished their housing and helped them become naturalized citizens, a process that took years. I was born here so I'm legal. They are both dead now, but lived most of their lives on that ranch afraid to leave in fear of being caught and sent back to Mexico. I decided anything would be better than ranch work."

"It's a lousy system, racked with corruption on both sides of the border," Draper said.

"Aye, that it is, but it's still the best country around."

"Can't argue that," Draper agreed.

"Hold the fort, Gary" Lopez said, "Mr. Draper and I are going to do some crime-solving work."

The front door to Sterling's house stood open. The first body lay in the doorway with the second in the middle of the living room carpet. A large pool of drying blood told Draper the house would require a new carpet. Draper followed Lopez into the kitchen where the third shooter lay. "You create all this *carnicería* all by yourself?"

"*Culpable de los cargos, sí*" Draper said.

"*Ah, usted habla español.* Lopez said.

"A little; comes from living in Arizona. Like most American's I'm too lazy to be fluent, I can understand the gist of it if you don't go to fast, but I'm more comfortable with English," Draper said.

Lopez laughed. "I'm actually more comfortable in English myself after all these years. In Montana, I don't get to use Spanish much until recently. Why don't you walk me through what happened here?"

Draper started from the beginning and gave the Deputy a rundown of events. It did not take long. When he finished the part about the shooting in the kitchen, the Deputy said, "No wonder Mindy was so shook."

"I didn't see a choice," Draper said.

"Doesn't look like there was one."

"You know any of these guys?"

"No, never saw them before, but the word on the street says Boulton has brought in some serious bad guys to guard that fenced compound he's got," Lopez said.

"Any idea what he's guarding out there?"

"Not a clue. We can't get on a place without a warrant, so I have no idea other than it looks suspiciously illegal," Lopez said. Lopez pulled out a cell phone and dialed. "Bill? Mario here, I've got three customers for you. Yeah; I'm over at Dean Sterling's house. No, they're okay, three strangers, died of GSWs, multiple in a couple of cases. Okay, we'll be here." Lopez hung up and turned to Draper. "Dr. Death is on his way with the wagon."

"Is he the medical examiner?" Draper asked.

"Not exactly, he's the coroner; handles most deaths unless there's a crime involved and then we have to get someone down from the Tri-State office in Lewistown. Probably be seeing them in this situation. No sense you staying around. Go take care of Dean and Mindy. I think they might need your services."

"Thanks, Mario. By the way, if you don't mind my asking, if anyone in your family is illegal, let me know, I'll try to help you out. Sometimes it helps to have friends in the right places."

Mario Lopez had stared at Draper a long moment without comment before he said, "I'm not going to regret telling you, am I?"

"I'm very discreet. I can't promise citizenship, but possibly a permanent visa. Family unification is a big political talking point these days."

"Thanks for asking. I'll think about it," Lopez said.

Draper walked back to the Sheriff's Office with a quick stop at his motel. Things were getting a little warm and he felt the need for a backup piece. Deep in his luggage he extracted a second Glock .40 in an ankle holster and then debated about a second .380 auto in another ankle holster. Most people searching assume a right-handed shooter; hence, the .380 was on his right ankle as a throw-away. The second Glock went on his left ankle because Draper was ambidextrous and could shoot equally well with either hand. He reloaded the nearly empty clip in his shoulder Glock and stuck a couple extra fully loaded clips in his jacket pocket. Feeling better prepared, he locked the room and continued to his destination.

Dean and Mindy Sterling sat alone in the Sheriff's small office when Draper stepped in. Mindy sat across from her husband looking about the same as anyone would who'd recently experienced a level of bloodshed that they didn't know existed other than in movies. Real violence tends to shock people into inaction, unable to move or react because their minds cannot comprehend what is happening. Draper could still remember the long-ago training where large numbers that could not withstand the pressure washed out. The Undersheriff's wife smiled at Draper, but it came hard, and more tears ran down her cheeks.

"I don't know what I'd have done if you hadn't been there," she said, between sobs. Sterling put his arms around her and did not say anything. Draper knew what he was thinking.

"You guys need to know this wasn't random. They weren't a couple of drunks that had stayed at the bar too long. These boys were professional killers. I do this kind of work for a living. I could see it in their eyes. That's why I shot the one holding you. I knew there was no negotiation. They were going to kill us both. I suspect though they thought I was your husband. I don't think they'd ever seen Dean.

"God, for moment there I thought you were with them and you were going to kill me," Mindy Sterling said.

"Understandable. You'd only known me a day. I had to take a shot, Mindy. I knew he was going to kill you. He misjudged how good I am. It was a risky move, but the dumbass hadn't cocked his gun which tipped the odds in my favor."

Mindy Sterling started to cry again and her husband tried to console her. Draper said, "She needs to get it out, Dean. Let her cry. She's had a rough evening. I stopped at my motel on the way over here and reserved a room for you two. Don't go back to the house for a couple of days until I can get somebody to clean it."

"Wait until the ME boys are done with it," Sterling said, always the cop.

Chapter Four

Eastern Montana

D raper was angry. He paced the length of his motel room wearing a new path in the thread-bare carpet for three hours. It approached midnight. Since sleep seemed out of the question, he checked his weapons and stepped out into the starlit night. The Lincoln was fueled as always, with the trunk loaded with armament. There was not a real destination in mind, so he drove north out of town toward the razor wire and chain-link enclosed encampment Boulton claimed was a working cattle ranch. There wasn't doubt that a few cattle lived there, but Draper felt it likely the bulk of the income came from a different source. He just did not know from what; at least not yet.

Draper parked across the highway from the entrance to the Boulton Land and Cattle Company and turned off all the Lincoln's lights. The first hour did not prove rewarding since only two cars passed his spot, neither of which turned onto the ranch road. By two a.m., he began to get bored and more than a little sleepy. Truth known, he had probably dozed, eyes half open, practice he'd learned in Southeast Asia years before. It required considerable practice and meditation training, but most trained snipers can sleep with their eyes partially open.

At ten minutes to three in the morning, two semi-trucks pulling forty-foot vans and running tandem, slowed to turn onto the ranch driveway. As Draper watched, both trucks stopped at the main gate for a couple of minutes. He could not see the drivers, but assumed they were known since the gate slid open and the trucks drove through. Draper stepped out of the Lincoln, went to the trunk and extracted his M4, laid it across the top of the Lincoln's roof and turned on the night-vision scope. He watched as the green and white lighted trucks drive past the main house and climbed a gentle slope toward the valley beyond. Draper knew from the flight he and Sterling made the day before that it contained a newly constructed metal building.

Draper put the M4 in the trunk, climbed back into the car and continued to wait. At ten after five while it was still dark, the two large trucks came out of the gate and turned north at the highway. Draper knew from watching the trailer bounce through the soft gravel they were now traveling without a load. Even before the two disappeared, four van-equipped trucks, smaller, not more than two-ton models, drove through the gate. All four continued to the highway and turned south toward town.

"I'll be damned," Draper said aloud to the empty car.

The first shades of dawn crept over Montana's landscape when Draper started the Lincoln and pointed it back toward town. On the way he dialed his cell and a grumpy voice answered, "Yeah?"

"Is that any way to treat a potential customer?' Draper said.

"If I'd a known it was you, I wouldn't have answered at all. What'd you want?" the voice said.

"You know anyone in Billings, Montana that will do cleaning?"

"Knowing you, there's blood involved. You do know that requires *Universal Precautions*, government paperwork and bullshit reports? How many did you kill?"

"Three, in a little town in Montana, called Highmore, north of Billings." Draper said.

"Cops involved?

"Yes. Do you know someone?"

"Of course I know someone. I'll have them there today sometime."

"Before noon," Draper said.

"That'll cost more."

"Of course it will." Draper gave the address.

"Get the hell off the phone so I can call."

"Nice talking to you, Pete. I appreciate it."

"Yeah, yeah, bullshit doesn't buy groceries. I'll send you a bill."

"And I'll consider paying it," Draper said, before canceling the call.

Small farming and ranching towns, like Highmore, rise early and by the time Draper entered from the North the sun had barely breached the horizon and there were already three dust-covered pickups sitting in front of the feed store. Likely strong coffee was available and agricultural talk flowed.

Draper stopped at the motel, showered, changed clothes, took a call from a cleaning service in Billings, arranged to meet them at eleven a.m. at the Undersheriff's home and walked to the Sheriff's office. Mario Lopez was manning Mindy Sterling's desk.

"You, my friend, aren't anywhere near as pretty as the lady that usually occupies that chair," Draper said.

"I know; all you get today is a grumpy old Mexican with a bad attitude. What the hell you want, Draper?"

"Dean around?"

"No, hasn't come in yet. What do you need?"

"Key to his house; I've got a cleaning crew coming from Billings this morning."

"What the hell are you, Santa Clause?"

"No, but when I make a mess, I clean it up. That is if the ME boys are done with it."

"They are, and it just so happens, I know where there is a key." Lopez stood and walked to a key lock box at the back of the room and returned with a single key. "You didn't get it from me."

Draper grinned. "What the hell was your name again?"

"Good, just keep forgetting it."

The cleaning company arrived at 10:45, a crew of three led by a middle-aged woman with a contractor's mind-set.

"You the guy?" she said.

"I am," Draper responded.

"You know we charge extra for blood cleanup, federal regulations, and all."

"I know," Draper said. "You do a good job and I pay promptly, that's the deal."

"That's one I can live with. What do you want?"

"Let me show you," Draper said.

They walked through the house and the woman made notes. "The living room rug has to go. Can't clean it with this much blood and besides can't fix that hole the cops cut into it. Same with the kitchen; those asphalt tiles allow the blood to seep down between the tiles, we'll have to take them up and replace them," she said.

"Do it. Work with the owners, Dean and Mindy Sterling, on colors and such. Put ceramic or porcelain tile in the kitchen. Anything they want in the living room."

"Gonna need some paint in the living room. Blood splatter on that one wall."

"Whatever it takes; send me a bill. Include a couple of new recliners and a couch."

"You must like these people, dude."

"I do. Oh, and change the locks, front and back to the new keyless entry type."

"We're on it, anything else?"

"Nothing, but there's a personal bonus for you it if you get it done quickly."

"You got it, here's my card."

Draper went back to the motel and slept fully dressed on the bed until after four. At four-thirty, he walked back to the Sheriff's office, returned the key to Lopez, and knocked on the wall of the Sheriff's private office. Dean Sterling sat inside staring into space.

"Those are pretty deep thoughts, my friend," Draper said.

"Hi, Draper, what have you been up too?"

"Nothing much, how's Mindy doing?"

"Better. I sent her to Billings with a friend for girl time and shopping. I hope we're still solvent when she returns. "Something tells me you haven't been idle." Sterling said.

"Some; spent the night watching the driveway into Boulton's place. It became pretty boring until about three this morning."

"Oh, yeah?"

"Two semi's with long trailers, running tandem that came from the north. Left about two hours later back north followed by four smaller vans that turned south."

"Sounds like a distribution center. Unload the big trucks into smaller trucks."

"Does, doesn't it? Question is what are they hauling?"

Sterling stared at the wall a moment before saying, "Drugs?"

"Seems likely; not much else in this world pays that well and has to happen in the dead of night. It also means these people are dangerous. I've dealt with them some and killing is a common trait."

"But up to lately, there hasn't been much. We've had more killings in the last week than we've had in the last twenty years. And you are responsible for a least half of them." Sterling looked hard at Draper. "Sorry, I'm a cop, Charlie. I'm naturally suspicious."

"No offense taken, Dean, I'd be concerned if you weren't."

"I also know that Mindy would be boxed in a funeral home right now if you hadn't been there. I'm torn between buying you a lifetime supply of beer and arresting you. It's a difficult choice."

"Know this, you are not alone. I have a cop friend in Tucson, Arizona who labors under the same burden. The good news is I've known him a long time and he hasn't arrested me yet, although he's considered it on a few occasions."

"So where do we go from here? The chances of my getting a warrant to search Andrew Boulton's property are slim to none. There's just no probable cause." Sterling said. "He claims not to know the three that came to my house so I've got nowhere to go."

"Nothing on them in NCIC?"

"Nope. It's as if they don't exist. The ME did mention, though not in writing, that he felt they were of Middle or Eastern European descent maybe even first generation."

"Russian?" Draper said when a bell rang in his head.

"He didn't say that exactly. There are lots of little countries in that area of the world after the dissolution of the Soviet Union."

"True," Draper said. "We could maybe learn something if we could get a look at Boulton's property."

"Does probable cause mean anything to you?"

"You may need a warrant, but I don't."

"Christ, don't say that! Now I have to pretend I didn't hear it," Sterling said. "You do know what B and E stands for? Breaking and entering is considered illegal."

Mario Lopez knocked on the wall and stuck his head in the room. "Dean, there's a great big black guy out front says he's Alejandro Jones, and he's looking for Draper."

"You know him?" Sterling said.

"I do. You mind if he joins us? He's with DEA," Draper said.

"Bring him in, maybe he'll arrest you and solve all my problems," Sterling said.

When Jones walked through the office door, the clearance between the top of his head and the doorjamb left little to spare. Draper stood and held out his hand. "What rock did you come out from under?" he said.

"Hard to find a decent sized one in this country," Jones said. "A little bird told me you'd pissed off half the county and if I didn't come to your rescue someone would try to plant you."

Draper laughed, "Already tried and failed. Dean, I want you to meet Alejandro Jones, biggest guy in all of DEA size-wise, but that's about all."

The two shook hands and Sterling went to get another chair. It was a tight fit in a small office so Jones ended up sitting in the doorway.

"So why are you here?" Draper said.

"Some son-of-a-bitch killed one of ours. You know we can't allow that to happen."

"Already took care of it," Draper said, "the asshole resisted arrest so I shot him."

"He was just an errand-boy. We want bigger fish," Jones said.

Draper spent the next hour bringing Jones up to speed. At noon, they moved to the cafe and continued. It lasted most of the day.

The conversation had slowed to a crawl when Jones said. "I think we should go back to the start. Whoever is behind all this has taken two runs at local law enforcement, my question is why? It seems counterproductive. Unless...," Jones paused, his eyes piercing through both Draper and Sterling, unless, its part of the plan. What happens if both the Sheriff and the Undersheriff are eliminated?"

"There'd have to be a special election," Sterling said. "Other than some law enforcement background is desired, but it's not required. Actually almost anyone can run, but they won't necessarily get elected."

"Here's what I'm saying." Jones said. "Let's say if someone wanted to have a shill in place, say as County Sheriff, the highest law enforcement presence in the area, a person that would control what laws were enforced and which ones were not. Wouldn't that be convenient for anyone running any sort of illegal operation?"

"Sounds a little like a conspiracy theory." Sterling said.

"Think Chicago here," Jones said, "only on a smaller scale, although I doubt the money involved is small. Why would they shoot the Sheriff, assassination-style at that? Wouldn't you be asking for trouble unless something else were involved?"

"Although I hate to admit you DEA boys might have a good idea, I'm beginning to see your point," Draper said. "So they, and for now we only have suspicions of who 'they' are, find a DEA agent in their midst, they've got to kill him, but the thought springs up that they could use it as a method to draw the Sheriff out in the open where our tree-line shooter can be ready. He has to take out the house owner also since they used him to get the Sheriff out there. Dead, they're both out of the way. A day later, they send three boys to eliminate Sterling because they need to force an election. Have I got that about right?"

"Why go after Mindy?" Sterling said.

"Make it look like collateral damage, or they planned a murder-suicide after a domestic dispute. In either case, they've eliminated you." Draper said. "If Jones' theory is correct, and I'm convinced it probably is that means you, my friend, still have a target on your back. You need to wear body armor at all times."

"I can take care of myself," Sterling said.

"No one can protect themselves from a trained sniper," Draper said. "With the proper equipment, which is easily available today, I could take you down from a mile away. Five hundred yards would be like shooting a whale in a backyard swimming pool from fifty feet."

Sterling looked at Draper and said, "I'm not sure why, but I believe you. I'm just glad you're on our side."

"Believe me when I say, if we are dealing with anything like the Mexican drug cartels, they have shooters as good and maybe better than me, and a lot younger with better eyesight," Draper said.

"You're scaring me," Sterling said.

"I hope so, my friend, you need to be scared. Go about your business, but I want you to be careful. Don't go anywhere alone; don't go outside without body armor on and be aware of your surroundings. Better yet, always have either Jones or me with you. Last of all, have Mindy do all the same things. One of the ways to get to you is to get to her. You know it, we know it and they know it." Draper emphasized every word while looking straight at Sterling.

"Amen," Jones said.

After dinner, with Jones registered at the now crowded motel, Draper retired to his room. They knew it would not be dark until almost ten pm. Eastern Montana's long summer evenings delayed darkness for an hour or more after sunset. Draper set his alarm for nine-thirty and promptly dozed off. He woke during a dream where Molly Henderson, the Sheriff of his home county in Arizona, his long-time friend and sometimes lover stood in the crosshairs of a sniper's scope. He could not reach her before huge bloody holes opened in her uniform blouse. Draper's eyes blinked at the grimy ceiling of his motel room with his body soaked in fear sweat. He glanced at the clock and saw 9:45 pm. He rose and went into the bathroom and turned on the shower. He stood twenty minutes letting hot water pound his face in an effort to wash away the nightmare. It only partially succeeded.

Jones stood by the Lincoln when Draper opened his motel door. He was dressed in camouflage-colored tactical clothing in contrast to Draper's dark t-shirt and blue Levi's.

56

"DEA must have a bigger budget than us independent folks," Draper said.

"Nothing but the best for us field folks," Jones said, "Got to have something to hide my masterful physique."

"Right, I forgot about that."

"Still the same plan?" Jones asked.

"Yeah, I've got nothing better. Let's go poke around and see what develops."

"I love poking around; makes me feel like a real detective. Like a big, black Sam Spade."

"Never work, Spade was a big, blond, white guy," Draper said.

"You sure? Bogart was short and dark."

"True, but in Dashiell Hammett's book the real Sam Spade was blond. Don't think you'd qualify."

"You're spoiling my fun, Draper."

"Hopefully we'll generate some fun before the night is over."

Draper drove beyond the entrance to the Boulton Land and Cattle Company about a mile where the tall fence made a corner and went west. A county road, gravel, but decently maintained paralleled the fence for a quarter mile before turning north. Draper pulled into a grove of Quaking aspen and killed the motor.

"Looks like as good a place as any," Draper said.

"It does," Jones said.

Draper opened the trunk and exposed two customized M4A1 carbines equipped with suppressors and night-vision scopes on the Picatinny rail. "I think it wise for both of us to be armed and wearing body armor."

"Nice, you have two of everything?"

"Just in case I have to work with an ill-equipped government guy on a tight budget, I carry extras," Draper said.

"I like a brother that comes prepared even if he's a honky."

"Glad you approve. How do you feel about walking? I figure it's a mile or so over that ridge."

"You mean there's no subway? Damn that's harsh." Jones lifted out the second M4, racked the slide to fill the chamber, and pushed the safety on. "Let's ride, cowboy," he said, "looks like a good night, moon's up and we won't need night vision equipment."

The walk took them southwest until they were in sight of the fence where they turned due west and began climbing the low hills. An hour later, they topped the ridge and found an opening in the trees where they could see down into the valley. Between them and the new metal building, the terrain sloped gently to the valley bottom, which was flat and forested with second-growth mixed Ponderosa pine and Douglas fir. On the west were steeper grades similar to the surrounding foothills. The east half of the valley extended a little over a mile south, Draper estimated, treeless and looking very much like a gravel-packed runway.

"Am I crazy or does that look like you could land a plane down there?" Jones said.

"Sure does look like it," Draper agreed.

'So, what you think we have?"

"If I was going to guess, I'd say something to do with drugs. Still, it smells of something else, because it appears too sophisticated for a run-of-the-mill drug operation.

"I've spent most of my career chasing two-bit drug dealers and the occasional heavy hitter, but getting close to the real operation is hard. There is so much money involved they can buy anything and bribe anyone they want with dollar amounts that would stagger the average person. In addition, those that won't play ball they kill without thinking about it. Cost of doing business."

"I know," Draper said.

They sat in silence several minutes, each puzzling over the sight before them. Draper was deep in thought when Jones said, "What the hell is that?"

"What?" Draper said his train of thought interrupted.

"Listen."

Draper listened. The mid-sized, two-engine executive jet sailed right over their position, wheels down on final approach to the open area below them. Suddenly, landing lights shone illuminating a mile-long runway. The jet, with full flaps down, slipped the plane sideways to lose altitude and line up with the runway. Draper could see two puffs of dust when the main gear touched. The plane dropped forward onto the nose wheel as the pilot applied brakes and came to a halt a quarter mile from the trees. The engines powered up and the plane did a sharp one-eighty degree turn and taxied back toward the big metal building.

"Son-of-a-bitch, nice landing," Draper said.

"How likely do you think that's a registered airport?" Jones said.

"Not likely at all. Whoever that pilot is, he had to have done that before. And he knew exactly where that runway was so they didn't need to turn on the lights until he was on final."

Both men watched the activity until Jones said, "That looks like criminal activity to me."

"It makes me want to get a closer look. My guess is whatever they are dropping off won't take long because he can't be off the radar very long without arousing suspicion. What do you bet they're dropping something or someone off and they'll take off again before long?" They switched on their night vision scopes on the M4s and watched the plane taxi up to the building.

"I'd give my left nut, but it would disappoint too many fine young ladies." Jones said.

"And who besides your mother and your sister would care what you did?"

"The numbers would stagger your white brain to numbness."

"Damn, and here I am without my cowboy boots, forced to wade around in bullshit."

When the jet came to a stop alongside the metal building, three men exited the aircraft and walked toward two others waiting. As soon as the men cleared the steps raised and closed. Draper and Jones watched as the plane taxied toward their end of the runway, turned, did a fast run-up, and began its takeoff roll. Midway on the runway the plane rotated, rose off the ground and disappeared into the night. Seconds later the runway lights went off.

Chapter Five

Boulton Land and Cattle Company - Eastern Montana

The sight of Pablo Elugardo Caldaron gave Andrew Boulton a twinge of fear. He could not help it since Caldaron, as head of the *Luces del Norte* cartel, was a man to be feared. Headquartered in the province of Tamaulipas, Mexico, Caldaron's reputation rumored that he personally killed more than fifty men, some of whom were his own family members. On the positive side, his organization was capable of supplying a wide variety of high quality drugs in quantities that made Boulton's greedy heart pound. He had made a deal with the devil he knew, but the devil paid well and gave him access to any number of young women willing to satisfy his carnal desires. His frequent trips to Eastern Mexico were always memorable. Caldaron stepped off the plane followed by his two bodyguards, a couple of hard-looking men, armed and able. They walked toward Boulton and Joey Diez, Boulton's ranch foreman.

"*Señor Caldaron, Pablo, mi amigo*, it is a pleasure to have you here," Boulton said, offering his hand. Boulton had hired a teacher to help him master Spanish, but despite the woman's best efforts, Boulton was a less than the average student and his limited Spanish sounded like a novice American. He learned most of his awkward language skills from Diez. Diez was useful that way and because he

61

was a tough ramrod and did not mind disposing of an occasional problem; bovine or human, it didn't matter.

"*El placer es mío, señor Boulton, ha sido un viaje largo y tengo sed y hambre,*" Caldaron said, pumping Boulton's hand and smiling, not because he liked the man, but because he had turned into a valued customer. "señor Díez," Caldaron added.

Boulton's limited Spanish allowed him to interpret the thirsty and hungry part as well as knowing that hungry included more than food and drink. Boulton had invested a tidy amount in a Billings prostitute venture that allowed him to import women from all over the country. It was a business enterprise that came in handy whenever Caldaron visited. "Come, my friend, we will drive down to the house, dine and enjoy the evening. Tomorrow is soon enough for business," he said.

After dinner, Boulton and Caldaron met in Boulton's study with the two bodyguards standing by the door. They started with glasses of forty-six year old Glen Garioch whiskey. Boulton watched as the older Mexican took his first sip.

"My friend, you have excellent taste in whiskey," Caldaron said.

"It comes from northern Scotland. Only three hundred twenty-eight bottles were released and I have five of them."

"What was the cost?" Caldaron said. "If you don't mind my asking."

"Not at all; it was comparatively inexpensive for fine whiskey, only twenty-six hundred a bottle. I have two bottles of The Macallan Fine and Rare Collection, 1926. It's sixty years old and set me back thirty-eight thousand a bottle. I propose we share one of the bottles when our little project is complete.

62

"It would be my honor, *mi amigo.*" Calderon said. "That brings to mind the purpose of my trip to your fine location. Calderon peered into his glass and let a moment of silence creep over the room before he spoke. An expert in using quiet as a form of intimidation, he said, "Some of my constituents have concerns."

"Concerns?" Boulton said avoiding the Mexican's eyes and looking into his next sip.

"The people who are helping us with finances are not happy with the delays."

"Just who are these people? We have always trusted one another, *mi amigo.* Why is it you come to my house and tell me you have crawled into bed with someone else? This is not like you, Pablo."

"The American government has made transporting product across the border much harder. Our revenues are down. Someone, we believe to be an American, destroyed millions of *pesos* worth of equipment down in Hermosillo that was destined to complete the southern project. In addition, we are yet unable to obtain land in Arizona. You can see why our northern project has taken on new importance."

"You surprise me, Pablo. I was under the impression this deal was between you and me. Now you tell me you have constituents. So tell me, my friend, who are these people and why do they have a say in our business?"

"I cannot."

"I'd say you'd better or I will have to take actions that neither one of us would enjoy. Take another sip of my fine whiskey, Pablo, and share your problem with me so we can solve it." Boulton felt certain his old friend was under pressure by another cartel; a continuation of the hundred-year-long war between the different factions in Mexico. He was unprepared for Calderon's response.

"They are Russian and they are very dangerous."

"Jesus Christ, Pablo!" Boulton said. "What the hell were you thinking jumping into bed with those assholes?" Boulton said nothing about his own Russian heritage.

"We've been doing it for years. At first it was only another source of financing; a way of growing our business. It just got bigger and bigger and when they offered to finance the southern project it seemed an easy way to go.

"How much do you owe them?" Boulton asked.

"Right now, with all the losses of the construction equipment, about two billion in American dollars. It is a small matter that we must deal with, but it hinges on our success here."

"That is a Texas-sized debt all right." Boulton said, enjoying Calderon's discomfort. He knew the estimates of cartel revenues ran near thirty to forty billion each year, but it was not all profit, and the cartels didn't work together, so some were doing better than others. If the *Luces del Norte* cartel owed the Russians two billion, he could see where they might be a tad concerned. Boulton's pleasure lasted for several moments until he realized his old friend was asking for help. Boulton felt himself rise to a position of power. Possibilities began to float through his mind in waves, supported by obscene amounts of tax-free cash and eager young women.

"There's another concern which is important to us. How are you doing helping our people control law enforcement in your county? We know from long experience that a hand in local politics greases the wheels of opportunity."

Boulton took a sip of his whiskey to give himself time to think. He rolled it around in his mouth savoring the taste, a light, peated mixture, with strong floral elements and deep, complex woody and earthy flavors that gave him a heady feeling. He plotted his next move carefully since he knew his companion was capable of most any act when provoked. Boulton leaned forward looking straight into the devil's eyes.

"Listen, Pablo, we are very close to gaining control of the local law. The Sheriff is dead and his chief deputy is a youngster with little outside training. He will soon suffer the same fate. Then we'll bring in our man. As for your other problem, I can see where it might be possible to assist you with financing the northern project in a way that may help you get out from under the foreigners."

They talked late into the night until the effects of good whiskey set in and Calderon's thoughts ran to carnal pleasures instead of business. Boulton knew the man well and was prepared. He had arranged things by bringing in two young women from his Billings establishment, both of whom he was positive would keep his friend busy for the night. The guest room's whiskey supply stocked, though not with the finest blends, but with those good enough for an already intoxicated guest. Boulton felt confident the night's activity would mellow his old friend's humor by morning. Boulton himself retired to his room alone, his mind running faster than Olympic sprinter, piecing together the beginnings of a plan that would result in his wrestling control of the northern project from his Hispanic guest. He did not sleep until the plan was rock solid and bulletproof.

At dawn, near five in the morning in Montana because of daylight savings time, Boulton rose and made coffee in his expansive kitchen. Making coffee stretched Boulton's culinary abilities, but after some experimentation, he could produce a reasonable product that most foreign guests would recognize. Coffee made, he laced his cup with good quality brandy at the fifty percent level, added coffee and moved to his office to drink it. During the night, he had put together a scenario wherein he could raise the necessary cash to fund the northern project. It involved a small group of acquaintances with more money than good sense. Players in financial transactions that bordered on risky but with obscene payoff possibilities, these individuals, had money to burn and dabbled in anything that would turn a buck. Boulton knew some of them personally, had slept with a couple of the female members, and knew he was dipping into dangerous waters. Risk was an aphrodisiac to most of them, a drug of arousal that was intense when you won and potentially fatal if you lost. By nine, a.m., he had raised two and a half billion on the phone with a handful of potential investors waiting in the wings.

Calderon was in the kitchen when Boulton went to refresh his coffee at nine-fifteen. The man looked like a hard-rode horse with Cushing's disease. "Pablo, my friend, how was your night?"

"Ah, Andrés, tengo que decir que la animación era el mejor de tus putas hasta la fecha. I was very pleased. Where do you find such women?"

"We are very selective for our best *amigos,"* Boulton said. "I believe I have good news this morning. What would you say if I took over financing of the northern project for, say twenty-five percent of the future profits?" Boulton watched the change in Calderon's eyes. He expected friendship to die when business rose. The old Mexican had negotiated with the best and his icy eyes brought tightness to Boulton's stomach.

66

"That is a kind offer, señor Boulton," he said, his words even, but there was no mistaking the threat, "however; you mistake me for a fool. Twenty-five percent is robbery. I should cut out your heart, but alas, you have been my good friend for many years. In order to live, you must accept no more than fifteen percent."

Boulton looked at the two bodyguards standing nearby with their right hands near concealed weaponry. He knew he was playing a dangerous game, but he also knew he could not give in too quickly to intimidation least he look foolish.

"You must be aware that I too, am not a fool. Why would I attempt to negotiate with the most famous and dangerous cartel leader in Mexico with nothing more than words? My man in the next room has the crosshairs of his .308 Winchester planted on the middle of your chest. You or your men even twitch and you will be dead. I'll take twenty percent because we are good friends."

The corner of Calderon's mouth rose ever so slightly. "I should have known, *mi amigo*, that you would be an asshole about business, but shoot me as you will, I cannot accept anything more than sixteen. My *constituyentes* would have my head on a plate if I did."

"Only because of our friendship I'll split the difference with you. Eighteen and we remain friends. Otherwise, you'd better send for your plane and figure out how you are going to settle up with your Russian buddies without my help. I will let you leave, but don't come back if the Russians let you live." Boulton put a hard edge on his answer knowing the old Mexican would only respect tough.

It had taken a long minute before Calderon answered and when he did, he grinned wide. "Andrew, you have learned. You negotiate much better than you did. Eighteen it is. Of course, I will expect the same treatment as always whenever I come to visit."

"I would give no less for my old friend. This afternoon after lunch, you shall see our distribution facilities. We've expanded to accommodate the increased supply load when the northern project is complete."

Boulton spent the afternoon showing Calderon around, highlighting the new expansion and improvements he had made in both distribution and handling. "Once the northern project is complete we will be able to move four to five times as much product into the states. Demand in the big metropolitan areas increases exponentially every six months with no end in sight. The new entitlement culture the government is promoting creates many new customers daily. We estimate that, in ten years, more than fifty percent of the U.S.population will be at least casual drug users in one form or another."

"Amazing," Calderon said, mentally calculating the cartels cut of the profits. "If what you say is true, *mi amigo*, we both will be very wealthy men."

"That's what the game is all about, Pablo."

After dark, near midnight, the same executive jet set down on the runway outside Boulton's new distribution building and the Mexican cartel leader and his two body guards climbed aboard. Once inside Calderon turned and stuck his head out the door. "Goodbye, my friend," he said, his voice low, even and cold. His eyes narrow slits of dark threat, he continued, "We have known each other many years and worked business together that has been mutually beneficial. I trust it will continue, but know that if you fuck with me I will kill you like a dog; painfully and slowly."

Boulton waited until the door closed before he muttered under his breath, "Asshole." His expletive floated away covered by jet noise.

***

Draper and Jones dry camped on the hill above the new metal building for two days. For the most part, the days were unremarkable other than the small trucks moved in and out of the building after the larger semis sat a couple of hours at two loading docks on the south end.

"Best guess?" Draper said.

"Without actually seeing the product, I'd say they are probably repackaging something into smaller, easily saleable quantities. Likely the smaller trucks are headed for larger metropolitan areas." Jones said.

"Likely destinations?"

"I'd say probably Denver first, then Chicago; stay on the Interstates, because it's faster, less chance of being noticed."

During the afternoon of the second day, Draper was able to take a high-resolution picture of Boulton's visitor. The distance made it grainy but with luck, they could find a lab that could enhance it enough to enable identification. He planned to email it back east as soon as he could get access to a computer.

"Now what?" Jones said.

"We wait and see if the jet comes back. I'd really like to get the tail number of that plane. That would help us find out where it's registered."

"My guess would be Mexico."

"I agree, but the number would give us a lead on ownership, though if I were a betting man, I'd pick some dummy company and a post office box," Draper said.

"You've been at this too long. You're getting cynical."

"No, realistic."

They spent until dark taking turns dozing. An hour and forty minutes after dark, shortly before midnight the jet roared over their hiding place and landed on the runway as it had two nights before. Draper and Jones were instantly alert.

"Suppose they are going to pick him up?"

"I'd bet on it." Draper snapped half-dozen pictures of the plane at different angles but could never get enough light on the tail.

"Damn," he muttered, "Just not enough light."

They watched the jet fast taxi up to the metal building, stop, and open the cabin door to allow the passenger to enter. There was a short discussion between him and the man on the ground before the door closed. The plane immediately started another fast taxi, lined up with the runway and began his take-off roll.

"You notice he doesn't spend much time on the ground?" Draper said.

"Yeah, why is that?"

"My guess, he's trying to avoid being off the radar for very long. That probably means he is from out of the country and not supposed to be landing here. Probably has an assigned altitude that hides him behind the mountains at least part of the time so they won't notice."

"Wouldn't doubt it," Jones said, "In my experience for every move we try they have a counter-move. We are hindered by we have to be legal and they don't."

"Nice part about being independent. Don't worry about that so much anymore."

"I've noticed that; makes me jealous."

"I sure would like to get a look inside that building," Draper said.

As they watched, a line of people left the building followed by armed guards. A group of ten by Draper's count walked single file down the road toward a group of smaller buildings that looked like railroad cars. Draper remembered similar units used long ago for Gandy dancer quarters by the railroads. They were like crowded bunkhouses with limited facilities.

"What the hell?" Draper mused. How'd we miss this last night?"

"Because nothing moved last night?"

"What does it look like to you?"

"Illegal workers come to mind," Jones said.

"What if the fence is to keep somebody in as well keeping others out?" Draper said.

As they watched, the line moved toward the cabins and looked as if small groups of two or three entered each building. Draper could not see for sure, but it appeared locked doors followed.

"I'd say they are using illegals to process the drugs into smaller packages. You see any children?" Jones said.

"No, too dark to distinguish between male and female, but based on size they look mostly female."

"You suppose they're trafficking in drugs and people?"

"I'd bet on it," Draper said. "The two go hand in hand."

"We need to get in there."

"And how do you propose we do that?"

"I don't know. You are the fire-eatin' white boy. You tell me.

"Right now I haven't a clue, but chances are when I think of something it won't be legal."

Several minutes of silence ensued. Draper rose and walked over to the fence after looking carefully in both directions for signs of cameras, infrared detection equipment, or anything out of place that might indicate a perimeter detection system. He could not see anything obvious, so he took out his keys and tossed them gently against the chain-link. Nothing happened. He stepped back to where Jones stood.

"So, now what?" Jones said.

"We wait and see if anyone comes to investigate. My sense is they likely spent all their money down by the highway and they supposed no one would bother to climb clear up here."

"And if someone comes?

"We'll know they're very careful and gaining access is going to take an army."

"And if they don't?"

"We go back to town and get a couple of shovels and dig under the fence."

"Dig?"

"Don't worry, I'll help. First we look for a likely spot. Somewhere the ground dips, even a little and they went over it without worrying about lowering the fence; someplace that wouldn't require a whole lot of digging."

"Okay, suppose we get in, and I assume we are going to try to get those people out, then what?

"Likely ICE will deport them. Better than being slave labor and maybe we get some intel on what the hell is going on in there."

72

They waited an hour. No one showed up or acted as if they had any interest in the fence. The moon rose and gave them enough light to explore. The terrain consisted of alluvial gravels deposited deep in ancient times by the Laurentide Ice Sheet flow; the same flow that eventually formed the Missouri-Mississippi river basin. Tightly packed clay and multi-sized gravels over granite bedrock would make excavation under the fence challenging, if not impossible. Draper knew they had buried the bottom of the fence to preclude digging underneath, but he did not know how deep or if they'd adjusted for minor terrain differences. It made him question whether his idea had merit. He concluded it did not matter; they had to try. At two in the morning, they began a slow careful walk following the fence east toward the highway. They slowly lost elevation until they reached a small saddle where the terrain made a change to uphill for a hundred yards or so before continuing down. About halfway, there was a dry creek-bed. It was obvious the grade change had presented a challenge to the installers and they had cut a triangular patch to cover the stress relief seam that ran up about six feet. Draper guessed the fence under the seam and over the dry creek was not very deep. That was his hope. He found a two-foot tree branch to use as a digging tool and began scraping the deposited creek bed gravel away. In minutes, he found the bottom.

"This is it," Draper said. The gravels here will be smaller and water-borne; should be easier to dig."

"I may be dumb, but why not just cut the wire? I'm pretty sure a good set of bolt cutters would do the trick," Jones said.

"No doubt, but they'd know in a heartbeat if they walked the fence that someone had cut it, unless...," Draper hesitated, studying the fence.

"Unless what?"

"Maybe we could just cut out the patch." It would be a little tight for you and me, but someone smaller could slip right through. Might have to dig down a little for the two of us, but it would be a lot less, and much faster. Then a roll of steel tie wire would repair it like new and they'd have to look close to see that it had been disturbed. I like it.

"Don't sound so damned surprised. I went to college, too, you know; even played basketball."

"Of course you did, being tall and all." Draper grinned at his friend.

"Next time we find a hoop I'll show you how it's done."

"You're on. But for now I suggest we get the hell off this mountain and come back tonight with wire cutters."

"Lead the way, chief."

It took over an hour to pick their way down the mountain through heavy brush and tall pines. The vegetation created dark shadows hiding the uneven ground. By the time they reached the Lincoln, both men were brush-wiped and tired.

"Being stealthy is a lot easier in the city." Jones said. "Dumpsters and garbage cans are a lot easier to see in the dark." And there are no biting insects and critters with big teeth."

"We didn't see any critters with big teeth," Draper said.

"Maybe not, but I'm sure they're out there. Every movie I've seen about the west has them."

"If you see one, no problem, just shoot his ass."

"Shut up and drive."

Chapter Six

Highmore, Montana

At noon the next day, Draper went to the Highmore hardware store looking for wire cutters and a roll of electric fence wire. The store was well-stocked considering the town's size and he found what he was looking for. Outside, his purchases tucked under his arm, Draper stood on the dusty main street watching the day's activity. His view included a regular round of long-load grain trucks dragging pups and pickup trucks with wiry-looking ranch workers. Their vehicles were mud-covered and cow-dung smeared. Body-dents were common with beds stacked with extra wood corner posts, barbed wire, steel tee posts and fencing tools. The men were either young and strong or old and bent from years of hard labor. In both cases, they walked tall and proud. The pace was steady, but not fast, as if time did not matter. Draper drank it in, enjoying what he saw and how easy they made it look, even though he knew, the work was long, difficult, and hard fought.

"You look deep in thought," a voice behind him said.

"I'm enjoying the town," Draper said to Mindy Sterling when he turned to see her standing in his shadow. "The peaceful facade masks what I know to be a difficult existence."

"It's not so bad. These are good people and fun loving. The hard work is just part of it."

"How are you doing, Mindy?" Draper asked, knowing the kind of near death experience she had sometimes left a detrimental mark on the recipient.

"I'm better; the first few days were difficult, but I have a great husband and he helped me through it."

"He's a good man, Mindy."

"I know that. However, I owe you my life. I understand that, too."

"No, you don't. I just happened to be there."

"That's my quandary. I've always hated violence. I had to accept a certain amount because of Dean's job, but he's never had to kill anyone."

"It might happen, though it's not likely. Many cops go through their entire career without ever drawing their gun. It's not so true anymore though."

"Would you buy me a cup of coffee? I'd like to talk to you."

"Absolutely," Draper said.

They walked together the short distance to the cafe in a pregnant silence. Draper was not sure what Mindy Sterling had on her mind, but he was certain she needed some convincing that violence, while to be avoided whenever possible, could, under some circumstances, be the only option.

The cafe was empty and Draper led the way to a corner table. A bored high school-aged server with wild pink highlighted hair, an arm tattoo and facial piercings in places that made Draper cringe, pounced on them with menus in hand.

"We just need coffee," Draper said.

The server returned shortly with glasses of water followed by dark black coffee. When they were alone Draper waited for his companion to start the conversation. She stared into her coffee cup several minutes. "I'm sorry to bother you with this," she said, her eyes welling with moisture and she dabbed them with a paper napkin. "Dammit," she said, "every time I open my mouth I start to cry."

"Nothing to be ashamed of," Draper said. "You had a traumatic experience, takes time to get beyond it. It helps to talk about it."

"I know." Mindy Sterling stared at Draper until he began to feel uncomfortable.

"Tell me what's bothering you," Draper said.

"I don't really know, I guess. Dean likes you a lot. He says you saved my life in a way few people could have. For some unknown reason, I need to understand how you could do that."

Draper debated a moment before telling her an edited version of the truth. "I was trained by the government a long time ago during the cold war. We were ordered into in places and situations where it was kill or die. The reasons were simple. The other person was the enemy. They taught us to kill in many different ways. Using weapons was only part of it." Draper stopped when tears began to roll down Mindy Sterling's face. "I'm sorry, but you asked."

"Have you ever told anyone else?" Mindy said.

"No, it's not something I want everyone to know."

"What about your lady friend, the Sheriff."

"We've never actually talked about it. Probably she has guessed some of it."

"You should tell her."

"I think her problem is her law enforcement experience. She's torn between loving me and arresting my ass. It's not an unusual problem for cops I know. I'm not sure Dean doesn't think that way."

"I believe I know how they both feel," Mindy Sterling said, her voice soft, almost a whisper. "I like you a lot, but you scare me about as much. I'm a happily married woman, with a husband who treats me like a princess; but occasionally, if I wasn't and he didn't, I might spend a bit of time wondering what it would be like to sleep with you."

"I'm going to take that as a compliment," Draper said.

"I meant it that way," Mindy Sterling said. "You've helped me understand. Thank you."

Draper watched her leave the cafe. He could not help a twinge of envy for Dean Sterling. His lovely wife had sand she only recently found. She held her head high, her back straight and did not look back; walking as if she was going to take on the world. Draper had no doubt she would.

The high school server came back and asked if he wanted more coffee. "Yes," Draper said, "and bring a menu. I think I'll have lunch." Draper was half through with his burger and fries when Jones walked in.

"There you are. Thought you'd died or something. Get a pair of wire cutters?"

"I did. It's been a busy morning. Between shopping, watching the natives, and entertaining a pretty lady. There's no rest for the wicked."

"I figured the first two. Tell me about the pretty lady," Jones said.

"I was standing innocently on the street when she propositioned me."

"In your dreams; I don't believe that for a second," Jones said.

"Alejandro, my friend, you know I wouldn't shit you."

"Yeah, only if you were alone or with somebody; who was she?"

"A gentleman doesn't tell," Draper said, enjoying the moment. "How about I buy you lunch instead?"

"Thought you'd never ask," Jones said.

Draper and Jones both returned to the motel after lunch to get some sleep. Draper stared at the ceiling thinking until four in the afternoon. He had not come to any conclusions and finally set his alarm for ten p.m. and went to sleep.

The alarm blared in his ear what seemed like only minutes later. Draper showered, dressed, strapped on his shoulder harness, checked the Glock, slipped into a windbreaker jacket, and stepped out into the night. It was fully dark and the northern lights blazed across the north horizon. It was a dazzling sight, one that he had not seen in years and he stood and enjoyed it a moment before knocking on Jones' door.

"'Bout time, dude," Jones said through his open door. "Thought you'd overslept."

"You ready or are you going to stand there and bitch at me all night."

"Of course, I'm ready," Jones said, "been waitin' on you."

Their travel followed the same circuitous route and took them to the grove of aspens where they parked previous night. By the time they were set the moon was up, though waning and the night seemed darker. Geared up with body armor, handguns, and an M4 carbine each, they started picking their way up the mountain. At ten minutes before midnight, they stood at the fence a little higher than their destination. They both spent another twenty minutes glassing the compound around the new metal building. No signs of activity appeared.

"Looks quiet; I hope we aren't wrong about what is going on down there," Draper said.

"I don't think we're wrong. I've seen a lot of drug operations and this one stinks of it. Even if it isn't drugs, I'd bet something illegal is going on.

"You up to a little look-see?" Draper said.

"That's what we came for. I've already tossed in my penny, so I guess I'm in for the pound."

"No law enforcement quandaries, misgivings?"

"Hell, no, I've been working undercover for years. I'm pretty used to doing whatever I want, even some things that might border on illegal," Jones said.

"Every killed anybody?"

"Yeah, in self-defense," Jones said, his eyes narrow slits in the dark. "Why?"

"How about on purpose?"

"None I'll admit to," Jones said.

"Good answer. I had to ask. We need to know we can depend on one another. We may get into a situation here where it might be needed."

"I'll follow your lead. You can depend on it."

"I knew that," Draper said, "just wanted us to be clear on it."

They followed the fence back to where they found the patch earlier. Draper used the wire cutters to surgically remove the patch and stashed the roll of electric fence wire in a rotted out fir downfall.

"What's that for?" Jones said.

"It's a roll of electric fence wire. We use that to repair the fence when we're done and hopefully they won't notice someone's used it to enter the compound. Confuse and mystify the enemy is rule number one in the covert handbook."

"There's a covert handbook?" Jones said.

"Sure, there is; the Feds have a handbook for everything. Also tells you how to wipe your ass with leaves when in-country."

"Dammit Draper, I find it hard to figure out whether you are bull-shitting me or giving me the straight skinny. A little less white-boy vernacular would be appreciated."

"Sorry, my friend; I'm not used to working with someone other than DeCollado."

"So where is that old Apache anyway? I thought you two were tied together like Siamese twins."

"Silly ass went and got married to the mother of a young woman we rescued from the cartels a few years ago."

"No shit?"

"Nope, he's sixty years old and never married; fell harder than an old tree in the forest. She's a little monied and last I heard they were gallivanting all over the world on a honeymoon. Nice lady though, long-time widowed and a little stiff, but he'll cure her of that."

"Well, good for them," Jones said.

Draper cut the last tie wire and the patch fell away leaving a triangular-shaped hole that looked a little tight for a couple of beefy Americans.

"You expect me to wiggle through that little hole? I'd get stuck and have to lay there helpless until some no-account bad-guy comes along and shoots my ass," Jones complained.

"That's why we brought along the GI shovel." Draper set the army surplus multi-purpose tool at ninety degrees allowing him to use it like a scraper. Dragging it toward him, he removed several inches of forest duff, skimpy topsoil and another four inches of tougher gravel subsoil until he was satisfied both them could shimmy through.

"Damn, you are multi-talented," Jones said, "You must have been a Boy Scout."

"The rewards of a misspent youth." Draper said.

"Someday you'll have to tell me about it. I thought only us black kids got into trouble."

"You didn't have a corner on that market."

"So, tell me," Jones said, watching Draper on his back, sliding under the fence using his elbows and feet to push himself through.

"We must have been about ten or so I guess and a friend had a grandfather who owned a beer distributorship. It was located on the main street of the town we lived in. The old man sat at an elevated desk in the narrow office area and one day he decided he could save money if he hired us kids to unload the semi-trucks full of cases of bottled beer. He offered us five cents a case; so on Saturdays and Sundays we'd unload beer. Well, the work of throwing cases of beer on roller conveyors and transferring them into a big walk-in cooler got boring. At first, we only stole one bottle out of every ten or fifteen cases but after a while, we were up a bottle every five. At first we'd stash them for later pickup but our downfall came when we started drinking them on the job. The old man was huge and the only time I remember his getting out of that chair was when we started losing cases off the conveyors and breaking too many bottles. I can still remember him coming out into the warehouse, mad as hell and yelling at couple of drunken ten-year olds. Funny part was he was madder about the broken cases than he was about us drinking. We lost our unloading job. We still got to load empties, but never again the full ones."

"And here I thought you were a saint," Jones said. "I grew up on the streets of south Chicago. I was probably ten before I realized not everyone was black like me." Jones talked as he wiggled his way under the chain link fence. "I sure hope nobody's shooting at us when we return. This little effort is going to make us easy targets."

"Remember that while we're inside. Let's make sure no one follows us."

They crept up on the railroad car-type buildings first since they were closest. The first two were unoccupied, but looked lived in. Personal belongings and packsacks were stacked between crowded army surplus cots covered with a single blanket and grease-stained pillows. Skimpy living quarters, Draper thought. Draper went in first on the third one following his M4 and scanning the inside with his night-vision goggles. Half-way through, he spotted a young girl, not more than fourteen or fifteen, Hispanic, with terror-filled dark eyes, lying on a cot clutching a ragged blanket under her chin.

Draper pointed the M4 at her and said, *"Muéstrame tus manos, niña, ahora!"* The girl quickly opened her hands and showed them to Draper. He reached down and pulled back the blanket looking for weapons. He didn't expect any but wasn't taking any chances.

"¿Dónde está todo el mundo?" Draper said.

"Ellos están en el trabajo de construcción importante" the girl said.

"What's she saying?" Jones asked.

"All the others are at the new building working." Draper answered.

"Why isn't she there?" Jones said.

"I'll ask her." Draper lowered the M4 and said, *"¿Por qué no estás con los demás?"*

"Ellos vienen a llevarme a la casa de putas Billings esta noche. ¿Eres uno?"

"No," Draper said, *"estamos aquí para ayudarle".*

"Okay, fill me in," Jones said. "I can't make out a word."

"Apparently, she's waiting for someone to pick her up and take her to Billings," Draper said.

"Even I know *casa de putas* means whorehouse. We got a little white slavery going on here also?" Jones said. "Christ, these guys are making me feel a whole lot better about breaking and entering. I used to be an honest cop before I met you, Draper."

"I know; assholes everywhere, what's a guy to do? She thinks we're the ones here to pick her up."

"I'd say that means we'd better get her out of here, pretty damn quick." Jones said.

"Or, we wait and kill them," Draper said.

"What about the other Mexican workers, won't that put them at risk?"

"What else we going to do? They come and she's gone, they're likely going to raise hell."

"Good point," Jones agreed.

Draper turned to the girl and said, *"¿Cuántos aquí hay de México?"*

"Nueve," the girl said.

"¿Cuántos en su familia trabajan en el edificio grande?" Draper asked.

"Nueve," the girl repeated.

"She says all the ones in the big building are in her family; nine of them," Draper said.

"Think we can get all nine out of here tonight? That's a crowd.

"I know; a bigger challenge than we counted on." Draper looked back at the girl and asked, *"¿Cuántos años tienes?"*

"Dieciocho," she said.

"I asked her how old she was. Thought I'd better check since any woman under thirty looks twelve to me anymore. She says she's eighteen," Draper said.

As they walked to the front of the building Jones said, "We'd better make up our minds what we're going to do."

"Don't think it's going to matter, Draper said. "Here comes a vehicle. Get ready. Let them get inside so we have them in close quarters. We want to do this quietly if we can. *Ir a la parte de atrás, ahora!*" he hissed at the girl and she turned and ran to the back of the building. Draper hugged his back against the wall and watched Jones slide behind an upright wooden locker. He took two gulps of air before the door opened and the first man stepped in and closed the door. He had his back turned when Draper grabbed him around the mouth, put his knee in his back and broke his neck. He slumped to the floor without making a sound.

"Jesus Christ, man, you kill him?"Jones hissed.

"That's what I tried to do. He left his friend outside; couldn't take a chance on him calling a warning. Get the girl while I take care of number two."

Draper stepped outside to a four-door Dodge pickup. The driver sat smoking a cigarette. "Hey, who the fuck are you?" the man said.

Draper needed to get a few feet closer so he said, "Your partner wants to try the girl out, you know, kind of initiate her to what's coming, easy like."

He'd almost reached the truck when the man said, "I don't know you, what the...!"

Draper reached through the open window and grabbed the man's shirt front and yanked as hard as he could. The effort slammed the man's head into the window jam and gave Draper time to open the door and drag the stunned man out where he could finish the job.

When he looked up Jones and the girl were standing outside the cabin door. "Let's drag the other asshole out here and make it look like they got into over the girl. Maybe the others will waste time looking around for her while we get away," Draper said, trying to catch his breath.

"Remind me never to get you pissed-off," Jones said. He stepped back into the shack and returned dragging the first body outside and dropped him near the driver. "How's that look?"

"As good as we can make it." Draper said. "Let's get the hell out of here and let the dust settle. While they were walking Draper explained to the girl who they were and where they were taking her. Draper was making up it as he went along since her presence and situation needed a complete change of plans.

"What are we going to do with her?" Jones asked.

"I'm working on that, but right at the moment I haven't a clue. All I know is we can't leave her here. I'm hopeful we can get outside the fence, repair the patch and get to the Lincoln before someone sounds the alarm."

"Damn, it's no wonder DeCollado went off and got married. Probably tired of savin' your ass."

Once they were out of sight of the railroad shacks, Draper stopped. Turning to the girl he said, *Quédate aquí. Vamos hacia el edificio de metal grande y ver si podemos encontrar a su familia.*"

"*¡No! Quiero ir con usted,.*" she said.

Even in the moonlight, Draper could see fire in her eyes that emphasized the determination in her voice.

"What?" Jones said, seeing the conflict between Draper and the young girl.

"I told her to wait here while we check out the big building and see if there is any way we can get the others out. She thinks she should go with us."

"Mind of her own, huh?" Jones said.

"Appears so, she seems pretty determined," Draper said. "Dammit, she's a problem and I don't see how we can get her and nine others out of here without some of them getting killed. Even one gets hurt and we can't risk the others to try and help them."

"Looks to me as if we don't have a choice," Jones said. "How about this, you stay here with the girl since you can talk to her. I go down to the building wearing my natural disguise so no one will be able to see me in the dark. I check things out and see what we're up against."

"Then what, you take on the whole crowd by yourself, as the Lone Ranger?"

"Hell no, though back in Chicago, one black against five white boys was just about even. Now that I'm educated I just text you on my phone and you come help me clean up."

"It's a good thing this young lady can't understand bullshit, she'd think you were just as crazy as I do."

"So, things go bad, you take her and light out of here." Jones stood and disappeared into the dark before Draper could reply.

"*¿Adónde va?*" the girl asked.

"*Él va a bajar al edificio grande y ver si podemos sacar a su familia,*" Draper said, responding to her question about where Jones was going. He told her the truth. He assumed Jones would look for a way to rescue her family. He did not have high hopes, even considering that Jones had proved to be a tough son-of-a-bitch in many ways. Draper doubted he could kill indiscriminately. He knew from experience it needed a special mindset and substantial training; unless, of course, you were a psychopath. As Draper remembered it, the psychopaths washed out early.

Chapter Seven

Northeastern Montana

The next hour was excruciating in Draper's mind. Time seemed not to move at all. The young girl sat quiet, staring at the large metal building below them as if she could somehow will her family up the hill. She hugged her knees wearing a thin cotton dress printed with flowers. It looked washed-thin and faded. Her long black hair fell across her face and she repeatedly tried to get it to stay behind her right ear. Under better circumstances, she would have been pretty, but on that night, she looked tired, helpless, and pathetic, yet Draper could see the hardness in her eyes. She shivered and Draper took off his windbreaker and handed it to her. She stared at his shoulder holster filled with Glock.

"*Gracias, señor,*" she whispered while putting on the jacket, "*¿Por qué haces esto?*"

She asked him why he was doing this and Draper took a moment to answer. "*Lo hago porque hay que hacer.* I do it because it needs doing," he said, noncommittal. "*¿Cuál es tu nombre?* What's your name?"

"*Maricella Abeja,*" she said.

"Well, Maricella Abeja, my name is Charlie Draper. *Bueno, Maricella Abeja, mi nombre es Charlie Draper.*" Draper stuck his hand out and she cautiously reached for it. She gripped it and gave him a bashful look before releasing it though she continued to stare at his face as if trying to read his eyes. Whatever she saw, it pleased Draper when she gave him a small hint of a smile. Then his cell phone beeped. When he looked at it, a text message read "Need interpreter."

Draper said to the girl, "Come on, Maricella, my friend wants us." She stood and took his hand without question and Draper lead the way down the hill toward the metal building. At the tree line he stopped, scanned the open ground he could see surrounding the building. There were not any doors on the side in front of him so he turned to Maricella and said, "Wait here, *espere aquí.*"

"*No,*" she said and gripped his hand tighter.

"Okay, but stay behind me. *Está bien, pero quédate detrás de mí.*"

There had not been any shooting so Draper had shouldered the M4 at the top of the hill. As a precaution, he drew the Glock. Maricella's eyes widened, but she followed tight behind him as a shadow. He quickly forgot her and concentrated on the corner of the building. He stopped with his back against the wall and checked around the corner. About seventy-five feet away, a walk-in door stood open. He took his phone out and texted Jones' number with "Where are you?"

Thirty seconds later his phone beeped and the text read, "Come on in, I left the door open."

When Draper stepped through the door, he quickly scanned the building while Maricella ran passed him toward a group of Hispanics seated on the concrete floor with their hands clasped behind their necks. The tall black man standing over them smiled at the girl as she ran to an older man and cried, *"Padre!"*

90

Draper walked over to the group. *"Usted puede poner sus manos hacia abajo. Somos amigos y nos vamos a salir de aquí. Debes darte prisa. Deja todo lo que no se puede llevar en sus manos."* Draper told them they could put their hands down, and that they were friends. He added they could take only what they could carry. A mixed group, male and female, old and young, they were dressed in thin work clothing, little defense against the cool Montana nights. When he asked, he learned they came from El Salvador. Behind the group where stainless steel tables, designed for commercial kitchen use, but here used to re-pack drugs. There were neatly stacked piles of baled marijuana, shrink-wrapped packages of different kinds of powdered substances Draper guessed were cocaine, heroin, and others. When he picked one up it sounded crunchy and he knew, the piles included the crystalline form of methamphetamines. In addition to being a well-equipped drug factory, the far end of building housed two long loading docks, capable of handling long vans while hiding the big trucks inside. Overhead doors down masked the unloading. The size of the operation staggered his imagination.

"This is without question a high-dollar business and the owners are going to be kill-crazy pissed when they discover their workers gone," Draper said to Jones. "Let's round them up get them to hell out of here. Any resistance?"

"Two that won't be waking up in the morning," Jones said.

Draper made no further comment as they pushed the group out the door and up the hill through the trees. It was a bit like herding cats, Draper mused since the group was ill prepared for a nighttime walk in the forest in a foreign country while frightened. Both Draper and Jones tried to spread them out so they wouldn't leave a trail a blind man could follow, but their efforts were hindered by the need to hurry. The duff and pine needle covered forest floor was slippery and both men worked at picking up the ones that fell and getting them walking again. It took forty minutes to reach the hole in the fence.

Jones scooted through first and began verbal encouragement of the group members. Draper crawled through last. Jones moved their charges back into the trees where they could not be seen and let them rest. Draper grabbed the electric fence wire and began the tedious task of repairing the hole. He felt encouraged by the lack of any sound coming from below and hoped the loss would miss discovery until morning.

They reached the Lincoln at four am. The first thing Draper did was call Dean Sterling's cell phone. When the Undersheriff answered his voice and attitude reflected a man wakened in the middle of a short night's sleep. He did not sound pleased. "What?" he barked into the phone.

"Dean, this is Draper. Sorry to get you up so early, but I need Mario Lopez's phone number."

"What for?"

"You don't want to know, Dean, just give me the number."

"Dammit, Charlie, I'm still the acting Sheriff, for at least a few more days. I ain't telling you shit until you tell me why."

Draper told him about his ten passengers though not where he picked them up. "I'll tell you the full story as soon as I can get them somewhere safe. We get caught now, there will be hell to pay, and you'll have bodies all over your county, including mine."

"Okay, Charlie, I'm going to trust you on this one since I owe you, but I'll call Mario and meet you at the Sheriff's office. I'll lead you out there since there's no way will you find it by yourself."

"We'll be there in thirty minutes," Draper said and hung up.

Maricella, with another older woman, sat squeezed between Draper and Jones in the front, while the rest sat packed into the Lincoln's rear seat like layered sardines. It was not comfortable, but no one complained, and if they did, Draper was the only one who understood. That required they speak slowly. The trip was short and he surmised they would all survive.

When Draper started the Lincoln and bounced out of the Aspen grove onto the graveled county road, Maricella said, "*¿A dónde vamos, señor Charlie?*"

"*Le estamos llevando a un lugar seguro donde usted puede descansar hasta que podamos averiguar qué hacer con usted,*" Draper said, struggling with a complicated sentence in Spanish.

"And this safe place where you are taking us is only temporary before they deport us?" Maricella said in perfect English.

"You speak English. Why didn't you say so before?"

"A woman doesn't reveal all she knows until she trusts the one asking."

"So, that means you trust me now?"

"I do; at least partially. I'll let you know when you are totally out of the woods." Maricella said.

"Any of the rest of your family speak English?"

"No. It was part of the Nun's training for girls. All of us had to learn prayers in English."

"I'm not going to lie to you, Maricella. We are going to have to turn you over to ICE eventually and they will likely send you back to El Salvador. There's not much I can do about that."

"Who is this ICE person?"

"It's a whole bunch of people anymore. It stands for Immigration and Customs Enforcement. They will probably fly you back home."

"I won't be able to stay?" Draper could hear the sadness in her voice.

"Probably not; the United States has a very complicated and antiquated immigration system overwhelmed by the number of people from countries all over the world who want to come here. Even those that do gain citizenship wait years for it to happen.

"You can't help us?"

"All we can do is save you from the mess you were in back there. When you get home and if you still want to come here, try sending me a letter in English and I'll see what I can do. No promises, only that I'll try, and it might take years. Remind me to give you my address."

"Don't worry, I will," Maricella said.

Dean Sterling sat in his county car with Mindy in the front seat with him when Draper pulled the Lincoln up behind. He got out and walked up to talk to the acting Sheriff. "Sorry to get you out of bed so early, Dean."

"It's going to take a long time for you to make it up. I haven't even had coffee yet," Sterling said.

"It's going to be light soon so let's get moving. Could you take a few with you? We're a little crowded in the Lincoln."

"Sure, Sterling said, "bring at least three, but explain to them they aren't being arrested."

"Thanks, that'll help."

Sterling was not wrong about the trip to Mario Lopez's place. Draper followed Sterling's cruiser south on the highway out of town

94

for a short seven miles. There they turned left onto an unmarked gravel road laughingly cautioned by a yellow diamond-shaped sign as single-lane with turnouts. Five dusty miles further confirmed the single lane, but not one turnout presented itself. Draper decided the prickly pear cactus covered rolling prairie on both sides gave drivers a choice of turnouts wherever needed. It did not take a genius to understand why most everyone drove battered pickups. At five miles, the road deteriorated into a two-path goat trail. A mile closer to low-lying foothills, they drove into the gated yard of a small homestead tucked into the mouth of a rock-lined gulch. The craftsman-style home, accented with a sloping front roof looked tidy, well maintained and inviting with fresh paint in a deep yellow. The other outbuildings, a small barn, chicken coops, sheds, and a metal building sat freshly painted with bright primary colors.

Mario Lopez stood on the front porch with his arm around a short, middle-aged, slightly heavy-set Hispanic woman with sparkling eyes, perfect olive skin, and long black hair.

"*señor Draper,*" Lopez said. "Estela, this is the big *gringo* I told you about. Welcome to my home," he said to Draper, Jones and Sterling.

"*Gracias por permitirnos venir a su hermosa casa, Estela,*" Draper said.

Mario's wife grinned at Draper. "*señor Draper,* based on what my husband said I expected you'd be taller and wearing a sword."

"When I call on beautiful señoras, I leave the sword at home." Draper said.

Her eyes never left Draper's face when she said, "You need to watch this one, Mario; he is a smooth talker also."

"Mario and Estela, I have a big favor to ask and if you say no I will understand. I couldn't think of anywhere else to stash the people we rescued." Draper continued to tell the story, albeit he left out the more grisly details. "These folks need somewhere safe to hide until we can turn them over to ICE. Don't worry; we'll do that in town so they won't know where we hid them."

"We can put them in the bunkhouse. That's where all the kids stayed when they were growing up," Estela said.

"Fantastic," Draper said. "The oldest daughter is named Maricella. She speaks English well and one of the old men is her father. Everyone in the group is part of her extended family. They've been held captive here locally and forced to labor in a drug distribution center just north of town."

"No shit? Here in Highmore?" Lopez said.

"You got it, right here in Highmore. Alejandro and I got them out tonight and the dealers are going to be kill-crazy when they find out. So it's important for both you and them that no one finds out where they are."

"We understand. Estela has been hiding for years. We know how to do it," Lopez said.

They spent the next couple of hours getting the group settled in. Maricella came up to Draper as they were about to leave and said, "Thank you, señor Draper, my family thanks you also."

"No thanks, necessary, Maricella. You have a big job ahead taking care of them and getting them back home safely."

Ready to leave, Draper and Jones stood by the Lincoln when Mindy Sterling walked up, her smile teasing. "Charlie Draper, you are something, a regular Lochinvar. I don't know when you have time to sleep. Rescuing fair maidens, slaying laggards and dastards at every turn, how do you do it?"

"Just lucky and I have good help. Alejandro here did most of the heavy work."

"What's going to happen to the young girl?" Mindy Sterling said, turning serious.

"She'll likely be deported," Draper said.

"Can't we do something?"

"Probably not; the best thing would require someone to sponsor her. Then maybe she could apply for what's called an F1 or a student visa. She says she's eighteen, old enough for college if she can pass the tests. She has to be at least eighteen to apply for citizenship." Draper said. "Adopting her would to speed up the process for a green card.

"Isn't there some kind of temporary visa?"

"Yes, but it's only good for six months, she wouldn't be able to work and she'd have to prove she could support herself." Draper could see the wheels turning in Mindy Sterling's head. "What are you thinking of?"

"Dean and I have been married almost ten years. We can't have children. I was just thinking."

"Think carefully, young lady. It's a long and frustrating process," Draper said. "I know because I've done it. You'll need a good immigration attorney and they don't come cheap."

"I know that." Without another word, she turned to rejoin her husband for the return to town. Draper watched her knowing she would not give up and that a bulldog was gnawing at his leg.

"Let's go back to town," he said to Alejandro, who watched without comment.

"I'm waiting on you, Lochinvar," Jones said. "So what did she mean by that?"

"It's from a poem by Sir Walter Scott, where a brave knight rescues his true love from marriage to a villain."

"Ah, that also explains the sword reference," Jones said. "Damn, Draper, you're a closet romantic."

"You repeat that in public and I'll shoot you."

"I don't know, the temptation might be overwhelming." Jones said.

"It appears the fair Mindy as been working on the temporary Sheriff."

"You think?"

"I think we should concentrate on disrupting the activities of some assholes," Draper said.

"I hear you, brother. Lead on, but first we need some sleep."

Draper woke to the sound of pounding on his door. It took a moment for him to come fully awake before he rose, and stepped across the room. His Glock and holster rig hung off a side chair. With his gun in hand alongside his right thigh, he cracked the door until the chain tightened. "What?" he said through the opening.

"Open up, Charlie, it's Dean."

Draper closed the door and unhooked the chain while standing in his jockeys and t-shirt. "Come in," he said walked back to the chair to retrieve his pants and re-holstered the Glock.

Dean Sterling stepped into the room and closed the door. "Sorry to have to get you up."

"No problem, what time is it?"

"Nearly four," Sterling said, "the chairman of the county commissioners just called to tell me they voted to hold a special election to replace Sheriff Hornsby. That goddamned Boulton talked them into it, said he's been contacted by a well-qualified candidate and wants a fair and impartial election."

"Who is the contact?"

"Says he's from Chicago; a guy named Robert Arcuni," Sterling said.

"So what's the problem? You are local, everyone knows you; should be a slam-dunk."

"There shouldn't be, but I don't trust Boulton any farther than I could throw him. He's got something up his sleeve," Sterling said.

"I know that better than anyone. He's running a major drug distribution network behind that damned fence, not to mention some human trafficking to boot. The guy's a low-life criminal."

"I'm not sure I want to know how you know that," Sterling said."

"Where do you think those Mexicans came from," Draper said. "Everything he's doing behind that fence is illegal."

"Easy for you to say, but I need probable cause to get a warrant. Chances are he's cleaned up that building and even if I could get a warrant, I wouldn't find shit."

"I know how hard it is, Dean, I'm just not used to working that way. So how do you suggest we find Boulton with his dick in the cookie jar; wait around while he dumps tons of drugs into the state?"

"How about the trucks, we could try and seize them doing something illegal, like speeding?

"Fine and dandy, they get a ticket for speeding. Where's the probable cause to search the truck? Any first year law student could get them out of that and you know it," Draper said. "A better idea would be I go out and shoot the son-of-a-bitch, drag his body outside and then you could declare the whole ranch a crime scene."

"Yeah, why don't you do that and then I'd have to arrest you. I wouldn't have to worry about Boulton, Mindy would kill me."

"Go pound on Jones' door while I get dressed. We'll go over to the cafe for coffee and food while we talk."

Draper was strapping on his shoulder harness when Sterling returned. "You got a permit for that cannon?"

"Yes, it's called Glock."

"Dammit, there's something else I have to ignore."

"Pretend you didn't see it, Dean."

"I've been pretending I didn't see a lot of stuff since you showed up."

Jones joined them and the three men walked the half block to the restaurant. The same teenager was waitressing and brought coffee without question. "Would you like menu's?" she asked.

Draper looked at the others and said, "Anyone eating except me?"

"Is the Pope Catholic?" Jones said.

The teenager looked confused, so Draper added, "Bring menus."

Draper ordered two eggs over easy, with hashbrowns and sausage patties. Jones looked at Draper as if he was crazy and said, "Breakfast? It's late afternoon unless you didn't notice."

"I just got up. That makes breakfast good anytime," Draper said.

They ate with sparse conversation. Finished, Sterling put down his fork and said, "So what are you two going to do?"

"What do you think we should do, Sheriff?" Draper said.

Sterling hesitated, looking at Draper as if he was trying to glean what he was thinking. "I'd follow one of the trucks and see where they go."

"That's what I'd do also," Draper said. "Excellent idea, we'll start tonight. The big vans come from the north. It's what, a hundred miles to the Canadian border?"

"That's about right and there's exactly nothing in between but prairie dogs and rattlesnakes," Sterling said.

Draper was silent for several moments thinking. "I think we need a road trip; see just where those large vans are coming from. A wild-ass guess says Canada, but there's a problem crossing the border. It's probably nowhere as difficult as the Mexican border, but I'd guess it ain't easy."

"Even so, wouldn't there still be a danger of catching a least a truck now and then." Sterling asked.

"That's likely," Draper said, "That's what we need to find out. I don't see any way other than following one of the empties and see where it goes."

"That sounds exciting. I'll need to go find a book to read," Jones added.

"You should be a cop. Each day filled with piles of routine paperwork and an occasional drunk. Bad guys used to be rare in this neck of the woods," Sterling said.

"I hear you," Jones said. "I worked a few years undercover for DEA until just recently."

"So, what's the plan?" Sterling said.

Draper considered how much he wanted to tell the acting Sheriff before deciding. "We park out at Boulton's place every night until a truck comes. We've put a crimp in their operation, but I don't think it will be down long. When one comes, we follow it and see where it goes. In the meantime, you start campaigning. Talk to everyone you know and convince them you are the best choice for Sheriff. Make Mindy your campaign manager. You need to raise money for signs, radio ads, newspaper ads, and all sorts of campaign materials. I'll start you out with a donation of five thousand dollars. If that's not enough, let me know." Draper pulled out his checkbook, wrote a check and handed it to Sterling."

"I don't know how I'm going to pay you back."

"You don't have to, it's a donation; tax deductible."

"Count me in for another grand," Jones said. "I'm not as wealthy as whitey here, coming from the Chicago ghetto and all, but I am willing to support you some."

"You just heard some first-class bullshit, Dean. See what I have to put up with?" Draper said.

"I don't care how he talks as long as his money is good," Sterling said. "Seriously, I thank you both."

Draper and Jones sat four nights across the highway from the entrance to Andrew Boulton's fenced enclosure. Three cars passed on the highway and nothing turned into or out of the driveway. Jones read three novels on his Kindle, sitting mostly silent while Draper alternately slept and read *Parallel Worlds* by Michio Kaku.

On the fifth night Jones observed, "We must have hampered their operation more than we thought."

"I guess so, but I still feel it won't take long for them to get back in operation. There's too much demand and way too much money involved," Draper said.

At one-thirty in the morning, the first truck appeared and slowed to make the turn. Both Draper and Jones were instantly alert. "Here's a truck," Draper said. "We got a live one."

As they watched, the truck turned and stopped at the gate. Several minutes passed before the gate opened and the truck continued into the ranch property.

"The last time it took a couple hours for them to come back out. I suggest we zip up to the Aspen grove and take a little hike," Draper said.

"I was afraid you were going to say that," Jones said, closing up is Kindle. "I was just getting to the good part."

"Time to rock and roll, Kemo Sabe," Draper said.

"I ain't no Indian brave, I'm a handsome man of color," Jones said when Draper started the Lincoln and pulled out on the highway.

"Suit yourself, cowboy, time to visit bad guys."

Draper turned at the county road and parked at the Aspen grove. They hustled over the hill to the fence and got a surprise. Armed guards patrolled the perimeter. They did not seem to pay any attention to the patch, but the timing of each watch left it only minutes unguarded. Nowhere near enough time to slip through.

"Looks like they're more careful," Jones said.

"Imagine that; it isn't like we haven't caused them grief. Let's hike farther up the hill and see if we can find somewhere to look down on the building area."

A half-hour climb put them higher up and able to see into the valley although the distance was greater. Draper estimated a quarter mile or so to the big metal building. As they watched a second large van pulled in and backed into the enclosed loading dock.

"Looks like they're back at it," Jones said.

"Seems that way, I wonder what they'll do for workers. Repackaging that much dope, would take some bodies," Draper said.

"What now?"

"We have some time, let's figure it'll take an hour to get back to the car before the second truck comes out. That gives us at least forty minutes to see if anything interesting happens."

"You have the patience of Job, my friend. Myself, I like a little more action. What the hell are you looking for?" Jones said.

"Anything that would give us information on how to take these bastards down; I don't know what that is yet but I'll know it when I see it. I learned it from DeCollado. He could sit on his haunches for an hour and study a mark on the ground without saying a word, but when he figured it out he'd lead you to whatever made it, man or beast. He can track a fucking snake through a buffalo herd."

"My early lessons ran more to jackin' cars and strippin' auto parts," Jones said.

"Good to have a trade to fall back on in case your present occupation doesn't work out."

"So what are you going to fall back on, Lochinvar?"

"No need to worry, always an abundance of bad people that need discipline," Draper said.

They had sat several minutes in silence before Jones said, "Well, look-y there; bodies."

"They imported a new crew; can't repackage without slave labor. I wonder if both trucks contain illegals."

"I'd guess probably both. They need product to keep moving also. I'll bet the illegals come packed in with the junk," Jones said.

Through a pair of binoculars, Draper watched a line of ten bodies prodded by rifle-carrying guards herded to the railroad shanties. Each person carried a small bundle of personal belongings. Best he could tell there were four women and six men, but their ages were a mystery at that distance.

"How many?" Jones asked.

"Looks like ten," Draper said.

"It seems their human smuggling activity is as profitable as drugs," Jones said.

"It doesn't look as if we slowed either one down."

Draper watched the line of bodies come closer. As they turned toward the railroad shanties, Draper said, "Shit!"

"What?"

"The last two in line look like young girls."

"No shit?"

"Not a bit; they're definitely in the right age group."

"Okay, so do we follow the girls or the drugs?"

"I think you know the answer to that question."

"Yeah, I do." Jones agreed.

Chapter Eight

Southwestern Montana

Draper and Jones were back in position an hour later. The Lincoln sat across the highway from the entrance to Andrew Boulton Land and Cattle Company behind a stockpile of winter road sanding material. Draper's wrist watch read three-forty and they sat unmoving while the two semi-vans turned north. Nothing turned south, not even any of the small vans. Draper considered it understandable since there had not been time to train the new workers to the point they could package anything. It worried him that there was no sign of the two young women. Either he had been wrong in his identification or it had been too late to send them to Billings. He felt positive that was where the two were headed. Draper's research of the local area told him Billings had long been the state's largest metropolitan area and served a huge area of farm and ranch country as well as being an industrial center. Oil refining and coal mining flourished, as well as many supporting industries. Until the early nineteen-seventies, a wide-open red-light district woke at dusk and did a brisk business serving miners, tradesmen, and businessmen alike. At that time, the city drew a line in the sand and forced the local law to shut it down. Like many blue-law efforts, it only moved the industry underground. By the turn of the century, as with most major cities in the new drug-fired culture, prostitution was alive and well.

"You don't suppose we erred in our decision?" Jones said.

"I don't know. I expected them by now though."

"Not too late to find the trucks if you stick your number twelve shoe into the carburetor."

"Let's wait a bit longer. Besides, cars don't have carburetors anymore," Draper said.

"I know that. I was boosting cars when you were just a babe in the woods. Know all about cars. That's called a figure of speech, in case you didn't know."

Draper ignored the barb. "Grab the atlas out of the door pocket and figure out how far it is to Billings. It'll be light in a couple of hours. That'll make it easier to follow them. I'm still hoping they'll show."

Jones was deep into calculating the mileage when Draper saw the gate open and a new-looking pickup sped through and turned sharply south on the highway. "Here they come!" Draper said.

As the pickup turned onto the highway under the lighted Boulton sign, Draper could see a male driver, a male passenger and two females in the back that appeared to be slumped against the doors as if sleeping. "Two assholes and two females in back; looks as though the women are drugged."

"I agree," Jones said, studying the pickup through the windshield. "Give them some space and let's go get them."

Draper waited until the taillight glow disappeared before pulling out onto the highway. When he punched the Lincoln, it jumped forward. At ninety miles an hour, he eased up and held it there until he could see the taillights again. Then he backed off and

108

settled in at a speed that matched his quarry. He wanted to lie back far enough so that his headlights would not be obvious. He hoped they would disappear on curves and hills in case their quarry was watching. He doubted they were that observant, riding as they were, complacent with two easy scores in the back seat, but he erred on the side of careful. Draper hoped it would make them careless. In fact, the idea beginning to to roll around in his brain, counted on it.

"How far is it to Billings?" Draper asked.

Jones opened the atlas and studied it for a few seconds before replying, "About hundred-fifty miles."

"It's near dawn, think they'll go the whole way tonight?"

"Hard to say, but I'd expect a stop, especially if the girls are drugged."

They drove better than forty minutes, though a dark and quiet Highmore, south into prairie country following the taillights of the quad-cab pickup. The highway swerved and dipped and the taillights appeared and disappeared with the terrain. The up and down, curved road fitted Draper's liking. It reduced the possibility that they would be spotted. At one point, a buck antelope jumped across the road in front of them causing Draper to brake hard. The animal only visible for an instant caused his heart to speed into overdrive.

"Shit, that was close," Jones said, "freakin' wildlife."

"An inch is as good as a mile," Draper said.

"If it's all the same to you, I'd prefer the mile."

An hour into the chase the highway made a sudden ninety degree turn onto a concrete overpass. In the dark Draper could not see what they were crossing, but assume a river or railroad tracks. Coming down the other side they passed a darkened bar coupled with a six-door building and a lighted neon sign that said BAR-MOTEL.

They almost missed it because Draper floored the accelerator when he couldn't see taillights in the distance. They came down the far side of the bridge approaching a hundred miles an hour when Jones said, "Hey, isn't that them at the motel?"

Draper glanced to his right and saw the two men walking toward the motel as if they already had a room reservation. His next response was braking, forcing the petal under his foot to pulse as the anti-locking feature held back the pressure. The Lincoln slid to a stop half in and half out of a fresh-mowed barrow pit.

"What?" Jones said when Draper opened the driver's door and jumped out.

"Need to get something."

Jones turned to watch Draper open the trunk, reach in for a second, and then gently close it. Back in the car, he withdrew his Glock and screwed on a suppressor. "Don't want to wake up the neighborhood," he said, "in case those assholes beg to be shot."

"Good plan, but then you get all the fun."

"You had your turn last time. Now it's mine."

Draper did a u-turn in the highway. The surrounding hills were prominent now as the sun began to chase away the night. By the time they returned to the motel the pickup was empty and they saw one of the men push a staggering young woman into unit number four.

"Looks like we're just in time," Jones said.

Draper turned the Lincoln around and backed in next to the light tan Dodge Quad-cab they had been following. He looked at Jones and said, "Ready for fun?"

"I'm following you. I want to see Lochinvar at work. Got your sword?"

"I do."

110

"So how do we get in?"

"I have a key."

"Really and where did you get that?" Jones said.

"Always take it with me."

"This I have to see."

"Look in the jockey box for a cloth-wrapped set of tools." Draper said.

"Jones looked and handed Draper the set. "This?"

"Yup," Draper said. "It's a master key to any older lock."

"Damn, you have all sorts of illegal talents."

Draper stepped up to the door and listened. The television, on loud to mask unusual noises, told him it would also cover his picking sounds. The old and well-worn lock allowed his slow rake of the pins to catch all eight on the first try. He put his hand on the knob, turned it and held it before looking at Jones and mouthing, "Ready?"

Jones nodded, withdrew a Smith and Wesson .45 auto, and Draper readied the silenced Glock. Then he pushed the door open.

The room had two double beds, a common arrangement with a bath, and one ass-worn wingback chair. An old television sat on a long dresser across from the beds. The decor was dated, stained and wafted the sour odor of unwashed occupants. The two young women lay each on the beds. Both looked as if they were sleeping. One man sat on the edge of the right bed lighting a joint with a wooden match. His friend stood next to the left hand bed holding the other woman's blouse and a surprised look on his face. He tried to pull a revolver tucked in his belt. Draper shot him, the Glock making a snapping sound, and the man stepped back against the wall. He stood only a second before slumping to the floor leaving a long, red streak on faded paint. Draper swung the Glock right until the second man filled his sights. The sweet smell of marijuana filled the air and its affects slowed the man's reaction time. His judgment impaired, his right hand moved awkward toward a chrome plated revolver on the bedside table. "Don't," Draper barked and when the hand kept moving his second bullet caught the man mid-chest.

"I don't know what you needed me for," Jones said. "Next time, I'll just wait in the car."

"Always good to have backup," Draper said. "Come on, let's carry the young ladies to the Lincoln and get the hell out of here." Draper took a minute to grab the first young woman's blouse and replaced it as best he could. It was not neat, but she would wake up covered.

"Don't have to ask me twice," Jones said.

Draper removed the suppressor from his Glock and holstered it. The suppressor slipped into his pants pocket. They had to carry the women out to the Lincoln as neither could walk. The one Draper held moaned and tried to struggle in his arms before falling limp again. With both in the car, Draper locked and closed the motel door after wiping both sides of the knob with his handkerchief.

"We are just going to leave them there?" Jones said, as Draper pulled out of the motel parking lot and headed back north on the highway.

"They'll be found soon enough. We're in a different county and I doubt the locals are going to look very far. Probably chalk it up to a drug deal gone bad. Since that one guy was smoking a joint, it's likely there's junk in the room somewhere."

"You think of everything, don't you?"

"Only way to stay alive," Draper said.

"What are we going to do with the two in back?"

"Much as I hate to, we'll have to dump them on Mario and Estela, at least temporarily."

"You're pushing your luck with them aren't you?"

"Probably, but we don't have a choice. If Boulton finds out where they are, it's likely, he'll act on it. He's got too much at stake."

"So, why don't we go shoot his ass?" Jones said.

"Believe me, I've considered it. I can't help thinking though there's something else afoot here that we're not seeing. We shoot him and in a week there will be a replacement."

"Like what? Aren't drugs and prostitution enough?" Jones suggested.

"You'd think so, but something's nagging at me and I can't put a finger on it."

"You sure you aren't over-thinking all this?"

Draper did not answer. He mulled it in his mind and much of what Jones said made sense. He pointed the Lincoln up the winding highway, his mind whirling trying to sort out what they knew. He could not shake the feeling, roaming around deep in the musty, cobwebbed reaches of his brain somewhere, that he had missed an important point.

"Doesn't it seem strange to you that they are taking a huge risk bringing in large quantities of illicit drugs and feeding a prostitution ring with young Hispanic women, just for the money?"

"Money fuels most crime. Believe me I've seen my share of drug dealers, killers and genuine punk-asses," Jones said. "Mostly it's about power, money and self-gratification; pretty basic."

Draper did not reply for over a mile. He looked back at their passengers to see the one he carried out of the motel staring back with dark eyes filled with moisture. He reached down and hit the child safety lock on the Lincoln not wanting one of their passengers to try to jump out. The girl's hair, dark with natural red highlights fell across a deep brown face reminding him of Central America. Two or three more years and she would be a beauty unless life robbed her of it. Draper hoped not, but considered it possible. Born in poverty, uneducated and unsophisticated to the realities of what she was facing, her chances on merely surviving, were slight. Draper pulled into a wide shoulder and stopped.

He turned to the girl and said, "*No te hará daño. Le estamos llevando a un lugar seguro. ¿Cuál es su nombre?*"

"What did you say to her?" Jones asked.

"I told her we wouldn't hurt them and that we are taking them to a safe place. I also asked her name."

The girl did not answer and instead grabbed the door handle and tried to open it. When it did not move, she started to cry. She sobbed quietly, barely emitting a sound as if the realization that her situation was hopeless made itself clear. The other girl still slept when Draper put the car in gear and pulled back onto the highway. "Don't think we're going to get anything out of her until we get to Mario's."

"Damn, you are a perceptive son-of-a-bitch, son," Jones said.

Over the next half-hour, Draper could feel the girl's burning hate on the back of his neck. She stopped crying and when he looked back she met his eyes with cold disgust and it made him thankful she didn't have a weapon.

"It's pretty obvious she thinks we're the enemy," Jones observed.

"Yeah," Draper said, "probably be a good idea to have Estela talk to her before we chance letting her loose."

"I think she likes me, but you, she wants to shoot," Jones said.

"I know; must be that gentle, fatherly image you have. More likely she remembers me putting her blouse back on and doesn't know who took it off."

Draper slowed when he thought he was close to the turnoff to Mario and Estela Lopez's home and almost missed it. Hard braking saved him from backing up, but not from a hard turn. Full daylight from a low sun sprinkled shadows across the landscape making the surrounding mountains stand out in relief. The forested slopes looked different from the bare Sonoran granite up-thrusts Draper loved, but each had their own unique magnificence. He wanted to stop, sit on a rock, and study the scene.

Once on the right road, the path led him straight in as there were no other possibilities that did not involve bouncing through the prairie. Mario stood by his pickup dressed in his Deputy Sheriff uniform. Keys in hand, Draper guessed he was about to depart to town and another day. Draper pulled up and stopped, rolling his window down.

"Why do I think I'm going to be late for work this morning?" Lopez said. He scanned the back seat without comment.

"Because you probably are going to be," Draper said.

"Think we should get Estela out here?"

"That would be wise."

Draper had hit the unlock button when he got out of the Lincoln more from habit than any other reason. Out of the corner of his eye, he saw both their passengers exit and the one who painted the back of Draper's neck with hate stares bolted, running full out, barefooted into the sagebrush covered prairie. Jones grabbed the other one and Draper jumped out and took off after the one running.

She had a twenty-yard head start. By the time he caught up to her, he felt five yards beyond winded. She whirled and hit his left cheek with a closed fist hard enough to hurt. Stumbling back, she tripped over a tall sage and fell flat. Draper, on his knees, because of the surprise blow and sucking in prairie dust, grabbed her left foot and held on while she tried to kick him. He lay there trying to catch his breath until Mario appeared.

"We're here to help you, Chiquita, we won't hurt you," Lopez said. "Don't be afraid." He repeated it in Spanish. *"Estamos aquí para ayudarle, chiquita, no te hará daño. No tengas miedo."* The girl lay in the dirt, her lower lip sucked in. Her tears, large and wet, became small puddles in the prairie dust.

Lopez looked at Draper and smiled. "Your cheek is bleeding, *mi amigo.*"

Draper stood and wiped his face. It felt sore and he guessed it would only get worse as the day progressed. "Tell her she'd better behave or I'll paddle her ass."

"No, you can tell her," Lopez said.

"I can't talk to her right now, I'm too damn mad at her. I do admit she's got some spunk." Draper rose and held out his hand to her and waited for her to respond. It took a couple of minutes before she reached up and took it. They walked back to the Lincoln and she stood defiant, her butt against the car's fender when Estela arrived.

"What are you men doing scaring these poor girls to death?" Estela Lopez said. "Come with me, girls. *Ven conmigo, chicas.*"

Draper watched Mario's wife lead the two young women back to the house. Halfway, the one that had slugged him turned and looked back, staring at the three men standing in deep prairie grass and scattered purple sage. She did not smile and her dark eyes were blank, almost unseeing. Draper hoped Estela could ease her back to trusting men again, but figured it might be a long, uphill road.

"*Buon Dio*, Charlie, you certainly like to stir up the ladies," Lopez said. "Want to tell me about it so I have an excuse for being late today."

"We had a choice to follow either the trucks or the girls, so, naturally we chose the girls." Jones said when Draper did not answer.

"Did Dean tell you what's going on at Boulton's place?" Draper said.

"He did when he promoted me to Undersheriff."

"Congratulations."

"Only temporary, all of us will out of work if he doesn't win the election."

"So, I guess we'd better make sure he wins," Draper said.

Draper slept until his alarm went off at ten pm. Silencing the noise, he studied the motel room ceiling while his mind inventoried the last week. His stats, even though he took points for rescuing the young women, came up short. It was apparent the drugs and human trafficking came in from the north. That suggested Canada, but he needed to know how they were transporting both across the border. Draper knew Canadian law differed in some respects from U.S. law, and they were dealing with a population one-tenth the size of the US. He felt it possible the new Canada Border Services Agency's responsibility for five thousand five hundred miles of common border stretched staffing thin. The border from Minot, North Dakota to Havre, Montana on both sides of the border ran mostly to rolling prairie and a sparse population of occasional roaming wildlife. That said it did not seem plausible that a continuous flow of unmarked trucks would not raise suspicion at any of the border crossings. Yet neither country had sounded the alarm. He continued his musing through a stinging hot shower, shaving, and a two-minute tooth scrubbing. Frustrated by a lack of progress, Draper dressed, hung his shoulder rig on, and filled it with Glock. He wanted coffee and food, but knew he would be going without since the restaurant closed at nine.

They sat two nights behind the gravel pile, watching a complete lack of activity on the road into Boulton's ranch. Boulton himself left and returned once during the first night, turning toward Highmore and coming back hours later. When dawn came the second morning, Draper sat discouraged by a lack of progress. Not a single car, truck or lost antelope used the driveway all night.

"Want to throw a bomb over the fence, just for fun and to get something moving?" Jones said looking up from an inch thick novel on his lap.

"Anything would help," Draper grumbled.

On the third night, they were in their chosen position a little before midnight. The first two hours mirrored the previous nights and boredom set in for both men. Jones read and Draper stared at the fence. Shortly after one am, a single truck appeared on the horizon driving a reasonable speed and slowed at the Boulton Land and Cattle Company turnoff. An unmarked forty-foot hard-side van pulled by a Volvo semi truck, identical to the ones they had watched before, it rolled clouds of prairie dust before stopping at the security gate. With only a moment's hesitation, the gate opened and allowed the truck to pull through.

"Want to bet on another one?" Jones said.

"You couldn't give me enough odds to bet against that; how about fifteen minutes or less on a second truck for a beer?"

"Only one beer? Hell, how about a six-pack?" Jones said.

"Okay, a six-pack it is."

Seventeen minutes later by Draper's watch the second truck arrived. They watched it mirror the first one and move through the security gate moments later.

"You owe me a six-pack, and don't try to make it cheap stuff either," Jones said.

"And you'd know the difference?"

"Of course I would," Jones said, "my mamma raised me to appreciate a sensitive palate. I allow only the best to cross my tongue. We going to sit here and wait or what?"

"Don't see much to be gained by going to look. We know the fence is being patrolled. Let's concentrate on where the hell the empties are going."

"You da boss man," Jones said.

Chapter Nine

Northwestern Montana

Following the second truck north required the same caution as tracking the two young women south. Draper stayed far enough behind so that his headlights appeared and disappeared with terrain changes. Highway 191 ran north through rolling pine-covered hills interspersed with undulating prairie and low glacier-formed moraines. Sight distance ran short due to the undulating terrain and Draper increased his speed in order to ensure he did not miss a turnoff. He knew they were approaching the Missouri River at the upper end of the Fort Peck Lake. The Missouri, in its relentless effort to move water toward the Gulf of Mexico, had, over eons of time, carved rugged, deeply engraved terrain on both sides of the main channel. Known as the "Missouri River Breaks," the Breaks extended hundreds of miles across mid and eastern Montana making an effective travel barrier between the northern and southern halves of the state. A bridge on Highway 191 is the only Missouri River crossing for a hundred miles in either direction.

An hour later, and less than five miles short of the Canadian border, they watched the truck turn onto a gravel two-lane road and disappear into the dark.

"Now what?" Jones said.

"I don't know. He's going to see us on that road and lead us around all night if he hasn't already."

"Okay, so what if we just wait a while. The amount of truck traffic they are causing should show up on the road. We follow the road that has the most use."

"Since I don't have a better idea, that somehow makes sense." Draper said.

They waited a half-hour before proceeding. Draper slowed their advance so as not to miss a turnoff in the dark. It turned out there were not many and following the most traveled route became obvious. At daylight, they had progressed about twenty miles roughly west of the highway turn off the highway. The road deteriorated to a single lane with prairie grass turnouts. They stopped at every junction and most showed rare usage.

The sun rose behind them showering the endless prairie with morning shadows. The grass and sage went on forever until it disappeared over the distant horizon. Strangely, Draper saw the view as captivating for reasons that escaped him. It did look as if not a single living thing moved in any direction.

After an hour of daylight, they had followed the road first northwest then southwest where the path made a confusing sudden switch in direction. After some discussion, they agreed it was because they were following an old wagon road and the crossing of deep gorges occurred only when the terrain allowed. Modern traffic followed the same route since it required minimal excavation cost. Back up on top the road turned due east. They inspected every turnoff and all were grass-covered and looked years without use.

"How far do you think it is to the Canadian border?" Draper said.

122

"You're asking me? You forget I'm a city boy. When we haven't seen a building in hours, I'm lost. I can tell you this, in another hour and this black Lincoln is going to require a wash job because of all the alkali dust."

"If you're a city boy, how do you know what alkali is?" Draper said.

"I got passed the third grade; I can read, you know."

"Right, my mistake," Draper said and went quiet. He braked the Lincoln, stopping in the cloud of white dust that had been following them. When it settled, the road straight ahead reduced to two tracks through prairie grass and the traffic turned north into a barbed wire fenced compound that contained a large metal structure and nothing else. They could not see activity so he continued forward driving slow so as not to make an obvious trail until they were out of sight of the gate and the building. He felt nervous that the car would stick out to any casual observer, but there was nowhere else to hide.

Draper pulled over into a wide area and with a little effort turned the Lincoln around for a quick getaway. Despite these efforts, he felt trapped.

"You know we're sitting ducks if anyone comes down this road and doesn't turn into that compound," Jones said. "You think it might be wise to have a couple of those fancy M4's of yours up here handy, just in case we have company?"

"An excellent idea," Draper agreed. "We may not win but it would be good to take a few bad guys down with us. I also think we should take turns watching the building until dark. Never know what might happen."

They both stepped out and walked to the rear of the vehicle. Draper extracted an M4 and handed it to Jones. He lifted out a second one and closed the lid. "I'm going to walk back and take the first watch."

"What kind of critters they have around here?" Jones said.

"Not much," Draper said, "rabbits, prairie dogs, an occasional coyote and, of course, rattlesnakes."

"Rattlesnakes?"

"Yeah, prairie rattlers can reach five feet in length. If you see two and they're discussing eating you there or taking you home, run like hell."

"Don't like snakes," Jones said.

"Just be careful where you step."

"That's everywhere, for Christ sake," Jones said.

"About right," Draper said. He left the car and walked the hundred yards or so to where he could see the metal building. Resting the M4 on a wooden fence post, he scoped the building and the area around it. His estimate of the distance to the structure ranged about two hundred yards and it duplicated the one at Boulton's ranch. There were two large overhead doors on the narrow side facing the gate and a walk-in door on the same side at the east corner. None of the doors stood open. Draper watched for two hours and saw nothing. Nighttime appeared the only period when there was activity. After two hours, he walked back to the Lincoln.

He woke up his friend when he opened the door. "Well," Jones said, "see anything?"

"Not a thing. I think we need to get into that building after dark unless you see something on your watch."

Dark in Montana's summer does not happen until after nine in the evening and by then both Draper and Jones were fighting boredom. They switched positions four times each and neither saw

124

any activity around the building. "Not a very productive day," Jones observed.

They waited in the car until eleven to allow the moon to shed enough light that they could avoid using night-vision equipment. Their initial approach required a little planning since there was sparse cover between the barbed wire fence and the building. They could only hunker down in the tall grass and hope the truck drivers were not very observant. At midnight, a truck arrived. Lying in the grass Draper studied the truck.

"Okay," Jones whispered "is he loaded or empty?"

"Near as I can tell, he's empty."

"And you know this how?" Jones said.

"I'm looking at the trailer's overloads. He's got an air ride overload system with a walking beam. The air system doesn't seem to move much and the whole trailer bounces when he's empty. Loaded heavy the walking beam would move more. We'll have to compare it to when he leaves."

"Where'd you learn all this shit, cowboy?"

"Misspent youth," Draper said.

The next hour dragged. Draper was reminded of the hours spent watching a target, waiting for exactly the right moment. Sometimes it took hours, even days. He had learned patience and the ability to sit motionless while scanning the killing field. He had not thought about it for years, but this night brought it to mind. He did not have a clue why it did since the prairie bore no resemblance at all to the jungle.

At thirty minutes passed one a.m. the left overhead door opened and the truck pulled out. Watching the overloads it was obvious to Draper that the truck was loaded heavy. The right side walking beam moved up and down yet the van body stayed level. After the truck had cleared opening, the door closed. The driver pulled forward to the gate, got out and opened it, drove through, stopped and returned to close it. With the gate secured, the driver re-entered the truck. The two observers watched the semi disappear down the road.

"He was definitely loaded," Draper said.

"If they are loading drugs here then some other trucks must be bringing the stuff in, right?" Jones said.

"That would be logical. The question remains how are they getting it across the border?"

"You got me on that one, my friend. What do we do now?"

"I want to get inside that building, but we have to wait for the second truck." Draper stared at the building as if willing it to tell him something. He received no response. "Does something bother you about an hour and a half the truck was inside?"

Jones did not answer immediately. "Is that some sort of trick question?"

"No. Think about it. It's a forty foot van. Do you see any vehicles around?"

"What's that mean?" Jones said, "Maybe they park inside."

"I guess that's possible, but why would they? The purpose of that kind of building is to warehouse something. Worker bees would usually park outside."

"Maybe with some sort of mechanical devise, such as a forklift, I suppose an experienced operator could load the van in an hour and a half. It would have to be palletized and ready to go."

Almost immediately, the second truck arrived, running empty, Draper concluded, since the trailer bounced on the rough road coming in. Everything was a repeat of the first truck. It came in empty and left heavy.

As soon as the truck's lights disappeared down the road, Draper moved. "Sit tight. I'm going to have a look inside." He set the M4 against a sagebrush and rose to a crouch and ran back to the Lincoln to retrieve his pick kit. He was back in minutes retrieved his rifle, and approached the walk-in door on the building. The door mechanism was a newer branded model, well-made and tight. It took Draper ten minutes to get all eight pins one by one, enough time to discourage the average burglar. When he turned the handle and pushed the door in, he saw a large dark room with what looked like a twenty by twenty-foot concrete cube twenty feet high sitting in the center. Automatic security lights at each end of the building cast shadows on an immense concrete floor marked with forklift tracks. Otherwise, the building sat empty. It startled Draper since he expected to find a building full of palate loaded drugs.

Since he could see the building was empty, he did not waste time or risk capture by entering. Instead, he relocked the door and pulled it closed. He signaled Jones to follow him and they returned to the Lincoln.

"Completely empty, how could that be?" Jones said, in response to Draper's announcement. They sat in the front seat watching an aurora build over the eastern hills as the morning sun began its climb in the sky. "It'll be light soon; I suggest we shag and find a motel to hold up in for the day. We come back tonight and watch again."

The second night was a repeat of the first. Two trucks came in empty and left appearing loaded. When Draper checked the building, it was again empty.

"That can't be," Jones said.

"You are right," Draper said. He did not express it, but the reason began to build in the back of his mind. Problem was, he would need proof to get anyone to believe it.

***

Andrew Boulton sat in an imported red leather armchair with his feet elevated on a matching ottoman. He wore private label, buffalo calf cowboy boots that set him back nine hundred dollars a pair. This set was one of ten in his closet. His right hand held an etched highball glass filled with an amber sample of one of his expensive Irish whiskeys, two fingers, no more. He sat across from a large man, middle-aged, work-hardened with enormous rough hands. The man squinted as if the light bothered him and his dark eyes showed no emotion. Boulton did not like him, but his talents were useful. His abilities included being a cold-blooded killer. Robert Arcuni would not have been Boulton's first choice, but when offered by the Chicago group it seemed prudent to accept. He liked whiskey, but in Boulton's eyes, the man was a lout and would not be able to tell the difference between quality bourbon and homemade rotgut. Boulton cringed every time Arcuni took a deep swallow instead of sipping like a true gentleman. If he had been able to get away with it, Boulton would have furnished the man cheap house brand booze.

"This goes down smooth," Arcuni said, "I suppose you paid better than a hundred dollars a bottle for it."

"More like a couple of thousand," Boulton said. "I asked you here tonight because I want you to understand our goals here."

"Fire away," Arcuni said. "I'm listening."

"You have two tasks; win the election, which means you have to convince the locals you are the man for the job and you will bring law and order to the county. Second, dig up anything you can on this Draper character and get rid of him."

"Does that mean kill him; just so we're clear?" Arcuni said.

"It does, but you make it look like there's no connection to our operation here. We tried to trap him at the Undersheriff's house, but that didn't work. You can do it any way you want, but make sure it is done before the election that is set for a month from now. We can use that to point out Sterling's incompetence at maintaining law and order. In the meantime, I'll be working on the local ranchers and farm owners. There are less than a thousand registered voters in this county and twenty percent are over sixty-five. We don't have to convince that many."

"Don't make the mistake of underestimating small-town conservatives," Arcuni said. "I was raised in the Midwest. There's nothing dumb about them."

"You let me worry about the locals. You get rid of Draper."

"From what I've seen so far, that might be easier said than brought to fruition." Arcuni said. He rose from his chair and placed his empty drink glass on an antique candlestick table without a coaster. "Don't you underestimate me, either, Boulton. I'm here to do the job. I take my orders from a lot higher up than you and if they'd sent me here to kill you, you'd be already dead."

Arcuni left, leaving Boulton alone and fuming. His anger directed more at himself that at his departed guest. When the Chicago boys had shown interest in his operation, he knew he making a deal with the devil. What they did not know was that they were a means to an end, not the final solution. Now he was not sure it had not been a mistake. He sat back in his five thousand dollar leather chair after pouring himself a fresh couple of fingers of first-class Irish whiskey and made a call on his smart phone.

***

Darchin Kazarian slept less than an hour when his white Apple iPhone, played an acceptable rendition of Verdi's La donna è mobile at three-thirty am, New York City time. It took effort to beat down the effects of an evening of fine bourbon and lengthy sheet wrestling before answering. The blond of the day, or was it an hour, since he was not sure and couldn't remember her name, lay face down trying to block the phone noise with a pillow. Darchin Kazarian had come to the United States on a student visa in 1999. He had not, and never intended to, attend school. The visa expired in 2001 and Kazarian made himself at home. By 2005, he headed an organization that controlled most of the drug and human trafficking on the east coast and he had begun to expand into the Midwest and had an extensive interest in Chicago. Nearly everyone in his upper management came from middle-eastern European countries. Most were illegals and involved in the crime business in one form or another. All were trained assassins and had little qualms with murder when necessary. "What!" he growled into the phone.

"This is Boulton, Darchin, we need to talk," the voice on the phone said.

Kazarian considered Boulton smart, ruthless and cold-blooded, all traits to his liking. The man was a distant cousin a number of times removed, and brought up not far from his own home. The man had middle European blood and upbringing, which made him a logical co-conspirator. They had common goals, with power and money topping the list. Boulton regularly sent large quantities of American dollars, which Kazarian knew was but a fraction of Boulton's total take. However, it added nicely to the master plan like a well-used glove. Boulton also kept his New York dealers supplied with high quality drugs and properly trained whores that sold as well as Grandma's hotcakes. Those efforts put bundles of American dollars in Kazarian's pocket. As long as it continued, Boulton could ask for any favor.

"Andrew, my friend, you sound stressed," Kazarian said.

"The boys in Chicago are getting a little big for their britches. The dumbass they sent here to run for Sheriff is uncooperative. He seems to think he's running the deal." Boulton said.

"You want us to eliminate him?"

"No, that would be inconvenient. If that resolved the situation, I'd have done it. I would prefer that someone from Chicago has a talk with him and let him know who runs things. I've spent considerable time, effort and money to make sure local law is on our side. Mr. Arcuni needs to understand that I'm the sovereign of this little part of the world and one word from me would result in his sudden demise."

"Andrew, as long as you continue to do your part, we are happy to honor your request. Is there anything else?"

"No, Darchin, as always we agree on what is best for everyone. You must come visit my humble home. I can offer the finest in Scotch whiskey, comfortable surroundings, and first class entertainment."

"Ah, my friend, I have read much about the American west, with its wide open spaces and sky that goes forever. We get the project completed and I will take you up on your generous offer."

Kazarian punched the end on the phone and immediately dialed another number. The voice that answered stumbled over the greeting as someone newly awake.

"Yeah, what!" the voice said, raspy from sleep.

Kazarian spent less than a couple of minutes describing what needed doing. The man on the other end confirmed the message and hung up. "Asshole," Kazarian mumbled.

"What?" the blond said next to him.

"It's nothing, honey, just business, nothing important that would interfere with you and me having a little fun."

"Again?"

"Damn right, again; the night ain't half over."

Chapter Ten

Eastern Montana

Draper and Jones drove back to Highmore in daylight, arriving at the cafe in between breakfast and lunch. They ordered coffee and Draper called Acting Sheriff Dean Sterling and invited him to join them.

"Okay, if I bring Mindy?"

"Absolutely," Draper said.

Draper and Jones had both downed their coffee by the time the Starlings' arrived. They all ordered lunch and while waiting, Draper outlined the last couple of days to the acting Sheriff.

"There's got to be a way they are getting the drugs and humans into that building," Sterling said. There are miles and miles of deserted border up there. Couldn't they just back two trucks together on each side and hand them over the fence?"

"I suppose that's possible, but it would be risky. Draper said. "They might get away with it for a while but, I know the U.S. Border Patrol well enough that while it might not look as if they are watching, I'd bet that they'd eventually spot it. They have drones, random flyovers, and helicopters, not to mention infrared cameras, and a host of sophisticated electronic detection equipment. It might be possible to evade detection for a while, but sooner or later the Border Patrol would catch on. They do a great job under very difficult circumstances. Unfortunately, their hands are tied by an overwhelmed court system that demands probable cause, and have to live with a whole host of hand-tying rules. It's not enough to find someone with their hand in the cookie jar; you have to wait until they actually eat the cookie."

"It's worse than that," Sterling said. "You have to see them actually swallow the cookie and even then some smart-ass lawyer will claim it was an accident and he didn't mean to swallow it."

"Or the cops forced him to swallow it," Jones said. Believe me; I've had some dangerous guys released because of insufficient evidence when we were sure we had them cold."

"Not to change the subject," Draper said, "how's the campaign going."

"We've been beating the pavement," Sterling said. "Everyone I've talked to claims they will support us."

"I've received the same support everywhere I've gone. We have signs up all over town and most of the county," Mindy Sterling said.

That's great," Draper said, but don't let up until the polls close. Every vote counts. And, Dean, watch your back. I don't trust your opponent any farther than I could throw him. We all think Boulton's got his fingers in Arcuni's pocket."

Draper and Jones sat alone after the Sterling's left, drinking another cup of coffee. Draper's cell phone rattled in his pocket and he answered it.

"Charlie, this is Mario. Estela just called and she wants you to come out to the house right away. One of those girls you brought in wants to talk to you."

134

"Any idea what about?" Draper said.

"No, she just said it was important."

"Okay, call her back and tell her we'll be out in about an hour."

"It's only twenty-five minutes to my place. I'd try to be there in fewer than thirty if I were you. Estela doesn't like to wait."

"Hint taken, Mario, we are on our way."

Draper and Jones pulled up to the Lopez front door and Draper looked at his watch. Thirty-four minutes since he didn't want to speed on the narrow driveway. Estela Lopez stood on the front steps of the Craftsman-style home. The steps led into a screen-enclosed porch that covered the full width of the house front. Inside, the home was sparkling. Bright colored pictures and small knickknacks from Mexico covered the walls. The decor was plain, yet dramatic and made Draper feel comfortable.

"Welcome to our home," Mr. Draper and Mr. Jones," Estela Lopez said. "Please sit."

Draper and Jones sat letting Estela Lopez guide the conversation. She faced them in a hardback chair, her hands clasped together in her lap.

Draper waited wanting her to lead the discussion. When she didn't start, he said, "Tell us what happened." He felt sure it wasn't going to be good news and assuming one or more of the young women had run away.

"Forgive me, *Señores*, my English is not so good."

"You do fine, Estela," Draper said.

"*Sí*, but I still think in *Español*. Mario is very good he helps me learn. He says you can speak *Español*."

"Barely," Draper said, "some phrases and a few words, just enough to get me in trouble."

"Good, but today I practice my English. We practice your *Española* another day."

"Mario said one of the young women we brought here would like to speak to us," Draper said.

"Yes, it is the one who tried to run away. I have talked to her and made her see that you were not trying to hurt her. Maricella has been a big help. She knows English very good and is helping me also."

Draper waited trying to arrest his impatience, knowing the Deputy's wife struggled to communicated with two very large American's, one white and the other coal black. Despite his total ignorance of how someone like Estela viewed the natives of her adopted country, he recognized that her devotion to people in a similar situation as hers was genuine. Draper respected her and let her find her own path. I did not take long.

"Mr. Draper, I have talked at length to Maricella. She says you both are good men and rescued her from a terrible fate. She says also that you did the same for the other two young women.

"We did only what anyone would do," Jones said.

"Maybe that is true," Estela said, "but I have trouble believing it. I know that if these young ladies are sent back to their homes their chances of survival are very slim. What defenses do they have? They are young, impoverished, and defenseless. I know of this because, without my Mario, I would have risked the same fate. I was raped by a neighbor at thirteen. When my father found out, he threw me out into the street like garbage. Nothing happened to the man who hurt me, but I spent the next four years in a Guatemalan *puta casa*.

Draper automatically turned to Jones and said, "Whorehouse."

"I kind of guessed that," Jones said.

"Mario paid *diez mil pesos* for me." Estela said.

"That's approximately ten thousand dollars American," Draper said for Jones' benefit. He grasped Estela's hand and said, "You were worth every penny."

"I won't let those girls be sent back to that life. I will not. I will hide them myself if necessary."

Estela's eyes shone with unreleased tears and determination masked her face. Draper looked in deep and defiance looked back. Draper saw strength resulting from a lifetime of struggle against unimaginable odds. There was little doubt in Draper's mind that he'd help, both financially and other ways. He wasn't sure how the 'other ways' would develop, but nothing was off the table. He knew that included the illegal.

"And I will help you," Draper said.

"What he just said includes me," Jones said.

Estella's tears, suddenly released as if the dam broke, ran down her face and dripped into her ample lap. Draper held her hand and let her shed the years of pent up emotion. After several minutes she said, "What can we do?"

"Worse case, you keep them here undercover until we can work on citizenship. That's your part of the deal. Our part is we will set up a monthly stipend to finance their needs. You name the amount and Jones and I will fund it. The others we'll have to turn over to ICE. We can't save them all."

"I know," Estela said. "I must go get the young ladies now; they want to talk to you."

"They?" Draper said.

"Yes, you two have developed quite a fan club," Estela said. "Wait here." Estela Lopez rose and left the room.

Draper could hear the front door open and close and Estela's footfalls as she descended the front porch stairs. Silence fell and Draper's eyes wandered throughout the room, its decor bright while at the same time calming. Lopez's wife had left her gentle loving touch on every inch, with straightened pictures, subtle colors, and hand scrubbed finishes. It had an effect almost like a psychiatrist's office, subtlety putting the client at ease and encouraging communication. Done intentionally, Draper would have been suspect, but Estela made it honest and soothing. She was gone less than ten minutes. She returned with Maricella Abeja and the young woman who had punched him in the chase across the prairie. Draper touched his cheek instinctively and the pain still residing there.

Maricella Abeja came straight at Draper, a smile on her face, wrapping her arms around him and kissing him gently on the cheek. *"Me alegro de verte de nuevo, señor Draper,"* she said, stepping back.

"And I'm glad to see you again, also, Maricella," Draper said.

Maricella touched his cheek, saying, "I was told about the helpless young lady who knocked down the fierce Charlie Draper with one blow. Does it still hurt?"

"No, I barely felt it," Draper lied. "And for your information, I stumbled on a sage bush."

"Poor baby, I will kiss it again and make it all better." Maricella's smile hinted at a seductive tease when her lips touched the sore spot a second time."

"That does make it better," Draper said.

"Let me introduce you to your attacker, who is now very sorry, since she mistook you for a bad man," Maricella said.

"Some would say she was only half wrong," Jones said.

"I don't need your help," Draper said to Jones.

138

"Charlie Draper, this is Celestina Vargas," Maricella said. *"Celestina, conocer Draper Charlie, un buen tipo.* I told her you were a good guy."

Draper reached his hand out, which the young woman sidestepped and put her arms around his neck. *"Lo siento mucho,"* she whispered. Draper had to bend forward in order for her to reach him. Even at that, she stood on tiptoes.

"No es nada," Draper said. "It is nothing."

"I have explained your proposal to the girls and they are willing to follow your instructions." Estela said.

"What about the other young woman?" Jones said.

"Like the others, this has been a terrifying experience and she just wants to go home with her family." Maricella said.

"Tell them ICE will treat them well. Deportation usually includes an airline ticket back to their native country. As long as they have no outstanding warrants or a crime history, it should be simple and straightforward. We will take them to the Sheriff's office in Highmore and make the exchange there," Draper said. He looked at Maricella and continued, "Your job is to ready yourself for citizenship and teach Celestina to speak English as well as you do. You can also help Estela with her English."

"We will do as you say, Charlie," Maricella said, her voice hinting at a tease.

"Damn straight you will or I'll come back and set you right, young lady," Draper said.

"Don't you worry, girl," Jones said, "he sounds tough, but in reality he's a declawed pussy cat with an attitude."

"I looked in that basket and I see two overgrown boys, trying to impress the ladies," Maricella said, "but I like it."

Draper made a phone call the next morning after Mario brought the illegal group to town and seated them in a row of straight-back wooden chairs along the wall. He did not call Immigration and Customs Enforcement. The number was one only he knew and the conversation was short. ICE showed up three hours later with a twelve-passenger van painted the green and white Border Patrol colors and occupied by two federal agents who spoke fluent Spanish. The uninvited guests heard their rights and then loaded into the van.

Draper watched them leave with Mindy Sterling standing next to him. She had stood silently during the entire process studying their faces, mostly blank and appearing resigned to their fate. The BP vehicle disappeared south on the highway before Draper realized his count was one short."

"The other young girl, the one who wanted to go back, wasn't in the group," Draper said, surprised he had missed it until after they were gone.

"I know," Mindy Sterling said. "I'm a dreadful woman. I'm going to be breaking the law for the next couple of years. Are you going to arrest me?"

"Hell, no," Draper said, "I have no authority to arrest anyone and it's unlikely you've done anything I'll have to shoot you for, so I suspect your secret is safe."

"Estella has agreed to keep her until she learns enough English and the people around town have forgotten today."

"I will pay for her room and board," Draper said.

"No, it's my responsibility.

"Maybe, but I can do it easier than you can. My occupation has paid well over the years." What else do I have to spend it on?"

140

"Young Lochinvar rides again?" Mindy Sterling said.

"Not so young anymore; my horse has tired bones and my sword has lost its edge."

"Poor baby," Mindy Sterling said. "Despite your many faults some of us still think of you as a friend."

Draper watched the Sheriff's wife walk away, standing tall and not looking back. She reminded him of someone in Arizona.

Acting Sheriff Dean Sterling and his wife moved back into their home the next day. The rooms where so much violence occurred looked different, masked by new paint, carpeting and tile. Mindy Sterling stood silent while making an unsuccessful attempt at fighting tears. She looked at Draper and mouthed a soundless 'thank you.' Most of the town arrived and quickly the women gathered in the sanitized kitchen while men and boys surrounded a galvanized metal horse trough full of ice and beer outside the back door. Draper and Jones arrived late having slept until far into the afternoon. They stayed only an hour as the townsfolk turned out enforce and there was not room to turn around. At six in the evening, they climbed into the Lincoln and Draper pointed it north. Neither man said a word until they had driven twenty miles.

"I'm still trying to figure you out," Charlie Draper," Jones said. "You remember the night we met? The night you had me trussed up like a hog-tied piece of dead meat while you went around shooting all the bad guys?" Jones did not wait for Draper to answer. "I thought you were one of the cartel shooters and I spent the time thinking about all the ways I was going to enact revenge on your sorry ass. It included every method of torture I could think of."

"You still mad at me, for Christ's sake? Get over it."

"Hell, no, I'm not mad. Although I should be; I told you I was a federal agent."

"I'm supposed to believe a gigantic black guy with an attitude working in a cartel-connected drug dealer's mansion in Phoenix, Arizona? You are lucky I didn't shoot you on sight," Draper said.

"You going to let me help you finance your do-gooder efforts or not?"

"No. I've got it covered."

"Though I am an extremely handsome black man, hounded by fine young ladies, I'm not poor." I have carefully saved my limited government stipend for an occasional philanthropic endeavor. You aren't the only Lochinvar riding the prairie, dude."

"I understand that, but there are plenty of needy folks around, get your own," Draper said.

At ten minutes after eleven pm, Draper turned the Lincoln onto the dirt road that led to the metal building hidden in the middle of endless miles of Montana prairie. At quarter to midnight, they turned around and sat in the same spot as before. They could not see the building or the barbed wire gate into the area, but knew they would see the glow of truck lights if one came. They relaxed falling into waiting mode, the nemesis of law enforcement everywhere. An old friend of Draper's had once described the job as "hours of boredom interspersed with short periods of sheer terror." Sterling expressed the same sentiment and Draper could relate since he hated the waiting time more the older he became.

Shortly before one am, they dressed in body armor, loaded, checked their M4's, and slipped through the barbed wire into the compound. Stationed and lying prone a couple hundred yards from the building's overhead doors, hidden by the dark and the surrounding sagebrush, they waited. Over the next hour two semi-trucks, twins to the ones they'd watched earlier, came in empty and left loaded.

"Same scenario," Jones said. "How the hell are they getting the stuff in there? They have to be bringing it in sometime. If this is strictly a transfer point, where are the incoming shipments?

"I've got an idea, but no one will believe it."

"You going to share?"

"Last year in Mexico we found a shipment of tunneling equipment in Hermosillo, Son, Mexico that appeared to be destined for a large project in the northern part of the country. The cartels were also trying to buy a large ranch in southern Arizona. Based also on some plans we came across the year before, the cartels planned a major tunnel, bigger than anything ever seen before that would provide a seamless conduit for drugs and human trafficking between Mexico and the U.S.

"A tunnel? I thought the tunnels under the border were mostly hand dug and easily caught by the Border Patrol folks with vibration sensors and all that other sophisticated equipment they have."

"True, but the plans I saw were much more elaborate, with ventilation systems, and a motorized train system, almost like a subway for freight," Draper said.

"Hard to believe," Jones said, obviously trying to wrap his head around such a large project. "If that were true, why aren't there drugs or bodies stored in the building? You looked and it was empty. Explain that."

"I can't unless they are storing them underground. There's a large concrete structure in the center of the building that could be an elevator shaft. That would fit with the plans I saw. We never considered Canada. We were thinking Mexico.

"Okay, let me get this straight. You're suggesting there is a tunnel from this building that goes north into Canada where there is another similar building and both have some sort of elevator access that allows transfer of drugs and humans across the border undetected, that it?"

"Pretty much," Draper said.

"Damn, I've been in this business a long time and that's the wildest theory I've ever heard. You must have stayed up night's thinking that one up," Jones said.

Draper lay silent a moment watching a full moon peek over the distant hills beginning its slow climb into the night sky. Everything he had heard about Montana was true. The sky looked huge, even at night, filled with glowing stars that that cast eerie shadows on the countryside. The moment the sun disappeared the temperature began to drop causing the dark to lie cold on Draper's back.

"You're right; the cost would be astronomical, though the engineering is available and actually quite simple. There are tunnels all over the world that are bigger, longer and a hell of a lot more complex. Everyone agrees that the cost is a big hang-up. I've seen the plan. I kicked it up the government ladder and no one could believe it. I'd bet anything they are languishing on some politician's desk, unread and ignored. Lazy bastards are too busy loading up on graft and making silly speeches.

"A bit cynical, don't you think?" Jones said.

"Cynical, maybe, true, but possible," Draper said.

144

"Well, then, what are we waiting for?" Let's go see if we can cause some disruption of their plans; maybe something will drop out of the tree."

An hour after the last truck left, Draper stood at the walk-in door with his pick tools in hand. Working only with moonlight, he again worked the lock pins. It took two minutes.

"Damn, you have to teach me how to do that sometime when we have an idle minute," Jones said.

"Can't, then I'd have to shoot you, locksmith rules."

"Right." For a shooter, you sure have a lot of moral hindrances."

"Can't help it, I had a saintly upbringing."

"Shut up and get us in," Jones said.

When the lock turned, Draper pushed gently on the door, opening it a crack to where he could survey the interior. As before, the building was empty of both materials and humans. They watched minutes and nothing moved. Draper slipped into the building followed by Jones. Draper went left and Jones slipped right following their M4's and proceeding with caution. They met on the other end. From there they could see the opposite wall of the concrete box in the middle held a double set of sixteen foot wide sliding doors that looked like two separate freight elevators. In between the doors was a single call light with a card slot.

"So, do we go?" Jones said.

"Too easily trapped; we have no idea what's down there," Draper said. "Need backup to take that risk. Besides, it requires magnetic card. Probably something the drivers have." Draper's eyes studied the concrete enclosure; certain it contained an elevator system. The size included enough height that it was likely a cable lift rather than a hydraulic platform type. Whether or not the deflector sheave was in the overhead or in a separate mechanical room, he couldn't tell but the overall height suggested overhead. Either way there was probably an access from the top. A fixed metal ladder on the east side confirmed his suspicion.

"You keep watch, I'm going up on top for a look-see," Draper said.

"Don't take too long. My thinking says we've been in here too long already. Too many fine young women would be disappointed if I got myself killed."

When Draper reached the top, he could see two round access covers located roughly in the center of each half of the concrete roof. He approached the nearest one and studied it. Hinged on one side and latched on the other with a half-inch steel cable attached to a steel arm that secured a counterweight. When he released the latch, the cover opened to ninety degrees, slow and silent. A levered safety switch turned on the maintenance lights and Draper peered into an enormous dark hole containing a deflector sheave almost four feet in diameter carrying what looked like three-quarter-inch steel cable. The depth of the shaft lay hidden in darkness, but he could see at least two hundred feet down. He racked his memory for long unused facts and gleaned a one that staggered him. This type of elevator had a maximum lift of somewhere between twenty-five and thirty stories, close to five hundred feet.

"Holy shit," he muttered, only half believing what he was seeing. Draper lowered the cover and climbed back down to where Jones waited.

"So, what'd you find?" he said.

146

"Let's get the hell out of here and I'll tell you in the car. You won't believe it."

Draper did not feel secure until they were back on the highway traveling south. After he had told Jones what he'd found both men rode silent until they reached the first town of any size. There they both rented rooms in a small family-owned motel.

"I could use some breakfast," Draper said.

"I thought you'd never ask, my stomach was beginning to think my throat was blocked."

They found a restaurant bustling with early-rising farmers and ranchers debating animal and grain prices over coffee strong enough to float rocks. Draper and Jones found an empty table in the back followed by inquisitive eyes. The talk did not stop but half the heads in the place followed the two strangers.

"Clear them county boys ain't seen too many handsome men of color," Jones said. The approach of a young woman in a fresh uniform blocked Draper's response. The other half of the heads followed her. She smiled and said. "What can I get you?"

Draper and Jones ordered after the young waitress brought them coffee. When she left, Jones said, "Okay, boss man, what are we going to do?"

"It looks to me like we are sitting on a potential powder keg." What we do next depends on decisions a tad higher on the pay scale than you and me. Anything we do could cause an international incident unless all the players are onboard. First thing I suggest is we both send what we know up the food chain and see what happens."

Chapter Eleven

Northeastern Montana

Draper received a return call at 1:06 p.m. The ringing cell phone woke him up and he took a moment to orient himself in the unfamiliar motel room. Punching send on the phone, he said, "Yes," and listened to a clipped and monotone voice for the next four minutes. The mostly one-sided conversation left him a little puzzled. He had not expected them to tell him to back off and not to contact the Canadian authorities under any circumstances.

"State has determined that they will need at least a month to work through the proper channels and ensure both countries are on the same page," the voice said.

"You do understand that we believe literally tons of drugs are being imported into this country, not to mention the illegal immigration and human trafficking involved," Draper said.

"We do, but these things take time. We will contact you when we decide how we are going to handle it. In the mean time do whatever you can to put them out of business from our end."

Draper alternated between dozing and pacing the small motel room floor until six pm when he went outside and pounded on Jones' door.

"You get a call?" he said when Jones cracked the door.

"Yeah."

"And what did they say?"

"I'm to follow your lead," Jones said.

Draper and Jones arrived back in Highmore a little after nine pm. It took less than a half hour of searching to find Robert Arcuni buying drinks for the locals in one of the two town bars. Pop's Place catered to young farm and ranch hands, mostly twenty-something rawhide hard kids still trying to convince the world they were tougher than most. Some were. The barroom's dimly lit decor included a mahogany bar top aged to a deep chocolate by decades of revelers. A thin layer of prairie dust covered any untouched surface and painted the old spurs, lariats, worn out boots, old carnival posters and an eclectic mix of other wall hangings. In one corner, carrying a vintage McClellan-style saddle and a work-worn snaffle bit bridle stood a fifteen and half hands high stuffed Palomino horse seated by a department store mannequin in cowboy dress. A little over the top even for Montana, the bartender, a tall hard-looking woman of indeterminate age stared at Jones as if she had never seen a black man. Her coal colored hair now peppered with gray, Draper didn't doubt her command of the bar and somewhere out of sight he would bet money on a squirreled away a solid ash head-knocker. A .45 automatic lying alongside the shortened baseball bat would not have surprised him.

"It don't wash off, mama, no matter how hard I try," Jones said.

"Don't expect it does," she came back with. "Don't see many of your kind in this part of the world. Suspect your money is as good as any. Watch your back in here though, might there be some that lack my easy going manner."

Robert Arcuni stepped up to the bar alongside Draper and said, "These men giving you a hard time, Angel."

"Not so you'd notice," the bartender said. "I was just about to buy my friends here a drink."

Arcuni stood an inch or two shorter than Jones and Draper guessed his height at close to six-foot. His frame came in large with arms that suggested a good deal of weight training. Probably strong as an ox, but not very agile, Draper thought, assessing the man as he always did in case things got sticky.

"My name's Robert Arcuni, and I'm running for Sheriff. I'd like to ask you for your vote since my experience and training are far beyond my competition."

"Tell me about your experience and training," Draper said, wanting to fill his information box.

"Former military cop, Chicago Police Department for ten years, and I know how to take care of assholes," Arcuni said.

"Chicago Police don't mean much if you never made it beyond street cop. Nothing against good street cops, but running a county Sheriff's department takes a little more finesse," Draper said, weighing the man's reaction, pushing a tiny bit. What he saw in the man's killer eyes told the story. Draper watched him grapple with rising temper, which made him vulnerable and careless. Draper stored the information for later use.

"If these boys give you any trouble, Angel, you let me know, and I'll take care of it," Arcuni said and walked away.

"There goes a dangerous man," Jones said.

"Dangerous no doubt, but the strings are being pulled from somewhere else."

Twenty minutes passed during which Draper and Jones and sipped a free beer each and studied the crowd by looking them over in the bar mirror. It consisted of mostly youngsters, passing the time over longneck beers, and lying to each other. The exception was Arcuni and a pair of heavy-set mobster types dressed in dark suits with matching ties. They stood out in a cowboy bar like two frogs in a sandbox. They were watching the bar patrons while listening to Arcuni. Together, like synchronized swimmers they pushed back their chairs and walked toward Draper and Jones.

The bartender slipped an eighteen-inch cutoff baseball bat into Jones' hand. "You might need this, handsome. I'd hate to see that pretty face all tore up."

"Thank ya, darlin'," Jones said and mouthed, "Brass knuckles," at Draper, "the one on the right and probably both."

"Both," Draper agreed.

"You figure trouble is afoot?"

"Probably, and I haven't finished my beer yet," Draper said.

"Hey, nigger, you lost?" the right side thug said.

Jones looked at Draper and said, "You hear an asshole, Charlie? I'd swear I did."

"You mean that pair of pencil dicks behind us?"

"Must be them. Don't see anyone else."

"You need help or can I finish my beer?"

"Finish your beer; I'll be just a moment." Jones turned, swinging the bat right-handed in one smooth motion, landing it across the man's upper arm and Draper could hear the bone crack. Draper watched in the mirror as Jones' left fist caught the second man's nose. Both men's knees buckled almost together and landed them on the sawdust-covered floor, one trying to protect his arm and the other capturing rivers of nose blood. Arcuni charged over clawing for a shoulder rig, but before he was half way, he stared into the barrel of Draper's Glock.

"I'd be very careful about your next decision, Mr. Arcuni," Draper said. I suggest you get down on your knees very slowly, with your hands behind your neck. Without doubt, the local law will be here in a moment and we'll let them sort all this out."

"I got me a silent alarm, they're already on their way," the woman bartender said, behind Draper.

Without taking his eyes off Arcuni, Draper said, "Appreciate the help."

"Saw this coming the minute you two walked in. I ain't no dummy," the bartender said. "Now that we're friends you both can call me Angel. The no-account you are pointing your gun at calls me by name but he don't have permission yet. After tonight, it ain't likely he ever will have."

Draper glanced at the door and saw Dean Sterling assessing the room from the doorway with his service pistol in both hands pointed at the ceiling. "Everything under control, Charlie?" he said.

"Probably better call an ambulance for the two in front of Mr. Arcuni; seems they've had an accident."

"Put your weapon away, Charlie," Sterling said, walking across the room. Deputy Mario Lopez stepped through the door behind the Sheriff carrying a Remington twelve gauge with a shortened barrel.

"I will as soon as Mr. Arcuni is relieved of his piece," Draper said, his Glock centered on Arcuni's chest.

"You know the drill, Mr. Arcuni, two fingers, very slowly and skid it out of reach," Sterling said.

Arcuni knew and lifted a chrome-plated Smith and Wesson .45 out, laid it on the floor and gave it a shove. His eyes stared hard at Draper who realized he was looking a man with no conscience, capable of any kind of violence and worse yet, unforgiving. He would not forget this night and his anger would only grow with time. Draper filed that away knowing that if there were a next time, and sure, there would be. He had better be ready. He stepped forward without looking at Sterling and kicked the weapon out of reach before leaning close to Arcuni. "We know what's going on with you and Boulton," Draper hissed, "Leave town now while you have the chance or I'll shoot you on sight the next time I see you." Draper stared direct into Arcuni's eyes, "You know I mean it, asshole."

"Fuck you," Arcuni spat through a curtain of anger.

Two hours dragged by before Draper and Jones where able to return to the motel. The two mobster-types were transported by ambulance to Lewistown; Arcuni was released since there was not a law against talking to idiots. Arcuni's only crime was not having a concealed-carry permit for the .45 allowing Sterling to confiscate it and give him an appointment with the local magistrate. The man did not appear concerned about it that told Draper there were more where the .45 came from. At the door to the Sheriff's office, Arcuni looked at Draper and said, "This ain't over, friend." Draper did not reply and watched the man leave. Draper and Jones left to fill out paperwork and record statements.

"I'd watch my back if I were you," Jones said.

"I'd bet we both are wearing Arrow shirts now, Draper said. "Nice move back there in the bar, by the way."

"Been a little harder without the bat; I own that lady one."

"That you do, 'cause without it I'd have had to help you."

"Doubtful; you white boys don't have the ghetto experience us black folk have. Probably get yourself hurt."

"Okay, I guess you two can leave. Mindy called and she wants you both to come to dinner tonight. Make it about six." Sterling grinned and added, "That is if you can stay out of trouble until then."

"We'll try." Jones said.

Draper locked the door on his motel room at twenty minutes past two am. His bones tired, he lay on the bed fully clothed and stared at the ceiling. A kaleidoscope of potential plans crossed his mind all of which he discarded as too dangerous, too limiting, or too illegal. The illegal part did not bother him as much as it created other problems without solving any real issue. Boulton's compound, a fort-like structure, sat secured on every front and heavily armed. Draper assessed every corner and could not see a way in that didn't carry considerable risk. The man appeared impregnable by any of the usual means.

Draper woke to the sound of pounding on his door. Sunshine streamed through the single motel window and when he looked at his watch and it read ten fifteen. He rose and went to the door and yelled, "Who is it?"

"Jones; you still alive in there?"

Draper opened the door and said, "What?"

"Why so grumpy this morning?" Jones said.

"My mind spent half the night looking for answers and found nothing."

"Well, I'm hungry. The restaurant is calling my name. Meet me down there and we'll talk."

"Give me a half hour and I'll be there," Draper said.

Draper showered in water only a few degrees above freezing,. It made bathing uncomfortable and hurried, but included the added advantage of waking him to the day. Dressed and armed. Draper walked into the restaurant forty minutes later finding Jones seated talking to Dean Sterling. Both were drinking coffee. Sterling looked serious.

"Glad you're here, Charlie. I need your weapon."

"Do I get to ask why?"

"Arcuni's body was found early this morning in the borrow pit next to the highway about two miles south of town. Know anything about that?"

"While that might have been on my list of things to do, someone must have beaten me to it." Draper said. How'd he die?"

"Large caliber bullet wound to the chest. Probably never knew what hit him," Sterling said.

"Understand why you might want my weapon, but I didn't do it. I did consider it, though, is that illegal now?"

"Don't mess with me Charlie, got to do my job."

Draper removed his Glock, dropped the clip, racked the slide to remove the chamber round, and handed the weapon to Sterling. "I want that back as soon as possible."

"Need your back-up also. You always carry a round in the chamber just walking around?" Sterling said.

"If I didn't your lovely wife would be starring at grass roots right now," Draper said.

"Point taken, Charlie, don't make this harder than it is. I don't like it any more than you do."

"I know you are just doing your job, Dean. I'm angry that I didn't see this one coming." Draper reached down and removed the second Glock from his right leg holster and repeated the unloading procedure."

"Jesus, Charlie, you are a walking armory; two Glock .40's?" Sterling said.

"White boys not as good at finesse as us blacks," Jones said. "We disarm the bad guys with colorful talk first and then we shoot them."

Draper sat staring into his second cup of coffee and forgot breakfast. Puzzled by Arcuni's murder, it eliminated his plan to use the man to get into Boulton's compound. That left only Boulton himself. Draper was considering the ramifications of running the gate at Boulton's ranch when the man walked into the restaurant followed by a hard case looking individual with dark eyes.

"Mr. Draper and Mr. Jones," Boulton said. "Ah, you have the new Sheriff with you, may we join you?"

"Free country," Draper said, curious.

"This is Joey Diaz, my ranch foreman." Boulton said, pulling back a chair and sitting. Diez took an empty chair from an adjoining table, turned it around, and sat without pulling it closer to the others.

Draper and Jones waited without comment for Boulton to continue. Sterling looked wary.

"As you probably know by now it seems the only opponent to Mr. Sterling's gaining election to County Sheriff has met an unfortunate end last night."

Boulton waited as if expecting Draper to comment and when he did not continue, "In any case, it seems Mr. Sterling has an uncontested chance to win the election. We, that is, Mr. Diaz and I, believe a peaceful gathering with our local friends for the general good is in the best interest of the county. Don't you agree?"

"I would if I thought for even a second you weren't trying to bullshit us," Draper said.

"Listen, I come in peace. I'm willing to open my house to you and Mr. Jones. Inspect all you want. The Sheriff is welcome, as well. You will see we are an operational cattle operation with absolutely nothing to hide. Mr. Diez and I will give you a personally escorted tour of our entire operation, and afterward you will have free rein to wander around for as long as you like. I will have to insist that Mr. Diez accompany you wherever you go, for insurance reasons, you understand, but you can decide what you'd like to see.

"That seems very generous, Mr. Boulton," Draper said.

"I think so, considering you haven't been exactly forthcoming about what your interest is in my humble operation, Mr. Draper. I'm interested in finding out just who you are."

"I'm nobody, Mr. Boulton, just a guy trying to help out a friend."

"You'll forgive me if I don't believe you. In any case after you have looked over my little operation to your heart's content, I'd like you to come to my house and we'll discuss the future of this county over some very fine Scotch whiskey."

"I think I'll decline, Mr. Boulton," Sterling said. "Political reasons I'm sure you understand. It would be awkward when I have to arrest you."

"You sound as if that's a distinct possibility, Sheriff."

"You never can tell, Sir. You will have to excuse me, gentlemen, County business, you know," Sterling said and left.

When Sterling disappeared out the door, Boulton said, "How about you two? Would you like a tour?"

"I think we would," Draper said, "When would you like us?"

"How does Friday afternoon sound? Say about three?"

"You're on. We'll be there," Draper said.

After Boulton and Diez left, Jones observed, "Left himself plenty of time to sanitize the place."

'Of course he did. Doesn't matter; I want to look the place over for its weaknesses in case we decide on a full assault. Might also be interesting to talk to him, get a feel for his thought process, and see if we can figure out what he has planned."

"He'll be trying to analyze us also."

"I know. Be interesting to see how he does it."

"It could be a trap also," Jones said, "bury us out in the middle of nowhere covered with lime.

"I thought of that also; we'll just have to be craftier than he is. It shouldn't be hard."

Draper waved at the teenaged waitress and she bounced over with a full fresh pot of hot coffee.

"Sweetheart, if you would bring me two eggs over easy with some hashbrowns and a couple of sausages I'll marry you tomorrow and disappoint every male in the county."

The waitress smiled as best she could with a mouthful of jewelry and came right back, "Sorry, Mr. Draper, I'm taken but I'll bring you breakfast anyway. But don't worry; if things don't work out, you're in the top ten."

"Damn, only the top ten?" Draper said to Jones after the young girl sped off.

"What'd you expect, old man." Jones said.

Draper ignored the dig. "Ever have a feeling that although things appear straight forward and simple, say Boulton's drug and human trafficking business, but something creeps around in your gut telling that you've missed something?" Draper said, more to himself than Jones.

"So, what's bothering you? I see a very sophisticated drug operation with a bit of human trafficking thrown in. What else could it be? There's certainly plenty of money in those two alone."

"Granted, but take the Mexican cartels for example. They're disorganized, fight with each other over territory and leave a path of violence that pales anything in modern history. Why go to the expense of building a tunnel when their current tactic of throwing shit against the barn and collecting what sticks is providing at least thirty billion a year in revenue. They have a socially disadvantaged country full of economically desperate and expendable people to act as mules for them. What's not to like?"

"What's your point?" Jones asked.

"What the cartels are doing along the Mexican border makes sense in a perverted way. Greed, opportunity and a huge neighboring country full of hungry drug users, low-level groups nearby willing to carry them and large organizations south of the border to fulfill the need. It's similar to the mobs supplying liquor in the thirties and arguing over territory. A completed tunnel between Canada and the U.S. only to move drugs and people doesn't compute. Why go to the expense and the difficult logistics of moving drugs and people across the mountains from Vancouver, British Columbia. The tunnel is isn't logical unless something else is involved."

"Why is it so tough?" Jones said, playing devil's advocate.

160

"Any contraband would have to come in through the port of Vancouver, which is located in an area with thousands of small inlets, waterways, and small harbors extending miles up the coast. It is an area difficult, if not impossible to patrol. The Canada Border Services Agency, similar to the U.S Border Patrol, while well organized an efficient, has an uphill battle just on numbers alone. In addition, the highways from Vancouver to Medicine Hat, Alberta are through rugged mountains, mostly two-lane, steep, and serpentine. A loaded truck could not average thirty miles an hour. Worse yet, Vancouver to Medicine Hat, Alberta is nearly eight hundred miles. From Medicine Hat to that building we found is another two hundred and fifty. Assuming the building on the Canadian side is twenty miles closer make it two-thirty. Over a thousand miles in any case; that's a hell of a drive with a load of contraband and especially with illegals on board."

"Even at fifty miles an hour average, that's twenty hours locked up in a truck. Not a pleasant trip," Jones said.

"My guess is they lose a few."

"So there'd be bodies buried somewhere around that building on the Canadian side, right?"

"That would be my guess," Draper said.

"What do you want to do?"

"I suggest we go have a talk with Maricella, see if we can get confirmation of our theory."

"Works for me," Jones said.

Draper and Jones walked back to the motel and fired up the Lincoln after Draper extracted a spare Glock out of the truck and filled his empty shoulder rig. Cold steel under his left arm removed the naked feeling that had plagued him all through breakfast. The drive to the Lopez place gave Draper time to form the questions he wanted to ask Maricella. He did not doubt that she would be able to shed light on the trip across Canada; if that was the way she arrived.

Maricella hugged both men, obvious in her joy to see them. "I'm always glad to see my American saviors. But I didn't come that way. I was brought across the southern border by a coyote. We were picked up by a twelve passenger van north of Nogales and transported to Phoenix. There we spent three days locked in a small van truck while they transported us north. They didn't let us out until we arrived at the place where you found me."

"Three days?" Jones said.

"Yes, they gave us two jugs of water and an empty five gallon bucket to relieve ourselves in. You can imagine what that was like by the third day." Maricella's face reflected the horror of that time in a way both Draper and Jones could only imagine.

"We were thinking maybe you came in from the north and we wanted to see if you could confirm they were using that route," Draper said.

"I didn't come that way," Maricella said, "but Selena did."

"Selena?"

"Yes, Selena Deferia, she was with the girl who hit you."

"Ah, the quiet one," Draper said.

"Yes, she told me she came through Vancouver, BC."

"I'd better get Estela to bring her. She's pretty traumatized yet. It was a rough trip in more ways than one, if you know what I mean."

"I can only guess," Draper said, not liking the image.

Maricella went after Estela and Draper and Jones sat in the Lincoln waiting. After fifteen minutes, Maricella returned. "Estela

162

has Selena in the house. She asked me to tell you to be gentle with her. She doesn't speak English and big ugly Americans frighten her."

"I will follow your lead. Let me know if I ask her something she doesn't want to answer."

Draper and Jones followed Maricella into the Lopez home where Estella sat next to a frightened Hispanic girl. Cleaned up and dressed in new clothes, Draper wouldn't have recognized her as the same young lady from the motel. She sat stiff, her eyes hollow, as if the light inside had dimmed and only time and a gentle hand would turn it back on. She glanced at the two men and could not look directly at them. Instead, she stared at Maricella.

"I will ask her the questions you want, since your Spanish leaves a lot to be desired," Maricella said.

"Ask her first if she came into this country through Canada," Draper said.

Maricella asked in Spanish and the Selena answered, *"No lo sé"*.

"She says she doesn't know," Maricella said.

"I got that. Ask her what she does remember."

"¿Qué recuerdas?" Maricella said.

The young woman looked at Draper and Jones for the first time. Her eyes traveled back and forth between them before returning to Maricella. *"Estos son los hombres que nos rescatados?"* she whispered. When Marcella nodded to the affirmative, the girl began a long narrative in Spanish. Midway Draper could see tears form in the corner of her eyes and by the end they were dripping off her cheeks. Several times she stopped, holding her face in her hands and sobbing. It was hard for Draper to watch and anger tightened his gut. He found it easy to imagine Boulton's face centered in the sights of his

Glock. The two men waited, sitting silent while the two women consoled the girl.

After several minutes, Maricella turned to Draper with wet eyes and said, "She first asked if you two were the ones who rescued her at the motel. She was kidnapped near her home in El Salvador, put on a boat with other victims, and transported to near Vancouver, BC, Canada. Apparently, there were about fifty on the boat, mostly young women. All were beaten and raped repeatedly over the course of the trip. Drugged early on, she says she remembers only the beatings and the rapes. At Vancouver, they were loaded into a small van and transported hours to a place with big doors into the mountain. Inside, they were loaded on a train-like thing. The trip was short she believes, but since she'd been drugged should couldn't tell for sure. At the other end, they went up an elevator and were again loaded into a bigger van truck and transported to a place where they were forced to re-package a white powder. She doesn't know what kind they were but only that the others said it was some kind of drug. After a week or so, two men came and drugged them again and the next thing she knew they're in a car and the other girl runs for it. I've told her the story of how you and Mr. Jones rescued them at the motel."

"Tell her the information she gave us was very helpful and that we will make sure at least some of the men who hurt her will be punished," Draper said.

"I can see where a little torture beforehand would make me feel better," Jones said, studying the floor.

Maricella told the girl with tears running down her face. She turned to Draper and said, "I believe I understand why you do what you do."

"Maybe one of these days I'll have you explain it to someone I know," Draper said.

Selena Deferia stood and stepped toward Draper and Jones. Draper was unprepared for her next move. She put her arms around his neck and kissed him on the cheek. "*Gracias, señor Draper*." she said and repeated the action with Jones.

Jones looked at Draper and said, "What do I say?"

"*No es nada*," Draper said.

Jones repeated the phrase with a south Chicago accent. Selena smiled and kissed him again.

On the trip back to town, Draper said, "You know I'm a tad bit jealous."

"Naturally, you would be, given my handsome features and dark suntan," Jones said.

"Is that the reason the young lady kissed you twice?"

"Of course it is. She couldn't help herself. It's a curse we men of color have to live with."

Chapter Twelve

Eastern Montana

D raper and Jones walked the two blocks to the Sheriff's house and arrived at two minutes until six. Mindy Sterling greeted them at the door and led them back into the kitchen. Maricella Abeja, Celestina Vargas, and Selena Deferia sat at the table with Dean Sterling. A longneck beer sat in front of Sterling with cokes in the hands of the young women. Mindy Sterling's face glowed like a new mother when she said, "Maricella, Celestina, and Selena are having dinner with us. I'm going to take vacation time next week so we can get to know one another. I thought we could run to Billings and do a little shopping."

After dinner, while the women cleaned up the dinner dishes, Draper, Jones and Dean Sterling sat on the back patio, a slab of cracked concrete that someone in past days had attempted with a limited knowledge of cement work. Lacking expansion joints and an amateur broom finish, nature had left its inevitable fingerprints. Like a number of the realities of life, the only cure would be to take it up and start over. Draper sat silent staring at the concrete while Jones and Sterling argued the merits or the lack of them of professional basketball. He felt good that Mindy Sterling was trying to make a home for the Salvadorian young woman, but had reservations as to its outcome. She was very young and only time would tell how much her psyche had been damaged. As he thought about it he became less comfortable about a trip to Billings. The exposure time was too long and protecting them would be difficult if not impossible. Draper resolved to delay the trip if not eliminate it until things were less dangerous. He interrupted a vigorous argument on the merits of a basketball rule he knew nothing about.

"I don't think Mindy should take the girls to Billings. It's too dangerous. The people we rescued them from will do anything to prevent any information about their activities from getting out."

"You need to tell that to Mindy," Sterling said. "I'm not sure she'd listen to me."

"How are you getting them home tonight?" Draper asked.

Mario is going to take them after his shift ends at ten."

Draper looked at Jones and said, "I think we should follow."

"Something bothering you?" Jones asked.

"Nothing I can put my finger on, just a feeling."

"One thing I've learned," Jones said to Sterling, "when white boy here has a feeling, best pay attention."

"You think there's some danger?" Sterling asked.

"Nothing concrete, just considering who we are dealing with, I don't think a little extra caution is out of line."

Draper looked at Jones and said, "How about you and I follow them home, just because it's a nice summer night and a drive in the moonlight would be fun."

"Won't be much moonlight tonight," Jones said.

"You noticed; all the more reason to be careful."

At ten-thirty, Draper and Jones sat in the Lincoln at the edge of Highmore. They had been there almost a half hour. Draper fidgeted, not a normal reaction and he resolved to settle down realizing there was probably a copious amount of tears shed at the Sterling house. He did not like the idea that the young women were exposed and was anxious to get them back undercover.

"Mindy Sterling is a strong-willed lady, might not be easy to dissuade her if her mind is made up."

"If I'm right about the potential danger, I don't think she'll argue," Draper said, fingering the police band hand-held radio Sterling had supplied so they could stay in contact with Lopez' cruiser.

At ten-forty-five, Mario's cruiser sped by and Draper waited until they were out of sight before pulling onto the highway. He waited to make sure no one followed. He almost decided they were good when a dark-colored Cadillac passed by with two occupants.

"Shit!" Draper said, pulling on to the highway with no lights. He used the highway side reflectors and the miniscule moonlight to keep the Lincoln out of the ditch and punched the accelerator until he could see taillights.

"What do you think?" Draper said.

"Two options; they probably don't know where Mario is going to turn off, so they'll wait for that. On the other hand, if that does not happen quickly they'll try to bump them into the ditch. Either way it isn't going to be easy to stop," Jones said, leaning forward into the windshield and studying the black highway. How close are we to the turnoff?"

"Not sure. It's too damn dark. My guess these boys will make their move at the turnoff. Mario will have to slow for that. I'm going to warn him off." Draper keyed the hand-held radio and said, "Mario, don't turn off, you have a caddy behind with two goons in it. We are going to intercept." He knew there was a two-mile straight stretch of highway ahead so he floored the accelerator and began to creep up on the caddy. "Hang on to your ass," Draper said, counting on the driver of the caddy to be concentrating on following the Sheriff's cruiser when he bumped the rear quarter panel in a classic pit maneuver. Ahead the Cadillac spun into a sideways slide and entered the ditch backwards coming to rest against a steel power pole. Draper wrenched the Lincoln's steering wheel, followed the Cadillac into the ditch, and stopped with the Lincoln's front end against the passenger door. Draper and Jones both exited weapons in hand as soon as the Lincoln stopped. The two in the Cadillac could not move. Draper opened the rear door behind the driver and shouted, "Hands behind your necks where I can see them or I'll shoot you dead where you sit." When both responded he continued, "Driver, turn around and climb over the seat. Passenger, you sit still until you're told to move."

Jones ran around the rear of the car where he opened the rear door and planted the barrel of his .45 against the other man's head. "Easy friend," he said, "be cool and you might live to see the sunrise."

When they had both men on the ground and zip-tied, Draper went through their pockets and found nothing. There is no wallet, no ID, not a scrap to identify them.

"Pro's," Jones said, looking over a blued SW automatic in .45 caliber, "weapon's been sanitized. Caddy's a rental."

"Where you two from?" Draper said.

"Пішов на хуй, мудак!" the passenger said.

"What'd he say?" Jones said.

"I think he just told us to do something impossible in Russian. The two languages are related. Seems we have a couple of real badasses here. I'm going to call Mario and have him drop off the girls and come back and give us a hand. Something very strange is going on." Draper retrieved the radio from the Lincoln and called Lopez.

The first done, he used his cell phone to call Dean Sterling. When the Sheriff answered Draper said, "Put that fancy badge on Dean and come south about ten miles on the highway. We've got a problem."

"What?" Sterling said.

"Everyone's okay but we've got two foreigners clowns out here with no identification, limited language skills, and the looks of hired killers."

"On my way," Sterling said. "Don't move anything until I get there. Are you secure?"

"For the moment, but I'm planning to get out the heavy artillery until help arrives."

"Please don't kill anyone unless you have to."

"Can't promise that but you can hope there's no backup for these clowns."

After ending the call, Draper went straight to the Lincoln's trunk and extracted two M4's and gave one to Jones.

"Dean and Mario are on their way. Anyone else, we shoot. I figure we have about a half-hour. You keep your eyes peeled for company and I'm going to have a discussion with our friends."

"You speak Ukrainian?"

"Not so much, but a little Russian," Draper said.

"Damn, you are a continuing mystery, cowboy, someday when we're alone and partially inebriated, you'll have to tell me the story."

"Keep a sharp eye out. We don't want any others invading our party."

Draper focused on the two captives. Lying in the long grass of a deserted highway barrow pit was not an ideal interrogation place, but Draper had no other option. He studied the two men and made a choice. His selection not based on anything scientific, but rather a wild ass guess enhanced by the captive's eyes. The driver's eyes moved, as if he were a trapped animal looking for an escape route, the fight or flight syndrome in full gear. The passenger's eyes, on the other hand, were cold, staring straight at Draper, as a diamond-back rattler might stalking a prairie dog. The driver would likely spill his guts given enough pressure, but probably knew little. The passenger responded to Draper's first question as if he knew English, despite answering in Russian, but looked toughest to break. Debate over, Draper touched the trigger on the M4 when the barrel end lay less than two inches from the man's left ear. The noise caused him to jerk sideways as the muzzle blast lit up the side of the Cadillac and a small hole appeared in the rear door. Draper followed the man's head with the barrel placing it hard against the bridge of his nose and said, "Next one goes into your brain."

"You crazy son-of-a-bitch, you almost blew my head off. My ear hurts like hell."

"Whoa," Draper said, "all of a sudden you can speak English. You should work some on your accent though, I guess southern Ukraine, more like Mykolaiv, not Kiev; less Russian influence. Here's the deal, you tell me who sent you and I'll let you survive in a country club American prison, or, if you like I can arrange for super-max where you'll learn about being some big guy's girl friend; your choice. Or, of course, you can try and run which in that case I'll shoot you before you make it a hundred yards."

"Fuck you, you don't dare touch me, I have rights. You mess with me and any decent lawyer will have me back on the streets in an hour. You have nothing. I'll say you planted the weapons we had."

"You know, you are absolutely right," Draper said, reaching in his pocket for a knife. He opened the blade slow, taking his time, deliberate, as if he had all the time in the world. He reached down, inserting the blade between the man's hands and slicing through the thick zip tie. The man looked at him incredulous, sure he'd won the war of words."

"Go," Draper said, "I won't stop you. Tell your friends though I'll be coming after them."

The man hesitated, climbed to his feet, and looked hate-eyed at Draper. "That's how it is, huh,"

"Yup," Draper said.

He went through the barbed wire right-of-way fence as if he had done it before, pushing down on the third wire and stepping over the bottom wires and ducking under the top one. Fifteen yards beyond the fence, Draper covered his back with the crosshairs of his M4. In the dark the light-gathering scope made the scene black and white, like watching a white shadow dart across a lit background. He was dodging back and forth, hunkered down as if he knew what was coming. Draper had the rifle laid across the Cadillac roof, solid, unwavering. He led the target just a hair and slowly put pressure on the trigger. The rifle jumped in his hands and the runner stumbled falling headlong into two-foot sage and prairie dirt. He did not move.

Draper walked over to where Jones held the second captive. "Turn him loose," Draper said, "let's see how far he can run."

"*Пожалуйста, я ничего не знаю.*"

"*Знание английского языка?*" Draper said.

"*Только немного.*"

"What's he saying," Jones asked.

"First he said he knew nothing, then, when I asked him if he spoke English, he replied only a little. He's scared and I think he knows more than he wants to admit. I think we should invite him to take a run through the fence."

"That was a hell of a shot on the last one."

"Misspent youth and a hell of a lot of practice," Draper said.

"Think he'll run?"

"No, I think it more likely he'll spill his guts."

Draper pressed the barrel of his M4 into the second man's forehead and said, "You want to run or do you want to talk to me in English?" He repeated it in Russian.

"*Нет, пожалуйста, я не говорю на английском, вы можете говорить мои, я расскажу вам все, что вы хотите знать,*" the man said. He continued in Russian, while Draper listened.

"What," Jones said when the man stopped.

"He says they were sent here by a guy named Darchin Kazarian, a Russian mob leader back east. They were here to kill Arcuni because he wasn't doing what he was sent here for. You and I including Dean Sterling were on the list not to mention anyone else who got in the way. A secondary objective was to get back or silence the Mexican workers we'd lifted."

"Holy shit," Jones said, "that's a blood bath."

"A little blood doesn't seem to bother them as long as they obtain their goal. I'm more convinced there is some purpose other than drugs and human trafficking. I have a feeling those are just a means to an end."

"Like what?" Jones said.

"If I knew that, we wouldn't be sitting in a highway right-of-way in the middle of the goddamned night up to our butts in Russian assholes and damp prairie grass."

174

They heard the siren and saw the lights of Dean Sterling's unmarked car long before it arrived. Jones and Draper re-stowed the M4s in the Lincoln's trunk and Draper locked it. A state highway patrol officer arrived from the south at about the same time. Sterling came out of his patrol car with his weapon out and crouched behind the front fender. The Highway Patrolman copied Sterling's weapon out behind the fender move. "Draper, that you?" Sterling yelled.

"We're secure, Dean, come on down. Bring your friend."

Dean Sterling did not say much until they returned to the Sheriff's office. The Lincoln was drivable, having sustained only minor front-end damage. The Cadillac came out worse for wear hitting the steel power pole. Draper drove the Lincoln back up on the highway and made room for a wrecker to retrieve the Russian's Caddy. They were standing on the roadside watching when Sterling said, "Where's the other guy? You said there were two."

"Over in that field there," Draper said, pointing.

"I assume he's dead."

"Probably is by now."

"You shoot him?"

"I did."

"Are you going to tell me why?"

"Tried to run away," Draper said.

Draper and Jones sat drinking coffee while Sterling sent Dr. Death after the body of the second Russian. The more talkative one sat on a dropdown bunk in Sterling's miniscule holding cage with his head in his hands. Draper could tell Sterling was upset because he had yelled at Mario Lopez. The Sheriff made a couple of phone calls before saying, "You two, over here." Draper and Jones moved their chairs over in front of the Sheriff's desk and sat. Neither one said anything, waiting for the Sheriff to open the conversation.

"I just got the County Attorney out of bed and he isn't a happy camper," Sterling said.

"I don't much give a shit how the County Attorney feels," Draper said. "The two we ran into tonight are Russian mafia and their goal was to kill Mario and the three girls. They'd already killed Robert Arcuni. Doesn't that worry you a bit?"

"How do you know that?"

"The one in the cage told me."

"How'd he do that, he can barely speak English? I can't understand a word."

"He's Ukrainian, but speaks mostly Russian."

"And how is it you can understand Russian?"

"Misspent youth," Draper said.

"Goddamn it, Charlie, don't get smart with me. The County Attorney wants me to throw you in with that Russian bastard and charge you with deliberate homicide. The other guy was shot in the back."

"He was running away, trying to avoid capture by a Federal Officer. The charge won't stick five minutes. Use your head, Dean, there's something going on here that stinks to high heaven. Ask yourself, why would two Ukrainian mobsters be interested enough in three Hispanic young women to want them dead?

Sterling thought a moment before he said, "All right, you tell me, why would they?"

"Because they knew or saw something that makes them a danger. The girls might not know what it is, but I'd bet the guy in the cage does."

176

The County Attorney arrived dressed for court in an expensive conservative suit, a crisp white shirt, and a yellow tie. Draper guessed his age at around thirty, shortly out of law school and not wanting anyone or anything to trample his political aspirations. He stood smug and confident, staring at the group as if he did not want to get too close and risk wrinkling the suit.

Jones stood and introduced himself as a DEA agent. Draper did not move.

"Is this the man who shot the suspect?" the County Attorney said before Sterling could introduce Draper. "Why isn't he in the cage?"

"He's a NSA fed also," Sterling said. "His name's Charlie Draper."

"You have some ID?" the county attorney said. "I want to see it."

"Yes, do you?" Draper said.

"What do you mean? Are you trying to be a smart-ass?"

"I mean exactly what I said. I don't know you from shit. You could be any dickhead on the street in a monkey suit for all I know. You asked to see my ID, but you didn't say please."

"I've seen his ID," Sterling said, trying to mollify the attorney. "Charlie and Alejandro, this is County Attorney, John Stafford.

The County Attorney stared a moment at Draper before turning to Sterling and saying," Okay, Sheriff, tell me what's going on here."

Sterling started it, outlining the parts he knew. "We suspect Boulton is running a drug and human trafficking operation out at his ranch, but other than the covertly obtained information Charlie and

Alejandro have supplied, we haven't a smidgen of evidence that we could use to ask for a search warrant."

"What about the people who supposedly these two have rescued?"

"None of them speak English."

"There is one," Draper corrected. "Maricella speaks fluent English."

"There's no collaboration?"

"No," Sterling said.

"What happened tonight?" Stafford asked.

Sterling reiterated what Draper had told him, with prompting from both Draper and Jones. County Attorney Stafford sat listening and as the night progressed, a look of concern replaced the initial arrogance.

"Mr. Draper, I do apologize, what I've heard so far scares me to death. Why do you think the Russians wanted with the three young women?"

"Call me Charlie, Mr. Draper died years ago. Jones and I have seen a large building up near the Canadian border that has an elaborate elevator system that goes underground as much as five hundred feet. It's likely at least some of the illegals were brought into the country through that route. Certainly some of the most recent drug shipments have."

"How did you find this building?" Stafford asked.

"We followed semi trucks from Boulton's ranch. They arrive empty and leave loaded, yet when we went inside, the building was empty."

"I'm not even going to ask how you got inside," Stafford said.

"Door was open," Draper said.

"Sure it was," Stafford said. "How did you get on Boulton's place or don't I want to know that either.

"Don't ask," Draper said.

"I don't suppose you two know anything about two dead junkies in a motel south of here, thankfully in a different county?"

"What motel?" Draper said.

"Never mind," Stafford said.

Draper could tell the young County Attorney was shaken by what he'd heard.

"How big an operation do you think this is?" Stafford asked.

"Conservatively," several billion dollars a year in drugs and human trafficking, and that might be low," Draper said. "Just what the Russian interest is, we haven't figured out."

"Best guess?" Stafford said.

"Hell, I don't know. Just a wild idea. It occurs to me that I've heard that the underwear bomber and the shoe bomber both crossed into the U.S. through Canada."

"That's true, but that was in Eastern Canada," Stafford said. "Montana seems like a long way around."

"Maybe not," Draper said. "The former Sheriff here was assassinated by a pretty good marksman. What was the purpose? Logic says it was a dangerous move, likely to arouse all sorts of questions. Unless, and this is strictly supposition, there was ulterior motive.

"Like what?" Stafford said.

"Going for the obvious, I'd say, make sure a new Sheriff put local law enforcement in the pocket of whoever is running this show." Draper knew he was barking up a dead tree, but it made sense to him.

"Somebody took a run at Dean's wife. I assume that was to scare him off."

Stafford looked at Dean Sterling and said, "Why am I just now hearing about this?"

"Nothing to tell," Sterling said, "Charlie handled it."

"More than one?" Stafford said.

"Three," Draper injected.

"Three? What the fuck are you, some kind of one man army?" The County Attorney looked at Draper with a head full of suspicion.

"I've had a little practice," Draper said.

"You know I'll have to check on you?" Stafford said.

"Be my guest, I'll even show you my ID which has a number on it to call."

"The guy in the cage, can he tell us anything?"

"Apparently he only speaks Russian; the only English I've heard is *I want a lawyer* with an accent so strong even that's hard. Draper here understands him though," Sterling said.

"Can you interrogate him?" Stafford said.

"I already have. To get more I'd have to use tactics you wouldn't like."

"And what tactics would that be, beat or torture him to death until he talks?" the County Attorney said, his tone bordering on sarcasm.

"There could be some of that involved, but I usually go more for subterfuge, in lieu of violence. Takes longer but the result is usually better. After I'm done I shoot them." Draper said.

"Don't get smartass with me; I'm trying to figure a legal way to handle this."

"And I just told you one. I interrogate him in your presence and we find out what we can. All legal like," Draper said.

"I want someone on my side that speaks Russian," Stafford said.

"I'd be concerned it you didn't," Draper said. "Get him or her up here as fast as you can."

Chapter Thirteen

Highmore, Montana, Antelope County Sheriff's Office, Jail

The Russian linguist from the University of Montana at Missoula arrived two days later after a six hour drive across the state. She entered the Sheriff's Office at nine am, wearing a dark suit with a jersey zip jacket and pencil skirt probably designed by someone famous as Giorgio Armani. Slim and taller than average, Draper guessed five-ten or eleven; she towered over everyone in the room except Draper and Jones. The jacket covered her arms down to the wrist and the skirt stopped at a respectable knee height. Her hair cut short but long enough to tie in a conservative bun in back exposed a scholarly face in keeping with her occupation. She carried an expensive leather briefcase, looked professional, competent and held a no nonsense approach. She did not smile when she stopped at Mindy Sterling's desk and asked for County Attorney John Stafford.

"My name is Cathleen O'Leary," she said.

Draper tried to guess her age but failed since he knew it could lie anywhere in a twenty-five to forty window. Taking the easy route, he settled on thirty-two while listening to the conversation between her and Mindy Sterling. He was sure she had stayed overnight in a motel in Billings because she looked too crisp for just having made a six hour drive. Sterling would know when the county received her consulting bill.

"Mr. Stafford just called and he's about thirty minutes out," Mindy Sterling said. "He had an early court appearance in Billings this morning that went long. He is on his way now though so please have a seat."

"Is there somewhere I can freshen up?" Ms. O'Leary said.

"Certainly, the ladies room is just beyond the cage," Mindy said, pointing at the hallway between the holding cell and her husband's office.

"Thank you," Cathleen O'Leary said and walked toward the back of the office. She looked quickly at the man in the cell, but otherwise strode eyes straight ahead.

Draper watched her until she disappeared into the ladies room approving what he saw. He was willing to believe before they even started that her language skills were top notch. He decided it probable that she even knew variations and multiple dialects common to that area of the world. He had no doubt the morning would be interesting. He wondered how much the suit cost, an idle thought with no answer, but if pressed, he would bet close to three grand. A vacant thought crossed his mind that the suit did not fit a college professor, but he dismissed it.

"You are staring," Mindy Sterling said, teasing Draper.

"Am not. I'm trying to determine whether she's friend or foe," Draper said.

"You mean she isn't the Russian linguist?"

"No, she's Russian all right. I'm just naturally suspicious."

When the tall woman returned she sat two chairs away from Draper without looking at him and began to paw through her briefcase. Draper watched until Mindy Sterling said, "Ms. O'Leary, the gentleman sitting next to you will be the interrogator and the man in the cage is the suspect."

"Thank you," the women said to Mindy Sterling and turned to Draper. "Charlie Draper," Draper said and offered his hand. She took it and Draper saw an apparently high functioning academic with brusque social skills.

"The county attorney didn't say, but I assume you teach at the University," Draper said, working on a conversation.

"Yes, I teach Eastern European languages," she said.

"How did you learn Russian?" Draper asked.

"My parents emigrated to the U.S. after the fall of the Iron Curtain when I was eight. It's my native language."

"Ah," Draper said, confirming what he already knew.

"*Как насчет вас? Вы американец, не многие могут разговаривать на русском языке,*" she said.

"*Я провел хороший немного времени в этой области, когда я был моложе. Изучение языка была часть работы,*" Draper said.

"Okay enough with the Russian," Mindy Sterling said. "What are you talking about?"

"Ms. O'Leary asked me where I learned Russian and I told her I spent a good bit of time in that area when I was younger. Learning the language was part of the job."

"You speak Russian very well Mr. Draper, hardly any accent."

"Thank you. I appreciate the compliment coming from a native expert. I have to ask though; O'Leary isn't exactly a Russian name," Draper said.

She hinted at a smile before answering, "My father changed our names legally because he didn't want anyone to know we were Russian. Why he picked an Irish name is anyone's guess."

An alarm went off in Draper's head. Not a loud one, but a tingle, and coupled with the expensive suit it was enough to put him on alert. "If you'll excuse me, nature calls. Be back in a second." Draper crossed the room, passed the cage, and entered the men's room. As soon as the door closed, he pulled out his cell and dialed information for Missoula, Montana. When the operator answered he asked for a number, received it and dialed the University's main switchboard. The voice that answered connected him to the Language Department's secretary. A woman answered and Draper asked if they had a Cathleen O'Leary on staff.

"We do, she's head of the Russian Language Section; a very competent young lady. Why?"

"Can you describe her to me?"

"Sure, about five-six or seven, dark black hair, pleasant features, dresses conservatively. You still haven't told me why you are asking."

Draper didn't answer. He slammed the phone shut to cut off the line and dialed Dean Sterling's number. When he heard the line open he said, "Don't say anything, our Russian interpreter is a ringer. I'm in the bathroom. I'm going after her, cover me but don't do anything until I do."

"To late," Sterling said.

"She's got a weapon on you?"

"Yes."

"Don't do anything until I get there."

Draper opened the restroom door with his Glock behind his thigh. He stepped out into the hallway and saw the Russian mobster dead on the holding cage floor. He knew then the woman would be a handful. The Sheriff's Department anteroom stood empty and

Draper's eyes went immediately to the Sheriff's office. Dean and Mindy Sterling sat on the floor with the tall woman shooter holding chrome-plated S&W automatic in a large caliber equipped with a suppressor. Draper knew then why he hadn't heard the kill shot in the cage.

"You should join us, Mister Draper," the woman said. Draper felt sure her plan included not leaving anyone alive. "Drop the weapon on the floor and walk toward us or I'll be forced to kill your friends."

Draper's mind raced, measuring the odds. He couldn't see an optimum outcome, so he decided on stratagem. He moved forward while placing the Glock on the floor. He rose and said, "Now what?"

"You are hard to deceive," Mr. Draper. "A worthy opponent, but if you miss behave I will have to shoot you."

"I'm certain you won't lose too much sleep over it," Draper said.

"Now remove your backup weapon, which I'd guess is on your right leg. Please do it very slowly."

Draper's mind calm, he plotted his next move. He removed the second Glock from its ankle holster and held it in loose with two fingers. He wanted her to concentrate on it, watching his action. Kneeling on the floor he made a smaller target.

"Drop it!" she said, and Draper threw the Glock at her. The underhand shovel toss sent the weapon toward her face and she reacted as he expected. She ducked and shot at him. Draper felt the two bullets pass next to his head while he pulled the .380 out from under his left pant leg and double tapped her chest high. She stumbled back a couple steps and Draper double tapped her again. To his right he heard Mindy Sterling scream. The Smith and Wesson dropped out of the shooter's hand and hit the Sheriff's Office floor an instant before she did. Draper retrieved the weapon and checked her pulse. There was not one.

"Son-of-a-bitch, Charlie; that was a risky move. She could have killed you," Sterling said.

"That was her intent. There's a difference between could have and didn't," Draper said. "There weren't too many options."

Tears flowed down Mindy Sterling's face, her face showing both fear and relief while she held onto her husband. "She was a woman and you killed her," she said.

"Not much choice. It was her or us. I preferred her. Besides, some people deserve killing. I'd bet anything the real Cathleen O'Leary is dead somewhere between here and Missoula. That put this one in a *deserves to die* column."

Sterling called in all the deputies and Mario Lopez arrived first. He had the Sheriff, his wife and Draper seated in a row before he went into the Sheriff's office and checked the woman's body. When he came out he checked the body in the cage and said, "You folks been busy."

County Attorney John Stafford arrived twenty minutes later to an office filled with confusion. "Sheriff, suppose you brief me on exactly what happened here."

Sterling sat with his arm around Mindy and told Stafford the morning's events. Stafford listened while staring at Draper. When Sterling finished the narrative, Stafford said to Draper, "I checked on you."

Draper did not respond.

"Seems as if you don't exist; that bothers me," Stafford said.

"What do you want to know?"

"You have to understand from my prospective. As County Attorney, it is my job to put away bad people as best I can. I'm not sure yet which category you're in. Since you've been here a lot of bodies have appeared, all of which resulted from violence."

"I can't help it if there are a lot of criminals around, but I'm not responsible for all the bodies. I didn't kill Sheriff Hornsby."

"Where is your black buddy this morning?" Stafford asked.

"He's out taking care of business. I was here, as you know, to interrogate the suspect."

Draper tried to be patient. County Attorney Stafford was tough, thorough, and direct, but after the third time repeating the same information, irritation set in.

"I'm not trying to tell you how to do your job, but it seems to me everyone would be better served if you'd get someone out looking for the real Ms. O'Leary. Chances are she's another casualty." Draper went to his packet and retrieved his ID. "There's a number on the back, call it. They won't tell you anything except to lay off me and start looking for the real bad guys."

"You won't mind if I determine that for myself; right?" Stafford said.

"Suit your own self," Draper said.

Draper watched Stafford's face move from smug to sullen as he listened to the call. He hung up and said to Draper, "Why didn't you tell me you were an attorney?"

"Didn't seem relevant, I rarely practice and I'm not licensed in Montana."

"Where are you a member of the bar?"

"Primary Arizona and thirty other states back east."

"You should have told me," Stafford said.

"Would it have changed anything?"

"No. I'm not fond of your methods. You leave a lot of unexplained bodies lying around."

"Don't feel bad, you have company in that boat. I don't shoot anyone who isn't intending to shoot me or an innocent," Draper said.

Stafford grumbled, but he accepted Draper's explanation of events when Sterling and his wife both confirmed his story. He instructed Sterling to put out a BOLO on the missing Russian linguist while the coroner removed the bodies from the Sheriff's office. "You," he said to Draper, "take Sheriff Sterling and Mrs. Sterling somewhere while Undersheriff Lopez takes care of things here. I don't want any problems."

Draper and the Sterling couple walked to the half block to the restaurant without words. The Sheriff and his wife held hands leading with Draper two steps behind, his mind racing and trying to wrap arms around want was going on. In Draper's head the smuggling of drugs and humans, while dangerous and profitable in spades, did not rise to the level of Russian assassins. The Mexican cartels did not have a problem with murder at any level. Their usual assassin choice ran to gangbangers; they had plenty of those hanging around and did not need outside help. So what was the Russian interest? He could not help remembering the two who took a run at him the previous fall in Arizona. They were Russian with some high-powered artillery. What was going on?

The cafe sat empty guarded by a bored teenager with multiple facial piercings. She smiled at Draper happy to see a customer. She grabbed the coffee pot and three mugs and bounced over to the table. "Hi, Mr. Draper," she said and poured him a cup of coffee.

"Hi, Brenda," Draper said.

She turned and said, "How about the Sheriff and Mrs. Sterling, what can I get for you."

"Just water, please," Mindy Sterling said.

The Sheriff ordered coffee. Draper considered suggesting lunch since it was an hour passed the usual time but held off deciding the morning's excitement had probably removed their appetites.

"Should I be jealous?" Mindy Sterling said.

"Jealous about what?" Draper said, confused by the question since it did not fit into the worry box he had open in his head.

"Young Miss Brenda seems to have taken a shine to you," Mindy Sterling said, teasing.

"I have that effect on babies and grandmothers; the ages in between, not so much."

"On a serious note, do you have any idea what the hell this is all about? I get the drugs and prostitution stuff, but where do Russian assassins fit in?" Sterling said.

"Don't know," Draper said. "I have some ideas but nothing concrete. Last year a friend of mine and I spent some time in Mexico harassing the cartels. While drug smuggling and human trafficking along the Mexican-U.S. border is like an open floodgate, most of the cartel efforts have been low-tech. They spend about the same amount of effort fighting each other over territory. There is considerable in-fighting, corruption, and greed that hinder a coordinated effort. It is a good thing; otherwise, the drug problem in U.S. would be even worse than it is now. We found a large stockpile of heavy structural steel in Hermosillo, Son, Mexico that included what looked like a segmented cutter head for a TBM. We destroyed most of it."

"What the hell is a TBM? The only TBM I know of is a World War II dive bomber," Sterling said.

"TBM in this case stands for a tunnel boring machine. Lots bigger than the dive-bomber you have in mind. It's a specially built machine for digging large tunnels like the Chunnel from England to France. The problem was the cutter segments only indicated a twelve foot diameter tunnel which seems too small for a long distance tunnel," Draper said.

"Why is that?"

"Long tunnels require ventilation and maintenance access. Not enough room in a tunnel twelve feet in diameter."

"You are saying they didn't actually build it?" Sterling asked.

"No, but that doesn't mean they won't keep trying. The monetary gain is too high not too." Draper said.

Sterling fidgeted his attention wandering. Draper could see it and was not surprised when the Sheriff said, "I've got to go back to the office. I'm the goddamn Sheriff, the County Attorney can't just kick me out of my own office," Sterling grumbled.

"He can if he wants too," Draper said.

"Well, I'm not going to let him. Can I trust you to take Mindy home?"

"Of course," Draper said.

The Sheriff stormed out of the cafe and Draper figured there was a potential for a confrontation coming at the Sheriff's office. Sterling had hardened some since becoming Sheriff and Draper figured it was near even as to who'd win.

When they were alone Mindy Sterling reached across the table and took Draper's hand. He could feel gentle pressure as she said, "Thank you, Charlie, that's twice you've saved my life."

"Didn't see any other choice," Draper said. "But I'm glad it turned out okay."

192

"Weren't you worried she'd kill you?"

"No, that was a given. None of us was destined to leave alive in her mind."

"You take a lot of risks; aren't you afraid of dying?

"Not necessarily, I enjoy living as much as the next person. Everyone dies; it's only a question of when. In this case, I knew she intended to kill us, so all options where on the table. I relied on her not expecting me to throw the weapon at her. I knew she'd shoot, I needed to get her aim off target long enough to shoot back. This time, it worked."

"But, you didn't know she'd miss."

"No, but if she hadn't we'd all be dead now.

A full minute went by with Mindy Sterling holding Draper's hand and staring at his face. "What?" Draper said.

"You are a complicated man, Charlie Draper, a mystery with no solution. If I wasn't happily married, you'd be first on my list."

"Does that mean I have to worry about Dean shooting me? I hope not, besides I'm too old for you."

"Not really, but you could adopt me," Mindy Sterling said, her eyes filled with probing devils.

"I already have an adopted daughter. I'd have to get her approval."

"Why am I not surprised?"

***

Andrew Boulton sat at his desk in his office staring at the far wall. The wall held a good number of expensive paintings he had acquired over a number of years. He did not fully understand French impressionist work, but if it had Monet, Seurat, or Renoir on it, he bought it. Any serious study of impressionism in art would have left him speechless. He selected his purchases at random with little thought of the subtle short brush strokes, stunning use of changing light, or the fleeting colors of day. None of this bothered him, since his grasp of impressionism was limited to having expensive art to impress friends, business associates and an occasional opponent. He did, however, on those rare occasions when he had nothing better to do and wanted to relax, enjoy a glass of fine whiskey and a moment to gaze upon his collection, because it tended to relax him. This night it was not working.

He shifted his gaze to the phone, lifted his glass of amber colored fire and took a sip. Coming from his 'good enough for employees and enemies stock' it wasn't to his usual standard. His ranch foreman, Joey Diez sat across the desk in a hard backed oak chair designed to discourage visitors from staying too long. Diez was useful in a limited way, since he had the morals of an alley cat and killed on command. He did know ranching and there was where Boulton depended on him the most.

"Just came from town," Diez said. "That Draper guy somehow got wind of the Russians."

"And, what happened?" Boulton said.

"He killed one and took one into the jail."

"Were they able to find the Mexican's?"

"Appears they did not; this morning Draper killed a woman assassin at the jail after she took care of the one in the drunk tank."

"A woman?" Boulton said.

"Yes, I don't know how but he somehow sniffed her out. The guy's dangerous."

"Or damned lucky," Boulton said.

194

Diez did not respond. He had his own dark thoughts on Draper which he was not about to disclose to Boulton, so he sat silent. "What are you planning to do," he asked.

"For right now, nothing; I've got him coming out tomorrow for a tour. I was hoping to get him off our backs," Boulton said.

"You could cancel the tour, press of business or something." Diez proposed. "Or...we could plan a little surprise for him and his black friend."

"Like what?" Boulton said.

"I recommend a little surprise, something that would necessitate a deep hole in the south forty. An old Hispanic proverb says, '*Mata a tu enemigo rápida y enterrarlo profunda*'," Diez said.

"Kill your enemy quick and then what? I didn't catch the last part."

"Bury him deep," Diez said. "The cartels live by that rule in Mexico unless it suits them to make a point. No reason we cannot apply it here. Same as we do with the Mexicans and sick cows that give us trouble only this time we bury them real deep. The Russians were careless leaving Arcuni's body out on the roadside. They deserved the trouble they got in town."

"Maybe so, but I trust we aren't going to make the same mistake."

Chapter Fourteen

Eastern Montana

D raper woke the next morning after a solid ten hours of sleep. He sat on the edge of the bed minutes in his jockeys and a plain white t-shirt, staring at the motel room wall and not seeing it. The Glock lay locked and loaded on the nightstand. His mind raked over the last week's events in detail. He knew he was right about Boulton and the ranch he owned north of town, but even though the man had invited them to inspect the place today, Draper had little expectation that they had find anything incriminating. They'd had too much time to sanitize it. Thoughts threaded through his mind in fleeting imagery. He knew Boulton was trafficking in drugs and humans, dabbling in prostitution, and responsible for more than a few deaths, but the tunnel up north screamed of a larger scheme, more dangerous and potentially devastating to the country. Draper had spent a lifetime fighting off the enemy. Or so he thought. Whether it was ideological, political, greed, corruption did not matter. The job was always basic. Find the enemy, kill or disable him and go home. It never changed, bad people propagated like rabbits and a new crop rose from the ashes of the last. This time it was different, more up close and personal, as if the enemy had bigger plans. He could not figure out what the plan entailed and it bothered him.

197

At nine am, after breakfast and many cups of coffee, Draper and Jones drove into the Boulton Land and Cattle Company driveway and stopped at the closed chain link rolling gate topped with razor wire in loose coils. He felt as though they were entering a super-max prison. A guard stood outside the small shack holding an AK-47 at port arms position. Draper considered seeing how long he could hold that pose, but rejected it as nonsense. The inside guard came to the Lincoln's window and said, "Identification please."

Draper handed him his Arizona Drivers License and Jones' license from the State of Virginia. The guard looked them over and said, "Are you armed?"

"Yes, both of us," Draper said.

"You will have to leave you weapons here."

"That ain't happening," Draper said. "Call you boss and tell him it's armed or not at all."

The guard pulled used his radio to notify Boulton. He listened and said, "When the gate opens proceed directly to the main house where Mr. Boulton will meet you."

"Got it," Draper said, putting the Lincoln in gear and watching the gate slide to the right.

"Has kind of a prison feel, doesn't it." Jones said.

"It does," Draper agreed. They drove the quarter mile distance to the house at a slow speed as both Jones and Draper scanned the surrounding hills and ranch buildings for anything suspicious. The main house was impressive. A two story timber framed structure with oiled cedar siding, it had lap type on the lower half and shakes on the upper. The roof coating looked like cement tiles colored to match the cedar siding. Ostentatious in every detail, the windows were large, the gables stood out and the roof overhang ran wide. The roofed

198

porch, spacious enough to list as an outside room, covered all sides of the first floor. Boulton stood at the front door waiting and only needed a white suit and a cigar to pass as a wealthy southern plantation owner. Instead, he was dressed in Wranglers and rolled over cowboy boots with a red western shirt with ivory buttons. A head-worn Stetson covered snow-white hair. A shorter man stood nearby who Draper knew to be the ranch foreman, Diez.

"Mr. Draper and Mr. Jones," Boulton said his voice warm as if greeting old friends. Welcome to my spread. Mr. Diez. will accompany you where ever you want and when you are satisfied we are a hard-working cattle operation, you must return here and we will enjoy some of the finest Irish whiskey this side of Ireland." No one offered to shake hands. While Draper knew Boulton was playing at a warm welcome, the air around him was icy cold.

"We'll see how it goes," Draper said.

They followed Diez who led driving a battered ranch truck that no longer resembled the original Ford pickup. The box removed and replaced with a small flatbed, it carried the usual farm and ranch tools and supplies Draper would expect with the back covered with steel fence posts, wooden corner posts, tools and dusty rolls of barbed wire. He held the Lincoln back to avoid the boiling dust behind Diez.

"I wouldn't trust the guy any farther than I could throw him," Jones said.

"I wouldn't either. Let's keep a sharp eye out."

"You think they might try something?"

"I'd be surprised if they didn't. Tried to disarm us on entry knowing we were Feds and probably carrying."

"Are you sure they know we're Feds?"

"I bet they have better resources than we do."

"Think we'll get out alive?" Jones said.

"No telling; best to have a plan, though."

"How about we crack Diez over the head at the first stop, bundle his ass up in some feed room, and snoop around on our own. Look where we want to look."

"Damn, I like the way you think. Let's do it. You want to lead or should I?"

"It's my turn to have the fun. You be ready to back me up, though you being kind of old and me being black and all, I doubt I'll need it." Jones said.

"Keep talking like that and I might shoot you instead."

"And send a covey of fine black ladies into mourning? They'd shoot you first at even the idea."

Diez pulled up to a long low roofed building with ten-foot side walls that Draper guessed was some sort of indoor caving shed. Diez got out of his truck and waited for Draper and Jones to join him. Diez headed to a closed walk-in door and while his back was turned, Jones sapped him, caught him before he hit the ground, and dragged him into an adjacent lean-to. Zip-tied and gagged, they covered him with a blue plastic tarp and weighted down the corners with straw bales. Satisfied the man was out of commission for a while, Jones looked at Draper and said, "Something tells me there might be a reception committee behind door number one."

"So, let's go look for door number two."

Draper and Jones walked the perimeter of the building using caution as their leader. At the far end were holding pens, a crowding line ended at a squeeze chute; a nice setup for working cattle. Large sliding doors provided access to the building for working indoors. In the center of one of the sliding doors a walk-in door allowing entry without opening the big doors.

"Not much doubt they run cattle. Those pens are in bad need of cleaning," Draper said.

"We open that door and they're going to see the light and know something's up."

"How about we leave them waiting, we go look over the building we saw that processes the drugs and see what we can find. They may not have secured it figuring we'd never get that far." Draper was not comfortable with hunting down waiting bad guys in a dark unknown building.

"You're not going to get an argument out of me," Jones said, "I much prefer bearding the enemy on our own terms."

"Amen, brother," Draper agreed.

They worked their way back to the Lincoln, got in with as little noise as possible, and drove away. Draper took the road that went up over the low ridge into the next valley where they found the drug processing building and the Mexicans. They passed the railroad caboose-looking buildings where they had discovered the young woman and a short distance later they stopped. The building looked different in daylight, bigger and well used. Truck traffic had beaten the narrow road into powder whipping up behind the Lincoln even at slow speed.

"Might be time to get out the big guns and body armor," Draper said.

Draper parked three hundred yards from the building while they dressed in body armor and retrieved two M4's from the trunk. The building looked quiet but neither man considered that a good sign. Draper drove to the edge of the building closest to the forest in case they had to use it for cover. They found same door they entered before locked and Draper spent less than a minute correcting it.

"Ready?" he said.

"Waiting on you, dude," Jones replied.

Draper threw the door open and waited and when nothing happened, he peeked in. The building appeared empty. The processing tables stood clean, wiped and shiny.

"Empty?" Jones said.

"Appears to be; cover me."

Draper stepped in, going low and sweeping the building with the M4. "Clear," he said and Jones followed. They spent the next several minutes searching every corner and crevice, M4's leading and finding nothing.

"Shit," Draper said, "We're going to look pretty silly if we don't find something. You go back and watch the road so no one sneaks up on us. I'll continue to look. Maybe we missed something." While Jones went to guard the door, Draper made a second slow walk around the perimeter of the building. He was almost back when Jones cried, "Here they come, Charlie."

There were four, heavily armed and accompanied by Andrew Boulton and Joey Diez. Boulton yelled, "You have been a very naughty boy, Charlie Draper, now I'm going to have to kill you."

"I thought that was the plan from the beginning."

"Of course it was. You surprised me; you are more resourceful than your predecessors. However, it won't matter. You can't stop us. You have no idea what you are up against. In fact, why don't you and your friend give up? I promise we will kill you quick since the plane will be here in minutes to pick us up."

202

"Enough talk, they spray the door with those AK-47s and we'll be sitting ducks. That ten gauge metal siding won't provide much protection," Jones said to Draper.

"I'll spray them first, that will give us time to get back into one of those loading docks. It isn't much but it's better than here. Go!"

Draper stepped to the doorway and stuck his M4 outside. He'd switched to full auto and emptied half a clip at the voices outside. He heard a couple screams and turned to follow Jones. Halfway to the dock pit he heard automatic rifle fire outside. When he dove over the loading dock, Jones said. "Hear that?"

"Yeah, I think they're cleaning up."

Draper heard the roar of a jet aircraft outside, but there was little he could do about it. He followed the sounds and figured they were landing. After several minutes, a second roar told him they were taking off and jumped onto the concrete floor and ran for the door. He could hear Jones right behind. He had wasted another short burst like the first as a safety measure before he looked. He saw four bodies on the ground. "Cover me, I'm going to check."

Draper ran toward the bodies following his M4 with a tight trigger finger. He stopped when he reached them and scanned the area around him. The plane was gone, Diez' battered pickup sat next to another Ford quad cab with its doors hanging open. Of the four bodies, two had entry wounds in their backs. Diez was one. The air was still with tomblike silence. Draper realized Jones stood behind him when he spoke.

"Not much of a retirement plan," he quipped.

Draper did not answer and pulled out his cell and dialed the Sheriff's office.

"Sheriff's office," Mindy Sterling said.

"Mindy, this is Charlie; I need to speak with Dean."

"Of course, are you all right?"

"Right as rain, my dear, let me talk to your husband."

There was a moment of silence before Sterling answered. "What's up, Charlie?"

"Grab all the deputies you can spare and get out here to Boulton's place. Boulton ran and we have four bodies."

"On my way," Sterling said.

Draper hung up and looked at Jones. "The place is sanitized but what would they do with the drugs and any Mexicans they had here. It's likely they'd kill the illegals, but I doubt they'd destroy the drugs. Makes sense they hid them."

"But where, there's nothing in the building?" Jones said.

"Maybe, maybe not, we have time before Sterling gets here. I want to snoop around a little."

Draper reentered the building wanting a second look when he was not continually watching his back. Jones followed retracing their steps along the walls. "Look for something unique or that looks out of place."

They reached the truck docks. Draper looked down into a pretty standard inside loading dock, bed height forty-eight to fifty-two inches and the floor fairly level which meant there had to be a grade correction outside to allow trucks to back into the lower level. The extended overhead door confirmed Drapers theory.

At the bottom of the dock there was a maintenance pit four feet wide and Draper estimated forty feet long covered with four by two foot steel plates for safety; again, usual warehouse construction. The two docks had a common truck parking area and Draper could not see anything unusual. The floor concrete blackened with truck tire marks looked like any other warehouse he had been in. He walked back to the maintenance pit, slid one of the steel plates aside, and looked into the hole. Down about eight feet, he could see water. Water in the wash pit made it look as if they had washed a truck in the last couple of days.

Jones walked up and said, "I didn't find squat; how about you?"

"Not so far."

"What are you looking at?"

"Just a wash pit, I guess."

"What else would it be?" Jones said.

"Nothing," Draper said and climbed back up onto the main warehouse floor. He stood a moment staring back into the dock.

"What," Jones said, "I know that look; something's bothering you, right?"

"Yeah, but it's just a little annoyance and I can't figure out what it is," Draper said.

"I suggest we take a look at the lower ranch buildings and see what we find."

"Makes sense," Draper said.

They walked halfway back across the floor to the entrance door they had used to come in before it hit Draper like a sack of rocks. "It's not deep enough," he said, more to himself than to Jones.

"What's that mean?" Jones said.

"It's not deep enough," Draper said again. "The freakin' pit's too shallow!"

"How so?"

"If it was just a wash pit it could be ten or twelve feet deep to catch silt and dirt washed off the truck. The deeper the better so they wouldn't have to clean it out often. If it's a maintenance pit it can't be so deep the mechanic couldn't reach what he wants to work on. A maintenance pit is usually about six feet so the mechanic can walk under the truck without hitting his head and he can still reach most everything. I didn't see any washing equipment, did you?"

"No."

"Let's check that pit and see just how deep it is."

"How are we going to do that?"

"If it's a maintenance pit there should be stairs at one end, usually on the door end."

Draper jumped down off the main floor to the dock level, walked to the overhead door end, and started pulling the steel plates aside. After two he said, "Ah, steps."

They removed four more steel plates until they could see the steps disappear into muddy water. Draper walked down, squatted at the last dry one, and reached into the water.

"Water's only about six inches deep and it feels like a concrete floor underneath."

Draper came out of the pit and he and Jones pulled four plates aside in the middle and four on the other end to provide light. Draper reentered and stepped into the water.

"Be careful there aren't traps or holes," Jones said.

"Damn right," Draper said. At each step he tested the floor before he put his full weight down. It took ten minutes to reach the other end. "There's a hinged four by four steel plate door here locked with a padlock. It's keyed. You'll have to run out to the Lincoln and get my pick set."

Jones was gone less than a minute, peered into the pit and said, "Found the key." He handed Draper a large set of bolt cutters.

"That'll work." Draper pinched off the lock and dropped it into the water. When he swung the door open, he noticed the backside was covered with a three-inch thick foam block. Behind the steel door, a second wooden door had a latch with a hook and eye set. Draper unlatched it and pushed the door in. He was looking into a black hole. He felt inside for a light switch and breathed stale air.

"Shit," Draper said, "look around up there for a light switch."

"Got it," Jones said.

The dark in front of Draper blazed light exposing a large concrete enclosed room and he could hear a ventilation fan turn on." His eyes fell on a group of people lying on the floor, none of them moving. Draper took little notice of the far wall, stacked floor to ceiling with shrink-wrapped bundles.

"Alejandro, I need help, there are bodies in here," Draper called, climbing into the room. "Call 911." He triaged by shaking each one and if he got any reaction he grabbed them up and carried them to the hole. Jones was there and took the first one without comment, a young girl. Neither man said a word while they worked, both knowing time was critical. Draper found two unresponsive and left them for last. As soon as they had them all up on the main floor, Draper said, "Check pulses, any that aren't breathing but still have a pulse start CPR. Any unconscious but with a pulse and breathing on their own let them go for the moment."

After twenty minutes both men were exhausted and they had six recovering and two dead.

"What happened to them?" Jones said.

"I'd bet carbon dioxide poisoning. No ventilation, your own breathing can kill you. You exhale carbon dioxide and it displaces oxygen, especially near the floor. It makes you sleepy, sometimes a little intoxicated, and you lie down. When the carbon dioxide level reaches high enough you die of oxygen starvation."

"How long does it take?"

"If the concentration of carbon dioxide rises as little as ten percent over normal, a person can lose consciousness in less than a minute."

"No shit?"

"That's why mining and confined spaces are so dangerous. Ventilation is critical. Why don't you call Dean and find out what's taking so long. I'm going to take a look at that room."

"You be damned careful down there," Jones said.

"Don't worry; as soon as you turned on the light a ventilation fan came on. As long as the door is open, it should be okay. I won't stay in there more than a few minutes until we can get it tested."

Draper waded back through the water to the still open steel door and climbed through into the concrete room. The air smelled fresher telling him the room had not been designed for human occupancy but rather to store illicit drugs. He took a hard look at the pile of plastic wrapped bundles ranging from small to large. He guessed the larger ones were marijuana and the smaller contained types that are more expensive. Based on what he had seen before, it looked like millions of dollars worth. Off to the side sat a nondescript wooden box about the size of a steamer trunk. It was not locked so Draper opened it. Inside were banded bundles of twenties and hundreds stacked to the top. Draper removed four bundles, stuck them in his shirt, and closed the lid.

Back up on the main floor Draper stomped his feet to shed water and walked to where one of the Hispanics was trying to communicate with Jones.

Jones looked at Draper and said, "I haven't a clue what he's trying to tell me."

"I'll give it a try," Draper said.

"*Entiendo un poco de español, pero habla lenta,*" Draper said. "I told him to talk slow."

The young Hispanic male began to chatter at a pace Draper could not follow and he held up his hands palms out and said, "*Despacio, despacio, por favor.*"

The young man seemed to grasp Draper's fumbling Spanish and, stopped. He looked hard at Draper and Jones before he said, "*No nos van a matar?*"

"*No, estamos aquí para ayudarle,*" Draper said.

"So what's he saying," Jones injected.

"He asked if we were going to kill them, I said no, we were here to help them."

"He believe it?"

"Probably not yet, but soon."

"What are we going to do with them?"

"Only thing we can, turn them over to Border Patrol. Can't save them all," Draper said. You stay with them; I have to go to the car for a minute. You get a hold of Sterling?"

"They are waiting on a search warrant."

"Figures," Draper said.

"What about the ambulances?"

"Same thing, guards at the gate won't let them in."

"We'll see about that. I'll be back in a minute," Draper said, grabbing an M4.

Draper reached the Lincoln and opened the trunk, hid the money he was carrying and slammed the lid. It took minutes to reach the front gate, where he jumped out with the M4, laid it over the roof pointing at the inside guard and said, "Ten seconds, that gate isn't open, I'm going to shoot your ass!" When the man tried to bring his AK-47 to bear, Draper shot him. Inside the guard shack he took a second to find the open switch and punched it. As the gate opened, Draper ran through following the M4. The outside guard dropped his rifle and ran. Draper let him go figuring the Sheriff's crew would pick him up eventually. There was not much of anywhere to go in the middle of hundreds of square miles of Montana prairie.

When he walked up to the ambulance, the driver said, "I hope you are the one that called."

"Close enough," Draper said, "follow the driveway passed the big house on your left, take the road that goes up the hill and over into the next little coulee. There's a big metal building with a tall, ugly black man, who needs your help. We have two bodies and six near asphyxiations. It's secure up there."

"I'm on it," the driver said and sped away.

Draper dialed his cell and when Sterling answered he said, "Dean, you are about to become the most famous Sheriff in fifty-six counties, with the biggest drug bust in Montana history. Come join us, the front gate is wide open."

"How many have you killed?"

"Only three so far today, but it's early yet. The bad guys killed a couple more, probably because there wasn't room on the plane and they didn't want to leave survivors. Have Mindy notify Border Patrol we have eight suspected illegals, two of whom are deceased."

"I'm on the way."

As crime scenes tend to be, the procedures to ensure a prosecutable case took hours and extended far into the night. Draper's temper felt short, and irritation rose more than once, yet he said nothing and let Dean Sterling proceed as required. He knew the efforts of dedicated law enforcement were frustrated by a snail slow and time-consuming legal system. He sympathized with them knowing the higher up the food chain you went the more complicated it got. A measure of how much criminals could get away with depended on how many expensive attorneys they could afford to buy. Draper knew Boulton had gotten away clean, if that was his real name. Chances were it was not and he was likely already in a foreign country somewhere sitting on a pile of money.

They were in the Sheriff's Office at quarter to four in the morning and Draper felt as though he had been without sleep for days. The six illegals were sitting on the floor of the holding cage, feeling, Draper felt sure, apprehensive, and tired.

"It's been a hell of a day," Dean Sterling said. "To bad Boulton got away, but what we have is going to count a lot."

Enjoy it while you can, we aren't done," Draper said.

"Somehow I knew you were going to say that."

"He's always the bearer of bad tidings," Jones said.

"This is only the beginning," Draper said. I'm afraid there's something else afoot here."

Chapter Fifteen

Atlanta, Georgia

A ndrew Boulton sat in a comfortable lounge chair in a downtown Atlanta, Georgia hotel executive suite on the sixteenth floor sipping Midleton Very Rare 2001. He stared into the amber liquid and swirled it around under his nose. At $139.00 a bottle, he considered it a bargain, since it slid down feather smooth. Saddened not in the least by his quick departure from Montana, he preferred the big cities as everything he desired was nearby. He grew tired of the ruse in Montana months earlier and considered the place barren, boring, and a type of exile. His friends and close relatives, motivated by political cause and ideology, held rabid dreams of destroying the U.S. Boulton's desires were more basic; power, money and pleasure, though the order changed from day to day. He ignored the fact the three were interrelated so changing the array did not matter. His fourth cousin, several times removed, Darchin Kazarian, sat across from him, also enjoying a sip of the Midleton. Boulton had not used his real last name, also Kazarian, for so long he now thought of himself as Boulton. He and Darchin had grown up on the Steppes of Middle European countries whose names changed at least once a decade depending on who held political power.

"It's too bad we had to abandon our little enterprise in Montana," Boulton said. "It was quite profitable."

213

"It became a liability when that fucking Draper started nosing around," Kazarian said. "If you'd kept you hands off those Mexican girls we wouldn't be having this conversation."

"So, what's lost; a little money and some drugs? It's nothing. We can replace that in a matter of days. The demand for drugs in this country is growing every day. The Americans are culpable for their own demise. Our plan will cause panic, kill millions, and result in economic collapse. What more could we want. Then we rebuild it into a communistic society of our liking. Besides, getting rid of Draper should be easy. It's not like we don't know where he is. We grab someone he cares about and make him come to us."

"You forget we've already tried that."

"True the man is damned lucky. However, what if we grab someone close to him, wife, child, whatever; someone we know he will come after. The man's a romantic fool."

"Maybe, but he's also very good and damned dangerous." Kazarian said.

Boulton decided to change the subject. His cousin, though useful in many ways, lacked the ability to see the big picture. The best there was at killing and making sure things got done at any cost, he lacked direction. That, however, fit nicely into Boulton's plan since he considered himself as the idea man. His grand plan was to become President of the United States; or maybe Supreme Leader of a new Marxism-Leninism type society. He felt the new drug-fueled, nanny state loving population was ripe for such a move. "How are we coming on *Pagun?*" he said.

"Very well, I think. The first of ten units are ready and soon transported by boat to a warehouse north of Vancouver, B.C. When it is off loaded, probably in the next few weeks, we will truck it across

Canada to our facility south of Regina, Saskatchewan. From there, bringing it into the U.S. will be easy. We'll use small trucks, one and a half or two ton van bodies will be work nicely. Can you imagine the government trying to round up every small truck in the country? That will be fun to watch."

"How soon will all the units be ready?" Boulton asked.

"If everything goes as planned we should have everything in place by July."

"Fantastic, that means we are ahead of schedule."

"Yes, it all hinges on this first load, but I don't anticipate any problems. We have been practicing for over a year without a hitch," Kazarian said.

"You make sure there aren't any," Boulton said, "We have too much invested to have it fall apart now."

"Rest assured, Cousin, everything will go as planned. I leave you now since I have much to attend to."

Boulton watched his cousin leave and when he was, alone he poured himself another couple fingers of the Midleton. He sat back and enjoyed the warmth in his stomach radiating outward. After a few minutes, he picked up the phone and called his favorite procurer. "Might as well have some fun," he said to empty walls.

***

Darchin Kazarian did not have any real purpose for leaving his cousin alone other than he had heard enough of Boulton's braggart talk. Of the opinion that if his lazy-ass relative would lay off the women and booze for even a minute, *Pagun* would be even further along than it was. He liked the name, taken from the Slavic God of Lightning and Thunder. He planned to rain lightning and thunder all right, in spades.

Kazarian left downtown and drove south on Interstate 75 toward the airport. He exited at 287 to the Old Dixie Highway and turned south into an industrial area with large warehouse buildings. His destination was one of the smaller units, little more than ten thousand square feet, but all of it open to twelve feet in height. It suited his purpose and the rent came reasonable. The parking was limited but he did not need much and there were two ten foot overhead doors. It was not much as metal buildings go, but adequate. He had two employees, relatives actually, with the same ideological bent that consumed him. Inside there were ten boxes, wooden crates eight feet by eight feet by eight feet. Nearby cascading sparks from a plasma cutter lit up the shop. Kazarian watched, fascinated by the precision machine cutting through quarter-inch steel plate. The actions of the machine were computer controlled and once completed the various sized items were picked by an overhead gantry crane. The crane moved the pieces to jigs that formed them into boxes so welders could tack-weld them together into two different sized containers, one large and another smaller that would sit on top of the larger one. Compete fabrication would happen on the shop floor with all the seams welded tight. The shop supervisor came over to Kazarian away from the shop noise.

"What do you think, boss?" he said. The man did not care what they were building as long as he could do it exactly as shown on the plans. Its final use was not concern. He enjoyed creating something, anything, as long as it needed his skills, which were mechanically adroit.

"It looks perfect," Kazarian said. You and your crew do excellent work."

"It ain't good unless it's perfect," the man said. "We don't do half-assed."

Very true, Kazarian thought, these men were old-country artisans who knew quality only came with care and time. It was the same with *Pagun*, not rushed, instead precise and controlled in order to accomplish the objective.

"These are the last two," the man said. "They should be ready to ship by the end of the week. Been meaning to ask, sir, what do we have coming up next? Need to consider how much re-tooling we'll need to do."

"Not to worry we have plenty orders coming in. It's only a matter of deciding which one we'll take." Kazarian was accomplished at lying, letting the words slide over his tongue with enough emphasis to be convincing.

Darchin Kazarian left the man with the excuse he had to make a phone call, which was true. He wanted to call his contact in Mexico at the first destination for the completed boxes to ensure everything was ready. Trucked from Atlanta to the Laredo, Texas border crossing into Mexico the wooden boxes containing empty steel tanks would not attract attention. The lading bill would read alcohol-distilling tanks. They looked and were at that point, benign. After crossing the border, the truck would travel to Monterrey, Nuevo León. At that location, the plant would fill the tanks before the final journey.

Kazarian dialed long distance to Monterrey, Mexico and waited while the antiquated exchange in Mexico completed the call. He imagined squirrels carrying little micro bites of information and stopping to rest every few feet all along the line. Finally, his party answered.

"*¿Hola?*" the voice said.

"This is Kazarian," he said.

"Ah, our friend in the United States, what can I do for you today, *señor* Kazarian."

"We will be ready to ship the first two boxes at the end of this week, so you can expect them somewhere around Monday."

Si, we are ready here also." the voice said.

"Have you made all the arrangements to ship them through Panama to our partner in Vancouver, B.C.?"

"*Si*, that is also in place. Do not worry, *señor* Kazarian, we are experts at this, we will use the very same process we use for the drugs."

"It had better work."

"I trust you understand that threatening us is not the best incentive. We respond better to a clean business deal and not so much to callous statements. You should understand that before you say another word. You need us, señor Kazarian, we don't need you."

Kazarian bit his tongue, wanting to lash out, but restraining himself. The man was right, much depended on the cartel to help with their project *Pagun*. The only safe way to bring the boxes into the U.S. was through Canada; he knew it as well as his co-conspirator on the phone did.

"Forgive me, my friend, I misspoke. This is a very important job and I have been receiving shit from higher up. I trust you will accept an apology. I understand it is to our mutual benefit that things run smooth," Kazarian said, while wanting to reach through the phone and throttle the man at the other end.

"And they will, *señor*, as long as you remember we also have a branch in the fire. The success of this project will benefit us both."

Kazarian did remember, though only enough to keep from lashing out at the man on the other line. He stabbed end on his smart phone, venting his anger on the unfeeling phone. He dialed a new number, one he knew by heart and didn't need to look up. The phone buzzed in his ear, ringing the party on the other end; twice. The voice on the other end said, "*Что?*" in Russian.

The conversation in Russian went lengthy as Kazarian updated his comrades on the events of the last few days. He could tell they were concerned and while he tried to soften the incident as best he could there was little doubt they were unhappy about the events in Montana. While his cousin did not feel concerned, the center of operations in New York fumed. His instructions were clear and immediate which left him little choice. He spoke a moment with the shop supervisor and returned to his car in the parking lot. The drive back to the hotel was uneventful. He dreaded what he had to do but it was not enough to keep him from completing the assigned task. When he parked, he tipped the attendant with an American twenty knowing it would close his mouth forever. At the sixteenth floor, he stepped off the elevator and walked to room 1604, slipped on a pair of leather gloves and inserted his key card. The door unlocked with a quiet click.

They were in the bedroom of the two-room suite; he could hear them as he screwed a suppressor on his Russian Makarov pistol, a short, easily hidden 9mm weapon with noteworthy short-range accuracy. He stepped into the bedroom. His cousin, distracted by coital effort did not notice the danger until too late. He mouthed "What the f...," but did not complete the sentence before he died. The muffled bark of the Makarov silenced the room. The woman looked around at him, surprise flowing over her face in the microsecond before the second nine-millimeter bullet entered her brain.

Kazarian spent the next few minutes cleaning. He did not touch the bodies, but instead wiped every flat surface he could remember touching. He had only been in the front room for an hour earlier in the day and hadn't touched much. His cousin had given him a key card so he wiped that as well and left it lying on a side table. His whiskey glass from earlier sat on the table where he'd left it. It went into his pocket. He was in and out in fourteen minutes.

Darchin Kazarian retrieved his car, thankful he opted for a luxury model since his destination sat eighteen hundred eighty miles away. The drive would take over twenty-eight hours plus the time necessary to pick up two shooters at the Kansas City airport on the way through. They would have to come sans any armament, but it mattered little as his trunk had extra stock.

Three days and hours of hard driving later, Kazarian and his two companions rented two motel rooms in Billings, Montana. They were sitting in a restaurant on King Ave West. The shooters, a pair of Armenian brothers recruited for their killing skills and not necessarily for intelligence, sat shoveling food down with little comment.

"The two we are after are a salt and pepper pair, one white and the other a very large black man. They will be hard to miss. The town is small and most everyone knows them. The county sheriff is a friend. He is a secondary target. The town of Highmore is about a hundred-fifty miles north of here. It's a couple hour drive but we can't stay any closer without being noticed. We'll operate only at night to lessen the chances of being recognized. You do what I say when I say it, understand."

Both men nodded, continuing to shovel food as if their interest waned at everything but their stomachs. Kazarian's temper flared but he tamped it down knowing the two might look too dumb to stack bricks, but in Russian circles, they came well recommended as efficient and deadly.

Big Sky Dead by Dave Folsom

Chapter Sixteen

Highmore, Montana

D raper and Jones had little to do for three days. County attorney John Stafford and his forensic team swept every inch of the Boulton Land and Cattle Company without finding anything of real substance. Customs and Border Patrol officials took charge of the six live Hispanics and two bodies for processing back to their native countries. They had a collection of fingerprints, none of which matched anyone in the FBI's IAFIS fingerprint database. They did have a nice pile of drugs with an estimated street value of close to ten million dollars and another eight million in cash. Draper sat across from Dean Sterling in his office.

"The Highway patrol at Billings notified us that they picked up the guard at Boulton's compound that you didn't shoot. He was caught trying to hitchhike on State Highway 191 near Missouri River crossing. He was tired, foot sore, near starving, suffering from exposure and he gave up without a fight," Sterling said.

"I figured as much. Wasn't likely he'd go far on foot wandering around in a hundred square miles of Montana prairie." Draper did not shed a tear at the thought of him spending the next ten years or more in the State Prison at Deer Lodge.

"So, now what?" Sterling asked.

"There's the little problem up at the border with Canada that needs to be resolved."

"How far from the border and what kind of a problem is it?"

"Remember me telling County Attorney Stafford that when Alejandro and I were following the trucks north out of Boulton's place they turned off the highway just south of the border and went west about ten miles or so to a big metal building out in the middle of nowhere."

"Yeah, I'm trying not to remember that you two clowns broke in," Sterling said.

"Didn't have to break in, the door was unlocked."

"Sure it was."

"The building was empty. But inside there was a large concrete box that looked like a freight elevator system," Draper said.

"So what does that mean?" Sterling said.

"It means that there is probably a similar building somewhere north of the border with a matching elevator system," Draper said. On the American side, we watched the trucks come in empty and leave loaded."

Draper felt the Sheriff studying him, trying to solve a mystery that appeared unsolvable. Like most dedicated law enforcement professionals, Draper mused, Sterling had reservations about his means to an end particularly when it did not always meet the letter of the law. "We took down Boulton, didn't we, isn't that enough?" the Sheriff said.

"It would be in most cases, but I think there is something more insidious going on, that the drug and human trafficking is only a means to an end."

224

"If you're saying the drugs aren't the reason for all this, then what is?" Sterling asked.

"That's just it, I haven't a clue," Draper said. "Up to lately, it was easy. The cartels in Mexico are disorganized, vicious, power-hungry criminals. Their motives, desires, and objectives are easy to understand when you think of the most basic of human needs. Don't get me wrong, the cartels have a death grip on Mexico, particularly the northern half."

"How were they able to do that?"

"It's complicated but, the obvious answer is a centralized government in Mexico City which has little interest in the rest of the country except as a revenue stream. There's limited industry, poverty levels that make the worst off in the U.S. look like millionaires, coupled with corruption, greed and political nepotism. It wouldn't be hard to predict the outcome under those conditions."

"The ones we've caught here though seem to be Middle European. How does that fit in?"

"If I knew that I wouldn't be sitting here talking to you. I will say I think Boulton might be a plant. Although he had no accent, I'd bet my first born Boulton wasn't his real name and I'm wondering if he might be Middle European," Draper said.

"Could be," Sterling said as his phone rang. He answered and listened silently for several minutes before saying "Sounds like our man." He listened several minutes more before adding, "Send them to us and we'll see if they match up with any we have. Thanks."

"That was Atlanta PD. They have a body whose name on the hotel register matches our BOLO for Andrew Boulton."

"Our Andrew Boulton?" Draper said.

"He's sending the man's prints. We'll see if they match with any we found at the house."

"Sounds as if he's dead."

"As a doornail, shot with a nine millimeter."

"Failure has consequences in the circles he ran in," Draper said.

"We'll see when I get the prints."

Draper met Jones an hour later at the cafe. They were drinking coffee when Draper's phone rang. He listened for a minute before grabbing a pen and wrote a date, time and a name on a napkin.

"What?" Jones said when Draper put his phone away.

"We have an appointment with the Canada Border Services Agency in Regina, Saskatchewan, tomorrow at ten in the morning."

Then Jones' phone rang. He answered and listened for several minutes before saying, "Are you sure that's how you want to play it?"

After listening several more minutes, he hung up and looked at Draper. "They want me to take lead and gave me a name and number to call."

"And you should. You represent a real U.S. Government Agency. I don't represent anyone who'll admit to it," Draper said.

"You okay with that?"

"Of course I am. You're capable and can do whatever we need to do to get the job done. Besides, the fewer people who know who I am, the better.

"What do I tell them?"

"Everything; we want them to find and destroy the twin building wherever it is in Canada. Here's the way we'll play it: Regina is a good six driving hours away. I suggest we borrow

Chauncey Flynn's 180 and fly. It's probably less than an hour and a half up and another hour and a half back. Do it in a day easy. Tell them we'll leave at seven in the morning tomorrow and be at the airport in Regina around eight-thirty. I better call Flynn and see if the plane's available first."

Draper called and it was. Flynn talked his ear off for close to ten minutes before Draper was able to break away. "He thinks he's part of a government covert operation and loves it," Draper said. "Anyway, we're in."

"He's not too far from right," Jones said. "You sure you know how to fly the damn thing?"

"Relax, I'm sure. I own a 182. The only difference is this one's a little slower and it's a tail-dragger."

Jones called the Canada Border Services Agency contact in Regina, Saskatchewan and arranged for someone to pick them up at the airport the next morning. Draper figured it would be a long but productive day. They arrived at Chauncey Flynn's farm within minutes of five-thirty the next morning. Jones grumbled about the early hour, mostly to jerk Draper's chain. Draper knew the man was only half joking though, since experience taught him rising early wasn't Jones' forte. Flynn had the 180 out, fueled and prepped. Everything Flynn owned shone like new boots and the 180 was not any different. Draper called Billings, filed a flight plan to Regina, SK, Canada, and notified APIS of their flight out of the U.S.

"We have to stop in Opheim, Montana on the way back for a customs check." Draper said.

"What the hell is Opheim?" Jones said.

"It's a little Montana town between here and Regina. Homeland Security wants to have a look at our cargo to make sure we aren't carrying any contraband. You have your passport card or a regular passport?"

"I've got both but only have the card with me. It's easier to carry," Jones said.

"That'll work, let's load her up and ride." Draper said. "You want to go around with me on a check ride?" he asked Flynn.

"No, son, I figure you know how to fly it, probably better'n me."

"I hardly think so, my friend, but I appreciate the confidence. I owe you one."

"You bet your ass you do. Wait'll you get the bill."

Draper did his run-up, taxied to the end of the runway and turned into a light wind. He noticed Jones had a death grip on the door strap. "Relax; this your first time in a small plane?"

"Yeah, does it show?"

"A little, are you concerned?"

"You sure you know how to fly this thing?"

"Absolutely; like I told you, I own one like it. I've got several thousand hours flying it."

"Well, then get this damn thing off the ground so I can quit worrying about it."

Draper set the prop and shoved the throttle to the firewall and the 180 rolled forward gaining speed. At fifty-five mph Draper began applying back pressure on the wheel until the plane lifted off the runway and began to fly. As always, Draper felt the elation that flying always gave him, the freedom of watching the ground fall away as if by magic. The trees, buildings, and people began to shrink, slow at first then faster until only the very large ground features remained. It never ceased to captivate Draper's sole.

The flight to Regina, Saskatchewan was short in terms of time so Draper set his assigned altitude on the autopilot at nine thousand feet. His cruising speed set a 165 mph; he estimated their flying time at about an hour and fifteen minutes. He looked at Jones, who was staring out the side window at the ground.

"Quite a sight, isn't it?" Draper said.

"It's amazing. I can see details I never knew existed. How hard is it to learn to fly?"

"Learning to fly a small plane like a piper cub for instance is fairly simple, just takes training and practice. This 180 is a little more complex but again it's a matter of good training and lots of practice. Like anything else, the more you do it, the better you get at it.

"What happens if the engine stops?"

"First, it's unlikely; private aviation is under strict maintenance rules that make that a rare occurrence. If it should happen, you practice dead stick landings as part of your training. It's not any different than a normal landing except you might not have an asphalt runway under you."

"That ever happen to you?" Jones asked.

"Long ago when people were shooting at me; we used to joke any landing you could walk away from was a good landing."

"Aviation is much safer in terms of fatalities than driving your family car. For starters, pilots are better trained and generally more careful." Draper said, but Jones did not look convinced.

Right at 7:30 am Draper called the Regina tower and received landing instructions. Minutes later, he was in the pattern following a small commercial jet. After touching down, he turned on the first taxiway and headed for the general aviation area. After clearing customs, they entered the main terminal were two plain-clothed representatives of the Canada Border Services Agency waited. After introductions, the lead representative said, "We've reserved a conference room. Follow us."

During the meeting, Draper listened while Jones briefed the Canadians. A couple of times he looked to Draper for agreement and when Draper nodded, Jones continued. Draper was impressed. Jones negotiated like a pro and did a fine job of belaying the men's skepticism. Draper also understood the Canadian's cynic responses. He shared some of their disbelief. The older of the two aked Jones unanswerable questions and Draper became conscious of the younger one staring at him. Draper guessed his age at somewhere around thirty-five, or sneaking up on forty. Old enough to be seasoned, yet still young enough to retain his youthful ideals. His partner was over fifty, hardened by a lifetime of chasing bad people and watching them get away with it. Draper felt certain he hated his job and wanted to be almost anywhere in the world except in an airport conference room with a couple of tolerable American cops with a wild hair up their butts. It became clear he was not buying a word of what Jones was telling him.

"You mean to tell me that some Russian terrorists have dug a tunnel from the U.S to Canada and the Canadian outfall is somewhere near here? What kind silly juice have you two been drinking?"

"Not near here, but in Saskatchewan near the border."

"Bullshit, I don't believe it."

"Believe it, we've seen it on the American side and there's nowhere for it to go except into Canada. All we're asking is that you go look and confirm there is similar structure on the Canadian side. You're looking for a large metal building or something similar, on a straight line north from the one in the U.S. The location on our side is such that we are certain it extends into Canada." Jones stared at the older CBSA official daring him to dispute his statement.

"There's no goddamn way I'm going to authorize a wild goose chance looking for some mystical building on your say so unless you can give me something more to go on than your intuition."

Concluding that the older CBSA official, a long time bureaucrat, wasn't about to endanger his job and reputation on the word of a couple of crazy Americans, Draper stuck his foot into the water, saying, "How about this? We have a plane capable of carrying the four of us. We go look, on our dime, you give us an hour a and half, and if we can't find anything we'll go home and take care of it on our side. Sound fair?"

"An hour and a half and you go home and say no more about it?"

"That's the deal. Jones and I will go get something to drink, be back in fifteen and whatever your decision is we'll stand by it." Draper felt certain he could make a phone call and create a flurry of embarrassment for the old man but hoped diplomacy would work instead. He stood and motioned to Jones, "Let's go find something to drink."

The Airport terminal was expansive and crowded. Draper remembered reading somewhere that the Regina airport was one of the busiest in Canada. Looking at the crowd of people moving through the building, most all dragging wheeled luggage, reminded Draper of a trip through Chicago's O'Hare terminal years earlier, packing heavy luggage like a rented mule, miles seemed, to the taxi pickup area. Watching a young woman sail past with rolling luggage prompted him to abandon his faithful old suitcase in the hotel room after purchasing a new set with wheels. That decision ranked right up there with the Magna Carta. They found a small sandwich and drink dispenser and each purchased a cola.

"That old fart is a tough nut," Jones said.

"Bureaucrat protecting his ass," Draper said. "I think he'll accept our offer because if we fly around for an hour and find nothing it'll make him feel he was correct to begin with. If we find something, so much the better, it'll confirm our suspicions and cover his ass."

"You think we'll find something?" Jones said.

"I don't know, but I hope so, although something just occurred to me. We've been thinking another building. Maybe it's something different on the Canadian side."

"Like what?" Jones said.

"Hell, I don't know, could be anything."

Jones and Draper walked into the conference room fifteen minutes later. The two Canadian officials sat across for one another, heads down in an intense conversation. It stopped when Draper and Jones entered the room. "What's your decision?" Draper asked.

"We are going to take you up on your offer. One hour and a half not a minute more," the older of the two said.

"Fair enough," Draper said, "Let's do it."

They walked back through the terminal to General Aviation and the younger of the two Canadians stepped up beside Draper. "I know you," he said, "took me until now to remember where. Kuwait 1998, I took a survival class from you."

"Learn anything?" Draper said.

"Must have; I'm still alive."

"There's that," Draper agreed.

"Seriously, it saved my life on a couple of occasions."

232

"That so?" Draper said, "What part?"

"The part about how to kill."

"Glad you were listening."

"Me, too," the younger Canadian said.

Any excuse to fly made it a good day, despite the reluctance of his two rear-seat passengers. After takeoff Draper set his GPS locator for an area fifteen miles due north of the metal building they had found in the U.S. Then he planned to turn due south toward the border, do a one-eighty turn and come due north ten to fifteen miles. Beyond that, he was hoping they'd see something to guide them into the object of their search.

Jones spotted the anomaly while Draper was busy staying on course and flying the airplane. "Charlie," he said, "look at that road. It seems a little well-traveled for out in the middle of nowhere." Draper looked and saw the same thing. He chopped the power a bit and put the plane into a shallow glide path to lose altitude. At two thousand feet he leveled out and banked the aircraft to get a good look. "Let's follow it and see where it goes."

"Your time is up, Mr. Draper; I don't see a damn thing unusual. Take us back to the airport." Draper could hear a twinge of satisfaction in the man's voice; certain he had won the point.

"One more minute, we want to check out that road. Then we'll return to the airport," Draper said over his shoulder. When his passenger voiced his dissent, Draper ignored him.

The road wound through the bottom of a deep gorge, cut three or four hundred feet deep in ancient times by melting glaciers. Draper stayed five hundred feet above the lip and followed its course a couple miles before they spotted their quarry. It wasn't a building.

"What the hell?" the older Canadian said, silenced by the view of what looked like a set of sliding double doors built into the side of the canyon wall. Its location hid it from view from almost any direction except straight on and the color of the doors blended seamless with the surrounding yellowish white clay. Draper looked at his GPS tracking and realized they had flown over it twice, but at altitudes above a couple thousand feet, it was invisible.

"I'm not sure what that is but it looks worth closer inspection. In fact, I'd bet if you kept watch on it you'd see small trucks coming in loaded and leaving empty. It that turns out to be true, it would be a good indication the other end of that portal comes up in our building." Draper did not need confirmation since he felt sure he was right. A tunnel of any size would mean almost any product, human, drugs or otherwise brought into the country would mean little or no risk. The unknowns scared the hell out of him.

Halfway back to the Regina airport the older Canadian said. "We need to get bodies into the place and find out what the hell it is."

"All due respect, sir, that might cost lives. We don't know how it's set up, what kind of protection there is, if any; or for that matter whether or not they even connect. Do I think so, yes, but that isn't concrete proof."

"What do you suggest?" the younger one said.

"If it was my tunnel, assuming there is a tunnel, I'd set up some sort of failsafe system with an ever changing code that had to be entered from either end. If the wrong code was entered it would bring down security doors that would trap whoever entered the code. Only one or two trusted individuals would be able to override the system."

"How do we get in then?" the older one asked.

"One or two people who know how to do covet operations, after a hell of a lot of recon. Maybe start with a driver and work our way up. They must have some way of notifying someone inside when they arrive."

"How do we know they'll tell us the truth?"

"Believe me, sir, Jones and I know how and I suspect your young assistant does also."

Chapter Seventeen

Northeastern Montana

After dropping off the two Canadian officials at the Regina airport, Draper refueled and prepared to return to the U.S. Shortly they were in the air and for the first few minutes, neither man spoke. Jones broke the silence saying, "You thinking what I am?"

"Depends on what heavy thoughts are rolling around in that head of yours," Draper said.

"Don't play with me, you know what I mean. I'm thinking why spend the kind of money to build a tunnel when the old methods of hiring cheap, expendable help to the dirty work is cheaper and the results similar. True, a tunnel would increase the volume some, but would it be worth it? My experience with drug trafficking tells me the cartels have much baser desires, like greed, power and sex. World domination isn't in their vocabulary."

"Keep talking," Draper said.

"Need a little help. Other than it doesn't make sense, I don't know where this is heading."

"Here are the questions rolling around in my feeble brain. Go a little farther and ask why the ranch? It's an expense that doesn't make sense. Why not process the drugs before they enter the country?

There is a lot of cheap labor in Mexico. What I think is that the drugs are a ruse, useful to defer expenses but not a portent of the real goal."

"And the goal is?" Jones asked.

"Terrorism," Draper said. "The U.S. is the big dog, and the mongrels are circling looking for a weakness. It's been coming for years.

"I thought the current administration removed that word from the dictionary."

Draper smiled at that thought. "They might have tried, but it doesn't change the fact this whole thing stinks of political violence on a grand scale. Why the sudden appearance of Middle Eastern criminals, a female assassin who speaks Russian and has no ties to the U.S. There's no record of her entering the country. Ask yourself, how'd she get here?"

"Through the tunnel?" Jones said.

"I can't think of another way. Coming through without impeccable paper work by any other means is getting harder by the day."

"Holy shit, they could bring in anything, any kind assassin, bomb, terrorist group, or whatever and it would be difficult or damn near impossible to detect," Jones said. "What are we going to do about it?"

"I don't know just yet," Draper said. "But I'd suspect they have a backup for everything. It only makes sense. Why risk everything on one place? This operation is too sophisticated. They abandoned Boulton's place without a whimper. I should have seen that before this."

"How do we find it?" Jones said.

"Don't need to. We go back to the building up north and wait for a truck."

Waiting became their nemesis; it threw boredom, anger, and frustration at them in an unveiled attempt at discouragement. It almost worked. Frustrated and angry, both Draper and Jones spent two weeks sitting every night at the metal building location they'd found in northeastern Montana. During their vigil the moon was at first waning until almost a sliver on a mostly ink black night, before beginning its waxing phase. After fourteen days with not a sign of a truck they agreed that they'd split up, one watching during the day and one at night. If anything appeared a cell phone call to the other sleeping at the motel would suffice. It was Tuesday night of the fifteenth day on Draper's turn at night watch when a truck finally showed up. Draper, alerted by the diesel rumble, watched as it entered the compound and backed slowly up to the large overhead door. The driver stepped out, punched a code into a keypad and the big door opened. Draper wanted to jump the driver, beat the shit out of him and extract the code, his employer's identity, the location of the new transfer point, and the name of the man's firstborn child. With considerable self-restraint, he did nothing, except watch.

As before, the loading took an hour and a half. The door opened and the truck drove to the barbed wire gate at the road; the driver got out, opened it, drove through and closed it, before reentering the truck and disappearing down the road. Draper followed. At the highway, the truck turned south toward Highmore. Twenty miles before Highmore, the truck's brake lights came on and Draper slowed, watching the truck turn left on to a county road. Draper waited slowing his Lincoln to a crawl until the truck disappeared over a small rise. Then he sped up and made the same turn.

In contrast to the Boulton ranch, the backup location was austere. No fancy buildings, no gated entrance, no security to alert law enforcement suspicions; just an abandoned farm house, two story four square model with cured lap siding long without a coat of paint and a roof with missing shingles.

"How far we've fallen," Draper mused.

The semi truck continued past the old house to an assortment of long unused outbuildings ten or more years beyond the deferred maintenance stage. One, a fairly large structure that had probably served as machinery storage in its prime, was now weathered to abuse on the sides but boasted a shiny new metal roof and a fourteen-foot overhead door.

"Bingo!" Draper said to the empty car.

Draper watched as the truck backed into the open overhead door until it disappeared and the door closed. "Nothing good happens in the middle of the night," Draper said aloud to the empty car.

He parked the Lincoln in the moon shadow of the old house and walked carefully toward the big shed. His path took him in a circle around the building looking at all sides for other entrances and found only old sliding doors, the barn type common in years past. Rust on the metal works indicated they hadn't been opened in years. The truck was inside two hours while Draper waited. When the truck left Draper walked cautious around the building looking for other entrances. When he could not find one he settled on the overhead and found it secured by a ten dollar padlock. He walked back to the Lincoln for his pick set and was lifting the door in minutes. He raised it only far enough to duck under.

Inside, he found pallets of sale-ready packaged drugs in cardboard boxes labeled with weight and drug name. "They're processing the drugs before they enter the country now," he said to himself. At the back of the building stood a newly constructed loading dock with a ramp to ground level and a shiny new Clark five-ton forklift. Seeing all he needed, Draper backed out and re-locked the overhead door. Back in the Lincoln, he called Jones.

"Rise and shine," Draper said, "we've got action."

"Finally," Jones said. "What happened?"

"Semi load of drugs picked up at the border building and I followed them to an abandoned farm twenty miles or so north of Highmore. I've got an old building here stacked cornucopia full of already street packaged drugs."

"No shit?"

"Verified," Draper said.

"Where do you want me?"

"I'll come pick you up in an hour or so and we'll come back here. I'm thinking we should highjack one of the smaller trucks. Rather make it disappear and see if that doesn't rattle their cage. However, anything's on the table if you have an idea. Drugs are your expertise."

"Sound like fun, I'll be here waiting." Jones said.

Draper picked up Jones and drove back to the new transfer site. Finding a site to view the old farmstead proved frustrating as the wide-open country did not allow many strategic points for observation. They ended up in a grove of young ponderosa pine and scrub fir mixed with quaking aspen. The only good feature was that it sat close to a quarter mile away with a slight chance of detection.

Draper would have liked closer, but settled because that was the only choice. The afternoon sun flirted with the mountains behind them by the time they settled in. The farm sat quiet and deserted on the Montana prairie. It looked forlorn in the distance, abandoned to the elements. The men took turns sleeping during the night, lying comfortable in thick duff and a soft layer of pine needles. At dawn, Jones drove into Highmore and came back with a cooler full of sandwiches from the cafe. Nothing appeared during the day and by midnight, Draper began to wonder if they'd misinterpreted something. To kill time, he dug a sniper's trench that allowed him to keep constant watch through the scope of his M4. The barrel rested solid on a five-pound sack of sand from the Lincoln's trunk. The M4's action set on three-shot burst, Draper felt confident he could take out any target in the area around the buildings. The range distance fell under five hundred yards, making kill shots easy. Darkness dragged through a two-hour period in the north unlike in Arizona where the dark crashed like a fire curtain. In Montana, total dark didn't occur until long after nine pm. At nine-thirty, two small trucks with van bodies showed up. Neither vehicle exceeded one and a half ton capacity. Small, but capable of a good-sized load, Draper figured the two together could haul all the drugs stored at the farm. He felt it likely they had driven to Billings carefully obeying every traffic law to avoid law enforcement. Draper placed the crosshairs of his telescopic sight on one of the men's center mass and caressed the trigger. So easy, his mind said, while judgment argued against action. His better judgment said not now, maybe later. Judgment won.

Draper continued to watch as the trucks loaded and closed the overhead door and left leaving an empty building.

"Now what, fearless leader; are we just going to let them go?" Jones said. "There's a fortune in illegal drugs in each van."

"I know," Draper said, "but if we stop them now they'll just change locations and all we'll end up with a lot of work for two truckloads of drugs. I think something else, bigger, much bigger is afoot. The drugs pay expenses."

"What are you, some sort of conspiracy theorist, Draper?"

"No, the Russian thing is bothering me though. Granted it would finance a bunch of covert activity but why?"

"You're asking me? I'm a poor black narcotics cop, just trying to survive from day to day. Talk to me."

The watch lasted most of the night until at four am Draper was about to give up the effort. He stood, stretched away aching bones when a full sized semi with a soft side van pulled in packing a tail-loaded all-terrain forklift. Both men dropped to the ground.

"What have we got here?" Draper whispered.

"This is a new twist," Jones agreed.

"Damn right," Draper said, "he's loaded heavy. His tandems aren't flexing a bit off the overloads." Draper watched through his scope while the truck maneuvered in the farmyard and backed up off to the side of the overhead door. Parked, the driver stepped out and walked to the side of the door where Draper knew the padlock lay. He unlocked the door and raised it to full height. Next he climbed aboard the forklift, lowered it to the ground and backed away from the truck. He parked the forklift, walked to the truck, and began opening the soft side. As it slid back, it exposed two large wooden crates.

"What the hell have we got here?"

Two big wood boxes," Jones said, stating the obvious.

The two men watched the activity below while the driver slid the forks under the first box, lifted it, and backed away loaded. His movements slow and deliberate, the driver moved the box inside the building and set it on the loading dock. He repeated the action with the second box. After completing his chores, he reloaded the forklift on the back of his truck, closed and latched the soft side and drove away.

"What do you suppose is in those boxes?" Jones said.

"I don't know but I'd bet by the end of day we'll know."

"Are we going to break in and take a look?"

"No need, I have a key."

"Forgot that," Jones said.

They waited until ten in the morning to ensure there weren't going to be visitors. They took an M4 each and enough ammo to sustain a firefight in case one ensued. Breaking in only took a minute for Draper to pick the lock. Rolling up the door exposed the two boxes. Close up, they looked even larger, Draper certain each would measure eight by eight by eight. Each dimension was double banded with three-quarter metal strapping tight enough they could not be moved. The boxes, built of four-quarter rough-sawn hardwood that Draper guessed was probably ash since it resembled oak but lighter in color. In any case, the boxes were hell for stout.

"Whatever is in them is well protected. If we cut the bands, it will still take a lot of work to get them open."

"Take a look at this," Jones said, walking around the first box. "It looks like an access panel."

Draper looked. The panel was close to twelve by twenty four inches and screwed on with one-way screws spaced about two inches apart. "Shit, whoever thought this up didn't want anyone to see what was inside. Those are tamper-proof or sometimes called one-way screws. They're commonly used in public bathrooms to deter vandalism; impossible to remove without the special extractor."

"Where do we get one?" Jones asked.

"Sheriff's Office might have one. It's not likely in a small office but worth a shot. If Dean doesn't have one, we'll have to make a flying trip to Billings."

Draper called the Sheriff's Office and when Mindy answered, he said, "Let, me talk to Dean, its important."

"Okay, just a minute," she said. Draper could tell she wanted to say more but the tone of his voice stopped her.

"What'cha need, Charlie?" Sterling said.

"Do you have a bathroom stall screw extractor?"

"Yeah, why?"

"Could I borrow it?"

"Sure, as long as you tell me what you're going to use it for."

"Do I have to?"

"Damn right, that's an important 'only authorized persons' type tool."

"Bullshit, Dean, you can buy them at Home Depot, but I don't want to drive all the way to Billings," Draper said.

"What about I bring it out to you, where are you?"

"You should see what we found, but you won't like how we found it."

"How'd you find it?"

"Don't ask, just bring the tool. We're about twenty miles north at an old abandoned farm house, on the right side.

"The Hirschman place?"

"Don't know what it's called, just bring the damned tool."

Draper hung up and looked at his watch. "I'm betting Dean gets here in less than seventeen minutes."

"Never happen," Jones said, "he'll fume, yell at Mindy, and he's got to find the tool; that'll be several minutes at least. Even Code Three he'd be at least eighteen, so I'll take that bet. What are we betting on, dinner?"

"Dinner's good though adding a beer or two before would be better," Draper said.

"Sounds good to me, though he'll never make it,"

Draper's watch read five seconds short of seventeen minutes when the Sheriff's unmarked sedan slid to a stop in a cloud of alkali dust. "Damn that dinner is going to taste good," he said.

Dean Sterling stepped out of his patrol car and said, "What the hell are you two into now. Dammit, you didn't break in, right?"

'The door was open, Sheriff," Draper said. "Isn't that right, Alejandro?"

"Aye, it was, God's truth," Jones said.

"Well, what the hell have you got here?"

"Don't know for sure, Dean, a semi unloaded these two boxes last night about four am. This morning we got to thinking about it and since the door was open, we looked them over. Seems suspicious and there's access panels on the back of each box but the screws are the one way type. Need to take a look-see."

"What do you think they are?"

"Not a clue. Only earlier last night we watched two trucks load up enough drugs out of this building to keep a user in juke for years. Don't think it was for personal use. Then these boxes show up. Wouldn't you think that would make a man just a tad curious?"

"Curious and illegal entry are two different things, Charlie."

246

"The door's wide open, Dean, let's go take a look. If it's nothing you can lock us up and throw away the key. Mindy'll let us out in the morning."

"Damned if I don't think she would. All right let's take a look."

It was not easy. Even with the extraction tool, the screws embedded deep in the hardwood came out hard and loosened only with considerable effort. Removing all forty fasteners took an hour. Draper took out the last one and pried the cover off. Dean Sterling shone his department flashlight in the hole and for what seemed like forever, no one said a word.

Dean Sterling finally broke the silence with, "Holy shit. You smell what I smell?

They were looking at a digital clock that read the current time in inch tall red letters. Below the time was another digital strip with zero dot double zero on it. They could see two separate steel tanks, tied together with an inch and a half quarter turn valve that was in the off position. Both tanks were enclosed in heavy mill plastic sheeting to reduce the smell. Below the digital clock a stainless steel, five inch diameter by four foot long cylinder lay tied to the lower tank. The smell of diesel fuel and ammonium nitrate fertilizer was unmistakable.

Draper pulled out his cell and dialed. When the voice on the other end answered he said, "I need a bomb expert on the phone right now, its urgent." Draper found it hard to remain patient while the other end transferred his call. After what seemed like an eternity, a voice said, "Describe it to me."

Draper did. His description detailed as he could make it he hoped it would spark action at the other end. When he finished the voice on the phone said, "It sounds like an ammonium nitrate and fuel oil or AMFO type that isn't mixed yet. The valve does that step. After mixing, this type of bomb only needs a booster to get the explosion started, usually common dynamite, and a blasting cap. Could also be a brick of C4. Can you see anything like that?

"No," Draper said." There's a couple of colored wires coming out of a small hole in the larger tank that are connected to the timer"

"Okay, it sounds like it hasn't been armed yet and from your description of the location it's being stored and that isn't the final destination," the voice said.

"Agreed," Draper said, "there are two more things you should know."

"What's that?"

"There's numbers on the boxes; big painted numbers. These two are nine and ten. To me, that suggests there are at least eight more boxes somewhere."

The phone went silent for a nanosecond, and then the voice said, "That's not good; what else?"

"There's a cylinder about five or six inches in diameter and four feet long tied to the bigger tank but doesn't seem connected to it."

"Holy mother..." the voice said, "Sounds to me that what you have there, son, is one hell of a big, dirty bomb that's going to need one hell of a DDH project."

"What the hell is a DDH project?" Draper said, unfamiliar with the newer government acronyms.

"Disarm, Dismantle and make Harmless, son, don't let anyone near that site until our people get there, understand. Secure with armed guards instructed to use deadly force if necessary."

"Let me let you talk to the County Sheriff. His name is Dean Sterling."

Draper handed the phone to Sterling and said, "They want to talk to you, but don't let them hang up until I talk to them again."

Sterling talked to the voice on the phone for over ten minutes while Draper paced. He had thoughts piled on other thoughts rolling around in his head and it took effort to organize them. He could not do anything about the boxes. That lay in the hands of the Sheriff and anyone else that he called on. In one ear, he heard Sterling call the County Attorney followed by a call to his Undersheriff.

Meanwhile, Draper had other fish to fry. He nodded to Jones and they left to climb back up the hill to where the Lincoln sat. Halfway up the hill he called Sterling's number but received a busy signal. Figuring that might extend far into the night and most of the next few days he called Mindy Sterling at the office.

"Sheriff's Office," she said.

"Mindy, this is Charlie."

"Hi Charlie, what's going on? I can't get reach Dean."

"He's busy with a big case. I can't reach him either. Would you tell him for me that Jones and I are going to see what we can do about the tunnel? Have him notify the Canadian authorities about the bombs."

"Bombs?" Mindy Sterling said. Draper could hear incredulous in her voice.

"Dean knows about it but it's keeping him busy at the moment."

"Is he all right?"

"Absolutely, he's coordinating an important crime scene or I wouldn't have bothered you."

"Okay, you and Alejandro be safe."

Draper hung up and he and Jones climbed into the Lincoln. They did not waste time talking as Draper turned north on the highway. They both knew where they were going and what they had to do when they got there. Draper's mind rolled plans around, analyzed them, picked them apart and discarded parts and adding new. By the time he turned off the highway onto the gravel road that led to the big metal building, he had solidified a plan.

"You going to share or do I have to follow you blind?" Jones said.

"When did you ever follow anyone blind?"

"Never, so tell me."

"Didn't you work for ATF when I met you?

"Yeah, but transferred to DEA shortly after. Didn't like bombs. What do you have in mind?"

"We wait for a truck. Disarm and disable the driver and get him to call the elevators. We go down with him and take out whoever is down at the bottom. I suspect some worker bees and a guard or two."

"We take out everyone?"

"Whatever happens; eliminate the worse and make harmless the rest, kill or subdue.

"You know that when those elevator doors open we'll be sitting ducks if there is any kind of warning system?"

"Fully aware of that, guess we'll just have to depend on full body armor, firepower and surprise. A bit of good luck would help."

Chapter Eighteen

Montana's Northern Border

They reached the metal building site a half hour before midnight. A full sized semi-truck with a soft side trailer arrived within the hour, minutes after they had finished dressing in full body armor, checking their weapons, including an M4 and two handguns each. Both added a couple of flash-bang grenades. In pockets and anywhere there was room were fifteen round magazines for the handguns and thirty round magazines for the M4's.

"You ready?" Draper asked.

"Ready as I'll ever be," Jones said.

"Okay, let's go grab that driver."

By the time they'd reached the building the truck was inside and the door closed. Draper picked the side door lock and they slipped in. The driver, content with his position had reentered the truck cab for a smoke before proceeding. Draper was alongside the truck's fifth wheel when the driver stepped out backwards to climb down from the cab. When his first foot touched the concrete floor Draper tapped him with the butt of his M4, not hard, just enough to daze him a little. His knees collapsed and he dropped like a poleaxed steer. Draper had to grab him to keep his head from bouncing off the hard floor. "What the hell?" the man mumbled, still rattled by the gun butt. His cigarette lay on the cement, smoldering. Draper stepped on it before dragging the stunned man over to the truck's front tire and propping him up.

Jones stuck the barrel of his M4 against the man's head and said, "My suggestion is you think about your next move because it will determine if you live or die."

"What'd you want?" the man mumbled, still unclear as to what had happened.

"You are going to tell us all about what you are doing here and what this building is for," Jones said. "If you resist or give us any bullshit you will be dead in a heartbeat; your choice."

"I'm just a driver," the man said, working his jaw in a futile attempt to stop it from hurting.

"Look friend, my buddy here wants to shoot you; but I can stop him and make sure you go home in one piece," Draper said, in a smooth, even voice, not friendly, but encouraging. "All you have to do is tell us what your job is and what you are supposed to do tonight and I'll convince my big friend here not to shoot you dead; fair enough?"

"I just drive, honest. I'm supposed to pick up a couple of big boxes and deliver it to a place north of Highmore, Montana. It's an old abandoned farm."

"What's in the boxes?" Draper asked.

"Hell, I don't know. I get paid to load and drive, not to ask questions. I haul them to the farm and dump them off. I don't know what happens after that. It's someone else's job. I have no idea where they go."

Fear ran rampant through the man's eyes. Draper could see it when he talked in short, hurried sentences as if talking fast would somehow delay what he felt convinced was inevitable. "I have a wife and two kids; this was the only job I could get and it paid good. I needed the money."

"What are you supposed to do now?" Draper said. Jones' M4 barrel still pressed against the man's forehead.

"Nothing," the man said, looking confused, "I just go down in the elevator and bring the boxes up and load them on my truck; nothing else."

"How do you get them on the truck?" Draper said.

"There's a forklift down there. I have to bring them up one at a time and then take the forklift back down and leave it there."

"Anybody else down there?"

"No, not usually, sometimes a couple of guards, that's all."

"How do you call the elevator?"

"There's a card, like a credit card. They leave it in an envelope hidden in a slot on the wall."

"All right," Draper said. "We are going to tie you up. You behave and you might see your family again. Fuck with us and you'll be dead before dawn."

"Look, I'll help you all I can, but I don't know much; this is only my second week on the job. Goddamn it, I knew it was too good to last."

Draper zip tied the driver while Jones went to look for the elevator card. He returned with a small brown envelope with a blank white plastic card with nothing on it except a magnetic strip.

"I believe this is it," Jones said.

They left the driver sitting on the concrete, zip tied hand and foot with his back against the sidewall. Draper and Jones walked to the elevators and Draper slid the card through its slot. Nothing happened for a second or two before a red light came on.

"You suppose that means the elevator is coming?" Jones said.

"I hope so, but be ready in case there's trouble."

They waited almost a full minute before the car arrived and the doors opened. It was empty. They stepped in and Draper scanned the control panel. There was only two choices; up or down. He selected down. The car sank, accelerating slow, as it came up to full speed, dropping almost a full minute before the brakes applied, and the car began to slow. Draper looked at Jones and said, "You ready?"

"Ready as I'll ever be," Jones said. What if there's an army of armed men waiting?"

"I guess we see how many we can take with us, I suppose," Draper said.

"Where we gonna take them?"

"Hell's fire, I suppose. Given our current record it might be our only choice."

"Hope they got women and beer there, then it won't be so bad." Jones said. The elevator stopped and the door opened.

There were two, sitting at a table playing cards, nothing in their hands but a lousy draw. They did not look at the elevator until the door was completely open and Draper and Jones stepped out. Then they moved in a desperate attempt to recover a sloppy guarding job. They were both dead before they reached their AR-15s. Once they ensured the men were no longer a threat, they cleared the room and found themselves alone.

Jones stared at the concrete roof over their head. Curved above them in a large arc with a twelve-foot radius, the circumference connected with the concrete floor leaving a twenty-four foot circle. The floor, bisected by a set of railroad tracks with a third rail off center of the middle running between the two outside rails. On the elevator side, cut into the rock, Draper could see a twenty by twenty foot room, apparently for storage. Two wooden boxes sat alone in an otherwise empty space.

"Holy sweet Jesus, there's your goddamn tunnel," Jones said, staring into the dark hole cut into solid granite with steel rails heading due north into Canada, "Them boys from the frozen north are going to shit when they see this."

Draper was more interested in the two wooden boxes. Identical to the ones they had found at the abandoned farm, he could not help wondering where the rest were. These two, numbered like the others with crimson paint indicating seven and eight. Logically that meant at least six more. That left a conundrum; where were the other six and was that the total or were there more? Draper's head hurt from all the possibilities and scenarios rattling around inside. He surmised that these two also were not armed, but he had no way of checking since they had not thought to bring the special tool. Looking around, his eyes settled on a Hyster 80-120 electric forklift. A brute of a machine, brand new with the paint still clinging to the forks and capable of loading up to six tons, it sat off in a corner of the storeroom, plugged into a charging station. The machine was overkill for loading drugs, but the wooden boxes, heavy as they were, would need a hefty loader.

"What if we load up these two and take them up to the warehouse above?" Draper said to himself, thinking aloud and not realizing Jones was behind him.

"Okay, then what do we do with them?" Jones asked.

"Jesus, don't sneak up on me."

"I'm too big to sneak anywhere; you were just deep in thought."

"You hear something?" Draper asked.

"What?"

"It sounded like a clank or metal on metal sound," Draper said. "There it is again."

"That time I heard it; could it be the train coming?"

The sound was louder by the time they situated themselves where they could watch the tracks. It was not a real train, in the sense of a railroad train; the engine looked more like a small donkey engine with small wheels, pulling two quarter-sized flatbed cars. Draper guessed they did not need a full sized train to move large quantities of drugs across the international border. The driver sat on a small seat to one side. He slowed the train to a stop, applied some sort of brake mechanism, and dismounted. He looked around as if expecting company and seeing none, shrugged and began walking toward where Draper and Jones stood hidden. He never saw the blow coming and slumped into Draper's arms unconscious. They zip tied him and dragged him over to where they had stored the two dead ones.

"Let's go see what we have on the train," Draper said.

The miniature-sized train had a wooden box on each of two flatbed cars painted five and six. "There's another pair," Draper said. Shrink wrapped on wooden pallets, blocks of different sized packets of drugs covered both ends of each flatbed car not covered by the wooden boxes.

"I suggest we move the two dead guys, the train driver, and the two boxes up to the surface. That way everything will look normal down here in case someone comes looking."

"What about the train?"

"We leave it here. If nothing else, it will slow any investigation. By that time we should have this place crawling with Feds."

"I was hoping you'd say that, 'cause I have to call this in. It's too big not too."

"I think that's the best strategy. Have them send in ATF also. Somebody has to deal with all these bombs and there's at least two more missing."

"What are you going to do?"

"I'm going after whoever is behind all this."

"You know how to run a forklift?"

"Yeah, don't you?" Draper said.

"Hell, no, I'm an undercover cop. No damned forklift license in my pocket."

"Well then, you keep watch and make sure no one shoots me." Draper said.

Jones made the first trip up to the surface with the bodies and the bound train driver. When he returned, Draper stopped unloading long enough to ask, "Everything okay?"

"Right as rain, except the two live ones bitched about having the two dead ones for bunkmates."

"Good, let them consider that for a while," Draper said. He had the drugs unloaded and stacked in the storage room. "Give me a minute and I'll be ready to start up with the first load of drugs."

He decided to leave the bomb boxes on the train and move them directly to the elevator. The boxes were heavy and needed an easy touch. He moved the drugs first, deciding a few minutes of practice would be worth the effort. After four trips to the surface, slowly adjusting to the machine, he relearned a long forgotten skill. The lift and his load just fit in the elevator cage. Jones rode the first load squatted on the machine's step. Draper had reservations that the elevator would lift the wooden boxes and the forklift but reasoned there was not any way to get them off at the surface without taking it along. The cables creaked and groaned more but rose to the surface without a problem. Sitting in the forklift seat, Draper stared at the wooden box in front of him and noticed something he had not caught before. A smaller word was painted underneath the red numbers, and Draper had to lean forward to read it. It said PERUN written in capital letters. "What the hell does Perun mean?" he said aloud. He studied the word all the way up until the elevator ground to a stop. He reached over and punched the door open button and as soon as the doors cleared, he drove out. Draper breathed a sigh of relief when all four boxes were safely stored on the surface. He took the forklift back down to the tunnel, parked at the charging station, and plugged it in. He took a moment to look around to ensure everything looked normal before entering the elevator and pushing the up button.

Draper stepped out of the elevator at the surface, surveyed the night's work, and concluded it was time to make some phone calls. He walked over to Jones sitting on a pallet of shrink-wrapped drugs with his M4 pointed at their captives.

"You know what Perun means?" Draper said.

"Perun?" What's it in reference too?"

"Damned if I know, it's written on the boxes all in caps."

"All I can think of is the Slavic mythical God of Thunder and Lightning. He rode a chariot pulled by a goat buck and carried an axe or hammer that he threw at evil people. He was similar to the Germanic God Thor," Jones said.

258

"And you know this how?" Draper said.

"Simple, took a course in medieval mythology, years ago in college. I didn't listen close since I didn't figure I'd ever need it for anything."

"Why'd you take the course?"

"Best of reasons; I followed a mighty fine young lady in the first day. She was interested in it so I went and signed up."

"So you wasted a bunch of money on a program you weren't interested in for a woman?"

"Seemed reasonable at the time, but I was younger then."

Draper laughed. "Well, it looks like it came in handy. What do you suppose the name means on the boxes?"

"Who knows, it could be code name for whatever madness these guys are trying to cook up.

"You might be right. Those boxes are dangerous. If that stainless steel cylinder is filled with radioactive material, they could be the so-called 'dirty bombs.'"

"That could cause a serious panic."

"It could," Draper said.

"Shall we call in the troops?" Jones said.

"I think it's time. Getting to the point we need the clean-up crew."

"You call your boys and I'll call Dean and have him notify anybody he thinks needs to know about this. Be damned sure the Canadian officials know there are probably two more boxes somewhere out there on the highway between here and Vancouver."

"We're going to need some ATF expertise as well," Jones said.

"Appears so," Draper agreed.

Draper left Jones to guard their stash and handle any political fallout that might occur. There was not much doubt that Jones' buddies at DEA and a crowd of other alphabet agencies would come running. Draper did not want any part of that cluster of real cops and federal agents.

***

Darchin Kazarian had been studying the town for two days, watching overt, but from a distance, careful not to stir up suspicion. Few people noticed the quiet man in a neat tailored suit sitting outside the restaurant for a few hours every morning after breakfast. He ate alone and seemed pleasant enough. Those that talked to him noticed a slight accent they could not identify, but paid it no mind since most of the strangers in Highmore in recent years were Mexican farm workers and he was not. Strangers in town were infrequent, so they gossiped about him in a casual way without caring one way or the other. Kazarian enjoyed the cat and mouse aspect of it, talking just enough to get them telling stories and then like a powder man loading a drill hole, slow and careful, he filled his mind with what he needed to know in little bits here and there until he had the whole picture. He was good at it and by the end of the second day he knew most of it. Draper and the big tall black man had been gone several days but no one knew where. Kazarian was anything but impatient and the Russian could talk a fruit vender out of his nuts. On the third day, he knew their strengths and especially their weaknesses. He watched a woman he knew to be the Sheriff's wife walk into the local dress shop with a young Hispanic looking girl. A passerby told him the young girl was the Sterling's new adopted daughter and he began to formulate a plan. From what he had learned from his cousin he felt certain if anything happened to the Sheriff's wife or the young girl, the tall

260

American would come running in an instant. All he needed was an opportunity, a moment of carelessness by the women and he would strike. Like a prairie rattler stalking a field mouse, he waited confident his chance would come. The Sheriff was not a problem because he left early every morning and returned home late at night leaving the women alone as much as twelve or fourteen hours. That left more than enough time to execute his plan.

On the fourth day, the tall American returned. Kazarian watched the man park a black Lincoln in front of the local motel. He did not go in and instead walked the block or so to the Sheriff's office where he stayed about an hour. When he left, he crossed the highway to the restaurant and entered. Kazarian considered his plan and began tweaking it, weighing risk and minimizing it at every turn. He finally settled on a window of opportunity where the women would be alone and the two men otherwise occupied. His mind racing, he debated on how to make that happen analyzing and reforming his idea multiple times. The Sheriff would be easy; calling for assistance at a remote location would take care of him. Late at night there was only one deputy and the Sheriff, if he was working late, which included most nights. He needed less than an hour for the plan's execution so the law did not need to be far away, just engaged. The question in Kazarian's mind became, when and how? He was still wondering when opportunity fell into his lap. The big American had retired to the motel when the Sheriff and the deputy came running out of the office, obviously in a hurry. The two jumped into a patrol car and sped down the street to the local bar. Never one to miss a chance, Kazarian followed. Inside the bar, confusion reigned. The Sheriff and the deputy were busy trying to talk down a drunk banishing a long barreled revolver. The crowd concentrating on the scene gave

Kazarian his chance. He pulled a Smith and Wesson automatic and aimed at the Sheriff. He held the weapon close and as he tightened his finger on the trigger, a nearby patron bumped him but he continued to shoot until the slide locked open. Then he turned and ran, stepping over frightened patrons trying to duck and cover.

His car a block away, Kazarian walked at a steady pace, not fast, more like he had all the time in the world. His demeanor calm, he felt nothing other than a determination to create a killing ground where he could take down the tall American. He had little thought of any others that might get in the way. His destination was the Sheriff's home where he knew the bait for his trap waited. He drove to the house and parked in the narrow alley in back. He reloaded the Smith and Wesson nine with a new clip and walked to the back door.

"говно!" he said, swearing in Russian when he realized the door was protected by an electronic lock and deadbolt No other option available and time running out, he ran around front and rang the doorbell and shouted "the Sheriff's been shot! Come quick!" He could see a shadow rise from the living room couch and run to the door. He had his hand on the knob and when he heard it click, he pushed in hard.

The force of the opening door surprised the girl and knocked her back. She tripped on an area carpet and fell. He was on her in an instant and when she struggled, he lashed out with his weapon, hitting her solid on the side of her head. She slumped still.

When Kazarian looked up, he stared at another woman in a long nightgown standing on the stairs above him pointing a small weapon. He fell sideways and felt a bullet whiz by his ear, followed by a burning sensation in his side as he double tapped the woman. She fell forward and slid down the stairs to the bottom and lay still, most of her body still on the stairway. He looked down at the bloody shirt on his left side where it hurt. The damned woman had shot him. He had never expected she would resist. The wound could not stop him though, not now when he was so close to success. Kazarian walked to the kitchen and found a dish towel and stuffed it into his shirt to stem the bleeding. He could see both the entrance and exit holes and knew it was superficial, a point that revived his confidence. It was nothing he could not handle. Emboldened, and without bothering to look at the other woman, Kazarian swooped up the young girl and exited the house. The town was quiet, though he could see red and blue lights flashing in front of the bar. He dumped the girl into the backseat of his car, tied her hands and feet with rope, and climbed in the driver's seat. In minutes, he was on the highway heading south. It seemed longer, but only twenty minutes had elapsed since he'd shot the Sheriff in the bar. He looked at his watch grinning despite the pain in his side. His plan had worked. There was not a doubt in his mind the tall American would come after him. That fact fit nicely into his plan.

***

Draper woke to the sound of pounding on his door. He grumbled, grabbed the Glock on the nightstand, and opened the door on the chain with his weapon ready. The strange face on the other side spoke in an excited voice, "Mr. Draper, Deputy Lopez sent me. He wants you. The Sheriff has been shot!"

"Where?" Draper prompted.

"I don't know, but he's hurt bad," the man said, looking confused.

"I meant what's his location?"

"He's at the bar. They're waiting for the ambulance."

"Okay, I'll be there in a few minutes." Draper slammed the door and jumped into his clothes, slipped on his shoulder rig and checked the Glock before holstering it. "Dammit!" he said to himself, unlatching the chain and piling into the Lincoln. It was less than a half block to the bar, but he did not want to have to come back if he needed more armament.

Pop's Place was a scene of confusion. The patrons milled about talking to one another while Deputy Lopez and the woman bartender were on their knees attending to Sterling. The Sheriff was on the floor with his eyes closed and unmoving. Draper kneeled down and said to Lopez, "How bad is it?"

"Bad enough," Lopez said, "I need my kit. I'm EMT trained but my kit is at the office. I've got most of the bleeding stopped but he needs surgery and it's over an hour away."

A local man ran in with Lopez's EMT kit and the Deputy began trying to start an IV. Draper's mind raced. "Anybody go get Mindy?"

"Shit no, been a little busy," Lopez said.

Draper touched him on the arm, "I know, Mario, you deal with Dean. I'll get Mindy."

The woman bartender looked at Draper with tears flowing down her face. "He was a good man, Mr. Draper."

"He still is and will be. Mario will make sure of it."

Leaving the bar, Draper felt cold in his gut, anger cursing through his veins with the knowledge that if anything happened to Dean he would hunt down the perp and extract pounds of vengeance. He was unprepared for what he found at the Sterling house. The front door was ajar. He pushed it open and saw Mindy Sterling lying head down on the stairway. Her eyes closed, there was significant blood.

He ran and felt for her pulse. He found it right away and took that as a good sign. A search located two bullet wounds, one high above her right breast and the other in her left arm. Both bullets had traveled clear through and looked worse that they probably were. In addition, she had a nasty abrasion on the side of her head, probably from when she fell down the stairs, he decided. Draper picked her up as gentle as he could and took her to the couch where he rearranged her nightgown for modesty and covered her up to treat for shock. Then he called Deputy Mario Lopez' phone. The bartender woman answered with, "Deputy Lopez' phone."

"This Draper, tell Mario that Mrs. Sterling has been shot twice also, she'll need to go on the ambulance, also."

"Just a moment, here's Mario," she said.

"Lopez," the Deputy said and Draper repeated his statement.

"The EMT's are here, but they only have room for one. We'll have to take her by car. Are you at the house?" Lopez asked.

"Yeah, I don't think she's critical but you need to look at her. I'm no doctor."

"Is she conscious?"

"No, she has a blow to the side of her head, also. I think she fell down the stairs."

"Any other injuries?"

"Not that I can see."

"Bleeding?"

"Some, but I've got compresses on the worst."

Okay, keep her lying down, and covered until I get there. You know how to treat for shock?"

"Yeah, that one I know."

"I'll be there as quick as I can. Watch for shock, monitor her breathing and heartbeat."

"Got it."

Draper hung up and scrutinized his patient. He took her pulse, checked her breathing and she did not appear to have symptoms of shock. He knew the critical hour was ticking for both his friends and it worried him. Mindy Sterling opened panic filled eyes. "Charlie," she said, "he got Maricella! I tried to stop him, but he was too fast. I think I hit him though."

"Don't worry, I'll find her, you just lie still and Mario will be here in a few minutes to take care of you."

Mario arrived and looked over his second patient of the night. "The wounds are superficial, but we need to get her to the hospital as soon as possible to avoid complications. I'll drive her, are you coming along?"

"I'd like to, but she told me Marcella was here and she's missing. Apparently the shooter took her," Draper said.

"Shit," Mario said. "You take care of that, I'll see to these two. Help me get her into the car."

"Mindy Sterling opened her eyes and said, "Charlie, please find Maricella."

"Don't you worry, Babe, I'll find her and take care of the asshole that did this. You hang in there."

Draper found a couple of extra blankets in the house and they used them to make the back seat of Lopez' cruiser a little more comfortable and strapped her in."

"I'll take care of her, you go do what you have to, Charlie," Lopez said. "Shoot him once for me."

"I will, guaranteed."

Draper watched the Sheriff's department cruiser fishtail a bit in the grass before it straightened and hit the street with full lights blazing. When it disappeared, Draper walked to the Lincoln.

Chapter Nineteen

Eastern Montana

"Hey, stranger, what's up?" Jones said.

Draper told him an abbreviated version, leaving out the details, but giving enough information that he would be able to follow up if things went south. "If something happens to me I want you to do the best you can to eliminate this bastard."

"Do you know who he is?"

"Not a clue, but I'm guessing he's from somewhere in southern Russia originally."

"That's a lot of territory, my friend," Jones said. "You think the girl's still alive?"

"Don't know; it's possible either way. She's the bait to get me in the open, I'm sure of that," Draper said.

"Well, you can depend on me to give it the old college try."

"That's all I ask. If I find out more about him and I'm still walking around I'll call you."

"Good luck, I wish I was there to help you, but this thing has turned into a nightmare. The bombs we have are all dirty and there's still two missing. I only hope to God there isn't more, and the Canadian authorities have slammed the door shut on anything coming into Canada. They're searching any truck that looks like it could carry one of the boxes across the country, but they haven't found them yet."

269

"Dammit!" Draper said.

"I know, as soon as we find those other two boxes, I'll be there to help you."

Draper's humor sank lower than polecat's tail after waiting two days and no phone call. He still felt the shooter would call, but angered that the man was playing with him. He knew it to be a ploy, a tactic to shove him off balance, make him careless, and mess with his concentration. Mario Lopez returned from Lewistown with news that both of the Sterling's were resting comfortable and prognoses were favorable. That news helped Draper's demeanor if not his patience. He sat in the Sheriff's Office after lunch on the second day grumbling at Lopez.

"So, I guess this makes you acting Sheriff," Draper said.

"Acting Sheriff, Undersheriff, Receptionist, and Janitor, my titles are longer than my desk," Lopez said. "Don't you have to go shoot somebody, somewhere besides here, preferably in someone else's county?"

"Nope, I'm waiting for a phone call."

"How about bothering the waitress at the cafe instead of me? I have real work to do and you sitting there makes me nervous."

"You need to learn patience, my friend, if you ever want to be Sheriff," Draper said, bantering because he was frustrated and worried.

"Patience my ass," Lopez said, "why don't you find some bad guys to harass and leave me alone."

The phone rang and Lopez answered it with a gruff, "Sheriff's Office!" His demeanor changed in an instant and a gray mask covered his face while he listened. "Thanks, Jake, keep me informed."

"What?" Draper said when Lopez hung up and stared into space, as if his mind floated in clouds.

"*Llueve mierda y luego la vierte,*" Lopez said to the wall, reverting to his native language when stressed.

Draper interpreted the phrase as 'Shit rains and then it pours' and felt a twinge in his chest. "What?" he demanded.

"Mindy is doing fine, but my friend there says the Sheriff is not so good. He's showing signs of an infection."

"That's not good," Draper said.

Being at loose ends bothered Draper more than he expected. Two days and no word made him wonder if he had misinterpreted the signs. Having pestered Lopez to the man's limit, Draper meandered down an empty main street in the throes of deepening dark, walking between silent stores with customers wanting. Ghosts of better times haunted grimy windows and long unlit merchant signs. They once shone bright, beckoning trade for thriving businesses since reduced to long forgotten storage. Draper stopped at one and peered through dirty glass into piled abandoned junk surrounding a grime encrusted '52 Studebaker Hawk with a missing windshield. One of its two doors hung open to rats, coons and a variety of other small creatures for warmth and hiding. He felt like the car; old, covered in dust and helpless. He turned away angry. Entering Pop's Place, he found the only place open a deserted establishment filled with a lonely woman bartender. She had aged hard, but Draper liked her after the incident with the former Sheriff Office candidate and more recently with Sterling shootings. She had cried over the fallen officer, something he had not expected considering her crusty attitude and rawhide tough exterior.

"What brings you in alone on a weeknight, Mr. Draper," she said.

"Nowhere else to go, I guess."

"Now that's a shame," she said, wiping the bar where it did not need wiping, mostly out of a long practiced habit and a need to have something to do. "Can I get you something?"

"Maybe a coke," Draper said, feeling he should donate to the cause if he was going to take up space in the bar.

"Nothing in it?" she said.

"No, I'm waiting for a phone call from an asshole."

"I understand. No word on that young girl of Sterling's?"

"Not yet. It's the waiting that is hard. I know he's doing it to get me off balance and it's almost working."

"You don't think he's killed her?"

"No, at least that's what I'm hoping. He has got an agenda; otherwise why come in here, a crowded business with lots of witnesses. He guns down the Sheriff, then immediately goes after his family. It smacks of him wanting me to come after him. That had to be the plan."

"Hadn't thought of it that way," she said.

"You get a good look at him?" Draper asked.

"I did. The barrel of that gun looked big enough to walk through. It was that stranger that been hangin' round town last few days. I don't know if anyone got his name. But I wouldn't have any trouble recognizing him if I saw him again."

"Can you describe him?"

"Like I'd seen him today," she said. "Medium height, maybe five-ten, sandy hair, kind-a foreign-looking in a way but I can't say just how; mean-looking though, tough, like he knew how to handle himself. Oh, and he had a scar on his face, you know, like a white line down his left cheek that wouldn't tan in the sun."

"Good eye for details there, young lady," Draper said.

"Call me young lady again and I'll think your making a pass at me. I've been tendin' this bar for forty-two years through two husbands, a handful of temporary boarders and a couple of no-accounts. I know bullshit when I hear it," she said, grinning at Draper and he knew he had made a couple points.

Draper's cell phone rang. He grabbed out his belt carrier and said, "Yeah?"

"I been meaning to call you," the voice said, "but I been busy. You know how it is with a new piece of tail, got to train them right."

"What do you want?"

"It ain't about what I want; it's about what you want. I've got this young lady, who I know you know is quite delightful, speaks very good English, but has a Central American accent."

"Quit dancing around, asshole, get to it," Draper said.

"Patience, Mr. Draper. The deal is I have her and you want her. Like a couple of businessmen. I have the commodity and you have the money. So bring me a million dollars and you can have her back, only slightly used. However, should you choose to try some sort of trickery, she might be much the worse for wear."

"All right, where and when?"

"Come to Billings. You have my number, call me when you get here and I'll tell you where."

"It'll take me a day to get the money together."

"You have five hours before I kill her." the voice said and hung up.

"Guess I have to go," Draper said to the bartender.

"Be careful; then shoot him once for me," she said.

"I'll do my best."

***

Jones was worried. They'd set up a command center in the large metal building and ATF people were busy dismantling the six bombs and carrying away the long stainless steel cylinders contained within. No one speculated or said a word but there was not doubt anywhere they contained radioactive material. DEA had charge of the tons of drugs found and they were busy with portable scales and field test equipment, sampling, weighting and inventorying the seizure. Jones had finished talking to his Canadian counterparts who were still looking for the two missing crates. He wandered over to where his fellow agents were working with the drugs.

"What's the count?" Jones said, his mind calculating how long it would take to drive to Billings. His eyes felt full of gravel and he could hardly keep them open. Looking at his watch it told him the reason for his discomfort. It had been close to twenty-eight hours since he'd slept more than a short catnap.

"We've only started and we have close to five hundred pounds of cocaine which on the street is worth something like fifteen million dollars," a supervisory agent said. "We haven't touched the rest. There's marijuana, heroin, a small amount of crack cocaine, and some other stuff that we haven't cataloged yet. It looks like we're going to be here a while."

"What are they going to do about the tunnel?" Jones asked.

"Beats the hell out of me, I've got my own problems, but I've heard some talk that the FBI and Homeland Security are scratching each other's eyes out trying to claim jurisdiction. Be glad no one else wants your part. Too much like hard work."

"You got that right," Jones agreed.

The younger agent looked at him and said, "Why don't you go out and crawl into one of our cars and get some sleep? Take my keys."

"Thanks," Jones said. "I guess I'll just do that."

***

Draper already knew that the drive to Billings was two hundred fifty miles in the dark with little additional time to watch for critters. The highways in Montana crawled with wildlife at night. Dodging deer, antelope and smaller animals represented nighttime recreation that Draper couldn't afford. He figured at least four hours baring any incidents with furry fauna. It wouldn't leave him time for recon which was likely intentional. He drove ignoring the nighttime speed limit hoping he did not draw a cop. He saw two antelope and a mule deer buck all of which took hard braking and lost time. The highway, a two-lane, barely one paving lift affair twisting and winding through ancient river created hills and valleys. The narrow roadway challenged the Lincoln's suspension and Drapers driving skills. He crossed the Billings city limits line at two-thirty am and pulled into a small subdivision with no street lights and few porch illuminations.

Draper opened the trunk of the Lincoln and began to dress in body armor. That complete, he selected one of the M4's and filled numerous pockets with clips for both his Glock and the rifle. He switched his concealed carry holster for a Falco fast draw model with an extra clip sleeve. He worked slow and methodical, checking every detail until satisfied before closing the trunk. He filled both ankle holsters and a side pocket of his pants held a sturdy knife with an eight-inch blade. Designed for close quarter combat with its blade

275

honed to a hair-splitting edge, it was capable of gutting a man from crotch to sternum with minor effort. He felt ready.

Draper did not waste time, but he did not hurry either. He learned long ago that hurry meant careless and careless could get one killed. The other reason Draper did not hurry was that he did not know where he was going. Montana is a huge state with many square miles of room to hide. Billings was the largest city and a huge metropolitan area by Montana standards. Given that fact, it did not make sense to rush since he could control the time because he was the one calling. Not for a second did he think the kidnapping of Maricella Abeja had anything to do with anything except to draw him out into the open where he was vulnerable. As bait for a marauding lion, the girl would be an incentive to draw him into an impossible situation where he would be a tied goat, helpless and edible. Finished, he sat behind the wheel of the Lincoln and called Jones.

"Jones." the DEA agent said.

"I'm in Billings, supposed to meet him here with a million dollars."

"Where the hell you going to get that kind of bread at night?"

"I'm not. Don't figure I'm going to need it either way; besides, I haven't got that much in cash. I don't think he's expecting it either."

"Be careful, man."

He had twenty-minutes left when he selected the number and hit send.

The phone rang three times and Draper had an instant of fear that he called too late. On the fourth ring, the man answered. "Did you worry? We've been having some fun together and I'm considering keeping her for a while longer. What do you think? Maybe a couple of weeks and she wouldn't care if you ever came to get her."

Draper sat silent for several seconds before he said, "Your call."

"What, you mean you aren't going to object? What the hell's wrong with you?"

Draper remained silent.

"Got nothing to say, big man?"

"Yeah, I do. Fuck you, asshole, call me back when you've got something to say," Draper said, and hung up.

Five minutes dragged by with Draper worrying that he pressed to far. Then the phone rang.

"You got the million?" the voice said.

"Yeah, you want it?" Draper was not above lying when the occasion called for it.

"Take Highway 310 up the Clarks Fork of the Yellowstone River to mile marker thirty-two. You'll cross the river right after Bridger. Then take the farm road to the left about two miles to an abandoned farm. She'll be in the house. Do as I say and come alone or she's dead."

"Got it," Draper said and hung up.

Draper had to turn around and drive the fifteen miles back to Laurel where Highway 310 took off Interstate 90 and followed the Clark's Fork of the Yellowstone River south into mountainous country. Just as he turned onto 310 his phone rang.

He almost did not answer but looked at the name to make sure it was not the shooter. When he saw it was Jones, he answered. "How's tricks?" he said.

"Rollin' along," Jones said. "Where you at?"

"I'm just outside of Laurel, turning on Highway 310 up the Clark's Fork of the Yellowstone." Draper said. "Little change of plans." Draper ran through his conversation with the shooter.

"I'm about twenty minutes to a half hour behind you. Try to keep a lid on things until I get there to help. I wouldn't want to miss all the fun," Jones said.

"Where'd you find a car?"

"Stole one from a fellow DEA agent."

"Isn't he going to be pissed when he finds it gone?"

"Not likely, they got enough work to do there to last weeks."

"Good to have help," Draper said. "You got equipment?"

"Some," Jones said.

"I'll leave the trunk of the Lincoln open in case you need more."

"Good, see you in a bit."

As described, Draper crossed the river and soon after, he found the Mile Marker Thirty-two turnoff. He stopped and studied a two-track road a minute seeing railroad tracks about a half mile distant and miles of rolling prairie that ran into larger hills in the far distance. He could not see a farmhouse but assumed it was ahead. After crossing the railroad, he stopped at the first knoll, shut off the headlights, and left the car. He took the M4 with him. He anticipated that his quarry would expect to see the car coming and would be preparing some sort of welcome. Draper planned walking the last mile would allow him the element of surprise. His night vision equipment gave him a view of the terrain in a mixture of yellows and greens. He stayed a couple hundred yards to the west of the road to mask his approach. Over the second hill, he could see the farmhouse, a small Queen Anne design, sadly abandoned and looking dark and forlorn through the M4 scope. It sat eerie quiet in drop-dead easy sniper range. He judged the remaining distance at a quarter mile or a little over four hundred yards. He subtracted another hundred yards by walking around the head of a small coulee running down to the east, found a clear spot and laid in the grass to scope the entire area. He removed a small sand-filled sock from one of his many pockets and tucked it under the rifle's forestock. Settled in he began a slow, systematic search of the terrain around the house. He spotted Maricella Abeja tied to a wooden straight-back chair seated on a narrow front porch. There were no signs of the shooter, but Draper was content with the knowledge he was around somewhere. He guessed it was a place very much like his own, high, concealed and able to view the house and the girl on the front porch. He asked himself where but did not get a satisfactory answer. Draper spent long minutes considering the options, not liking any. He could only be certain that wherever his quarry hid, it included crosshairs focused on the young woman.

Studying the girl through the M4's telescopic sight, Draper could see her struggling. Her hands behind her tied somehow, gagged and blindfolded. Lowering the view, he could see her bare feet tied to the front legs of the chair. A plan began to form in his mind. He reached into a side pocket of his pants and withdrew a muzzle suppressor for the M4. Guiding the weapon under his left shoulder until he could reach the end of the barrel, he screwed on the suppressor. If he had to shoot, he did not want the muzzle blast to give away his position. Back on point, he studied the young woman and the chair, debating.

A hand touched his shoulder followed by a whispered "Charlie" and Draper froze. "Jones?" he whispered.

"Who the hell'd you think?" Jones said.

"Damn glad to see you, my friend."

"What do we have here?"

"Maricella's tied to a chair on the porch of that house. I don't know where the shooter is, but he's not far away. I'd bet pretty close, where he can see her. It's a good bet he's got eyes on her through a riflescope."

"What's the plan?"

"I'm debating shooting the left rear leg off the chair and tipping her over. I'm betting before he can react she'll be on the floor behind that post and a much more difficult target. If you can get into place beforehand, maybe you can spot him and either shoot his ass or cold cock him."

"Lot of ifs in that plan," Jones said. "Besides we need to grill him a little and find out how many bombs there are and where they're at."

"As long as I can get Maricella out of her alive and unharmed, you can have him for as long as you like. You got a better plan?"

"No, sadly, I don't." Jones whispered.

"If I give you ten minutes, do you think you can find him?"

"Only need five, my mother was part Cherokee and I'm black; he'll never see me coming."

"Don't underestimate this bastard. He's a cold son-of-a-bitch," Draper said. Jones did not answer and disappeared into the dark. Draper waited ten minutes with the crosshairs of his M4 centered on the closest rear leg of the chair inches under Marcella's butt. Impatience won and he took a breath, held it and slowly increased pressure on the trigger. The M4 jumped expelling its load and the chair leg exploded under the young woman. As she was falling, a shot rang out to Draper's right a couple hundred yards away. The muzzle flash shone in the dark and Draper glimpsed a momentary outline of a prone shooter. He was up in an instant, running towards the flash. Halfway there he heard grunting and a sharp outcry and then silence. Two more steps and Jones' voice called out, "Got him, Charlie."

"You secure?"

"Yeah, sorry it took so long but I didn't want to kill him until we found out the location of the other boxes." Jones had his foot planted in the man's back and his M4 pointed at the back of his neck.

"Hands behind your back, asshole," Draper said, pulling out a handful of zip ties. The man's hands bound, Draper used three ties to secure his ankles. He would not be able to run only walk using a prison shuffle. There was not any doubt in Draper's mind the man knew how.

Finished, Draper said, "You bring him down to the house, I'm going to check Maricella."

"Go," Jones said.

Draper bounded down the hill as fast as his night-vision equipment would allow. He was panting by the time he reached the porch and knelt alongside the girl. "Maricella, its Charlie," he said, his tone gentle and concerned.

She murmured something unintelligible and Draper began stripping of the rag blindfold and gag off. Her hands and feet tied with cheap three eighths inch manila rope that dug harsh red abrasions on all her extremities. Draper knew it had to hurt and sliced through it freeing her. She reached up grabbing at his neck and pulled him close. He held her until the sobbing subsided. He spoke soft, reassuring, while she dampened his shirt. Then he noticed the blood on her nightgown. "Maricella" he said, "are you hurt?"

"My butt hurts," she said, her words muffled by his shirt. "Charlie how's Min...Mom? The man shot her."

"She's fine, honey," Draper said, "She in the hospital but she'll be fine."

"But...?" What aren't you telling me?"

"He had shot Dean before he went to the house; he's in the hospital also."

"And...?" she said, gripping Drapers's arm.

"I'm not going to lie to you, Maricella, he's hurt bad, but he's getting the best of care."

Draper scooped her up and carried her into the house looking for somewhere to lay her down. The only thing in the front room was an old brass bedstead with a dirty cotton-ticking mattress with no covering. He decided it would have to do and placed her on it, but she would not let go of him. "I've got to take a look, babe, you're bleeding."

She nodded and whispered in his shirt, "Don't worry, you won't be the first man to see my ass." Draper thought he heard a giggle mixed in with sobbing.

He rolled her over on her side slow and saw a damp blood circle about three inches in diameter. "I'm going take a look now," he said, picking up the nightgown and inspecting underneath the blood spot. High on her right cheek was a sizable sliver from the chair buried deep into her flesh and protruding about an inch. He laid her gown back debating. They were over an hour from medical care so he questioned the choices. Moving her would only increase the damage.

"Am I going to live?" she said. The old Maricella began to immerge and she had stopped crying, but she still held tight to his left hand.

"I think you're going to make it.

282

"What'd you think?"

"Well, it's a pretty big sliver.

"No, silly, about my ass?"

"It's nice," Draper said.

"Thank you. What are you going to about the sliver?"

"As soon as Jones gets here, I'll have him go get the Lincoln and its first aid kit. Likely though, I'm going to have to pull it out before we move you."

"God, when he shot the chair I thought for sure I was dead."

"He didn't shoot the chair, Maricella, I did. I was trying to tip you over so he wouldn't have a clear shot at you."

Maricella did not answer, she only stared at Draper, and tears welled again. "I guess it worked then because he missed."

"Yes, he did. There wasn't time to do anything else."

"I know you did it to save my life, that's all I need to know. I'm not even mad about the sliver."

"You might be when I pull it out."

Draper could hear low noise outside and moved to the door to look. Jones was outside with his captive who would not climb the stairs. "Make him get down and crawl," Draper said.

"You heard the man, crawl," Jones said. When he did not move Jones butted him with his M4 stock, hard, knocking him down on the steps. "I said crawl, asshole!"

A three by eight foot trapdoor sat on the left edge of the room's floor, probably leading to the cellar, Draper surmised. His interest was limited to the heavy iron forged lift ring, long ago used to lift the door. He dragged their captive to the door, tied him to the round iron handle with a zip-tie, and blindfolded him with the same rag he had used on Maricella. Draper enjoyed the poetic justice besides being handy. Maricella lay on the old bed and stared at him.

"How's our girl?" Jones said.

"Alive," Draper said.

"I see that, any injuries?"

"I've got a chair sliver in my butt but other than that I'm good," Maricella said.

Jones looked at Draper for explanation and did not get one. Instead, Draper said, "Need the car and a first aid kit. She won't be able to go anywhere until I pull that sliver out."

"Be my pleasure, be back in a jiff," Jones said and turned to the door.

Draper sat next to Maricella and took her hand. "As soon as I remove that sliver we'll move you to the car and let you rest in the back seat. Jones and are I going to have a little conversation with our captive before we leave which might be a while so you try to get some sleep while we're busy."

"No!" Maricella said. "I want to watch, I want to see you punish him. If you kill him, I want to see him die."

"No you don't; it won't be pleasant."

"Charlie, he raped me, many times, he shot my mother and may have killed my new father. I want to see him find out what it's like." She started to cry again, big tears, that streamed out of dark eyes that Draper knew had seen horrors even he could only imagine. "He wasn't the first, but he's the one I can get closure from."

"I have to tell you, he isn't going to leave here alive. Are you okay with that knowledge?"

"You just watch me," Maricella said.

284

"Remember much of intense interrogation is psychological, so don't pay too much attention to what we say."

"I told you, Charlie, I'm not a virgin in more ways than the usual. I grew up in Central America, there isn't much I haven't heard or seen."

Draper looked into dark brown eyes aged far beyond her years and said, "Okay, you let me know if you'd like to go to the car."

"I will."

Chapter Twenty

Southwestern Montana

J ones came back with the car and entered the house carrying the first aid kit. Draper sat on the bed holding Maricella's hand. "Everything go okay?"

"Right as rain," Jones said. "I got the kit so you can doctor our patient."

"Good, how about the tools?"

"I got them, too. I think we're going to have some fun with our friend here." Their captive tried to squirm around to look but could not. His hands tied close to the ring and his bound feet prevented movement.

"Relax, friend, we'll get to you in a moment," Draper said. He turned to Maricella who was staring at the prisoner. "Don't worry about him; we need to get that sliver out. Are you ready for it?"

"As much as I'll ever be," Maricella said.

Draper wished he could cover her legs to make her feel less exposed, but he had nothing. Looking at the injury told him he did not have much of a sterile field to work in so he poured alcohol into a 4x4 bandage and wiped it around the wound as best he could. He did the same thing to a pair of pliers. Most of the initial blood removed he studied the wound closer and decided it was not as deep as he'd first thought. Its entry was parallel to the skin rather than straight in.

With a handful of 4x4s ready, he grasped the exposed end with the pliers and when his patient yelped, he pulled. Using 4x4's to slow the flow of blood he pressed hard for several minutes. When the flow subsided, he bandaged it.

"You okay, Maricella?" Draper said.

"Yeah, is it out?"

"It wasn't as deep as I first thought you should be fine. We'll take you to the emergency room in Billings as soon as we're done here. You sure you don't want to go to the car?"

"No," she said, "I want to see him suffer."

"Where'd you get to be so bloodthirsty, girl," Draper said.

"I told you, growing up in El Salvador wasn't easy," she said. "I've seen my share of blood."

Maricella reminded Draper of his adopted daughter, Gabriella, beaten, raped and abused through most of her adolescence, after she was rescued some kind of inter strength rose to the surface and healed her. Draper hoped Maricella would find that same resolve. She showed the signs, he decided. If she did, Draper was sure Dean and Mindy would have a lot to do with it.

In the meantime, he had loose ends to tie. "You let me know when you've had enough and want to go to the car, okay?"

"I will," she said, "but don't count on it."

Draper said to Jones, "Let's do it." Both men knew intense interrogation involved more subtlety than violence. Jones started, almost as if they'd played the game before, which they hadn't; at least not together.

Jones walked over to the prisoner and said, "We could save a lot of time if you'd just spill your guts and tell us about the whole plot. What do you think?"

The man said nothing.

"Think you're a hard case, do you? Let me tell you something friend, my partner and I have a hundred percent record with hard asses. Every one of them ended up begging like little girls."

The man looked at the floor and said nothing.

"Should we start with his eyes or his manhood," Jones said to Draper.

"I've got a big knife," Draper said drawing the weapon out of his body armor while standing where their prisoner could see. He reached out, hooked the man's shirt with the blade tip, and ripped upward toward his throat. The cloth separated and the tip left a red line of blood on his chest.

"Any idea how long it takes for a man to bleed out?" Jones said his voice low and conversational. "No? Well, it depends whether it's a lot of little cuts or one great big one. I think we'll start with a lot of little ones."

Draper cut another section of the shirt leaving a longer, deeper cut on the man's chest. As a ribbon of blood ran down inside his shirt, Draper laid the knife across a long white facial scar on his right cheek. "Somebody's cut you before, right?" Draper allowed a long pause. "What's your name, friend?"

When the man remained stoic, Draper changed tactics. "You know the door you are tied to? Well, that goes down into a dirt cellar. Folks used to use them to store canned goods and such. It's damp and cool down there. Of course, they'd have to put up with rats, an occasional coon, maybe a skunk or two. Did you know rats and coons like blood? Yeah, they do, especially the rats. They'll come up slow at first, then, as they get more emboldened, they'll start chewing on you; especially eyes, they like eyes."

The man responded, "You don't fool me; there isn't a damn thing you can do to me. Play the psychobabble all you want. I know you'll eventually have to turn me over to the real police. Your justice system will spend lots of time plus a ton of money before I end up in a babysitting prison with three squares a day and all the television I can stand. You think I'm afraid of that? Guess again. There will be hundreds more like me coming and finally we'll take down your country. So fuck you."

"No," Draper said, "Back at you." He turned to Jones and said, "I'm going to the car and get some rope. I think we'll hang him right here and now. He's not going to tell us anything, so we might as well get it over with."

Draper saw a hint of doubt melt the man's defiance, not enough yet, but he could see it slip a tiny amount. Without a word, he went outside and walked to the Lincoln. The rope in the trunk was a long ago afterthought and he'd carried it around for years without using it. He retrieved it and returned to the house. Silent, he gazed up at the ceiling where long ago fallen plaster had exposed a rough-cut rafter. He tossed a three-loop coil up over the beam and grabbed the end as it fell through on the other side. He looked around for a chair. He saw an old wooden one, identical to the one he shot from under Maricella. He pulled it over in front of their prisoner and sat. Holding the loose end, he waved it in front of the man's face.

"Anybody ever show you how to tie a hangman's knot?" Draper said.

When the man did not answer, Draper continued. "You start with two equal sized loops; then you coil the loose end around the middle until you have eight or ten coils. Most people think it's thirteen, but all authorities on the subject recommend eight, so we'll go with eight. Then you pull on the other loop until it cinches down on the rope's end. See, a perfect hangman's noose." Draper held the knot close to the man's face. "Now it's important to line the coil up with an ear so the neck will break clean, but we're not going to worry about that since we've got nowhere to drop you. You are going to die very slowly because we'll take you to the edge, let you recover a bit and then do it again, and again. Most we've experimented on can last an hour or more. How long do you think you'll make it?"

"You can't just kill me." Earlier it would have been a statement, but now it became a question.

"Sure we can," Draper said. "We've got nothing to lose. We know you have at least ten large bombs set to go off in various cities in the U.S. We want know where and when. Otherwise, you die."

"I'm not telling you shit!" He looked surprised that Draper knew about the crates.

Draper slipped the loop over his head, tightened the knot and jerked on the rope, hard. Only then did he remember his captive was tied to the cellar door. "Oops," Draper said, faking an apology and reaching to loosen the knot. "Forgot you were tied to the door, friend."

Draper began again after cutting the zip tie through the door handle. He started slow this time, putting ever so slight extra pressure on the rope until the man's struggles included coughing and gasping. He continued the effort until the man's color turned an ashen gray and his eyes began to bulge. Then, he loosened the knot and let him recover a bit. After the third time, the man he held up his hand in surrender. "No more, I'll tell you, please stop," he gasped his voice raspy and almost unintelligible.

"Your name and where you're from and then tell us where each crate is going and what numbers the numbers are on the crates," Draper said. "Now, or I'll jerk you clear off your feet."

He began the list, not asking how they knew about the crates, eventually spilling it all while Jones made notes. As soon as the man finished, Jones stepped outside to make a call. The ten included all of the largest cities in the U.S.

Draper took off the rope, pulled it up through the ceiling, and looped it up into a coil for storage. Darchin Kazarian, he had said his name was born and raised in that part of the former Soviet Union now called Kazakhstan. Kazarian lay quiet, still coughing and trying to recover. Draper went to the bed, scooped up Maricella, and carried her out to the car. Jones saw him coming and opened the back door and Draper deposited her on the rear seat laying her on her good side. "Satisfied?" he said.

"I'd be happier if he were dead, but yes, it helped," Maricella said, but there were tears at the corners of her eyes. Draper knew she had been hurt both physically and emotionally. Not as tough as she claimed, Draper admired her fortitude. Not many young women could have endured what she had and survived it untouched, if any at all. He wanted to hold her, protect her, yet he could not. Mindy and Dean Sterling would have to do that.

"I'll be just a second and then I'll take you to the hospital in Billings."

Draper walked back into the abandoned house, its bones showing from years of neglect. At one time children played in these rooms, parents loved on the old iron bedstead, and laughter rang between the eaves. Those days fell many years past. This day a murderous man laid zip tied on the once polished fir floor. The same

292

man who had dumped tons of drugs on the country and planned a wave of death and destruction he could only imagine. It surprised him the depth of anger welling in his breast. He'd spent a lifetime in dangerous covert work and this day he felt tired, his weary carcass testifying to his advancing age. Still, the anger raged. Their captive, revived from his ordeal, stared at Draper with hate-filled eyes, again defiant, convinced that he'd won. A quick search of their man's pockets revealed a pocket worn wallet and cell phone. Draper pocketed both, before dragging him off the cellar door, grabbing the old cast ring and lifting the door. The opening exposed a set of stairs, its steps long rotted, and lying in debris-covered yellow clay at the bottom. He turned and grabbed his captive and pushed him off the edge. The six-foot drop knocked the wind out of Darchin Kazarian and he lay gasping in a cloud of long undisturbed dust.

Draper waited, his anger unfulfilled until his captive opened his eyes and stared up at him, defiance returning. It was easy, Draper decided later, almost natural, he drew his Glock and shot the man in both knees; multiple times each. He dropped the cellar door closed and walked out. The man's screams followed him until he closed the door on the Lincoln.

"Did you kill him, Charlie?" Maricella asked. Jones sat wordless in the front passenger seat.

"Not yet," Draper said, "but soon."

"You should have brought her in sooner," the emergency room doctor said. He stood arrogant and young, still filled with medical school pieties and the belief that because they were doctors, they knew everything. Draper let it slide knowing someday, some time he'd lose a patient, and it would shatter his arrogance.

"Did the best I could," Draper said. "We were hours from medical care."

"Actually, you did quite well. The wound was clean and blood loss minimal. Overall, she should be fine. We did see some unusual bruising. You know how that happened?"

"Not any more than she does," Draper said. I just picked her up."

"She tell you anything?"

"No."

"Since there are indications of a crime, I have to notify the police."

"Do what you have to do, Doc," Draper said.

The police officer was a young detective in plain clothes and belt badge, not much older than the doctor. Draper told his story, the one he and Maricella had worked out on during the ride in. They dropped Jones off at his car and he was long gone back to the northern part of the state. The locals were suspicious but stymied. After five hours at the hospital, they were on the way back to Highmore.

Maricella sat upright in the front seat during the drive. Draper could tell her injury pained her, but she gritted her teeth and said nothing about it. Instead, she seemed intent on Draper.

"Thank you for killing him," she said after a half hour of silence.

"He needed killing," Draper said.

"Is that the justification you use?"

"Something resembling that," Draper said.

"I think you are right. He needed killing."

294

During the ride, he told her about the drugs and the crates full of ANFO and the potential destruction they might have caused. Draper thought she should know, hoping the information would help her heal.

"What's ANFO?" she asked.

"Ammonium nitrate fertilizer and fuel oil, mixed. Same stuff Timothy McVey used in Oklahoma."

They rode silent for a quiet half-hour. Draper could tell she was thinking, processing all that had happened. He wanted to ask a question, but waited long enough to give her space.

After dodging a buck antelope intent on crossing the highway, Draper said, "How old are you, Maricella?"

"I think I'm about eighteen," she said.

"You don't know?"

"I don't know when my birthday is so I picked a day when I was young so I could tell people when they asked. I don't know the year I was born, so I'm guessing."

"How about we make it today? As in today is the first day of the rest of your life. Somehow, I think it's going to be a significant improvement over anything up to now. You can pick the year."

Maricella grinned. "I like that," she said.

She sat quiet, staring out the window while musing in her head and Draper let her be. He did not have a clue what mysteries roamed around in a young woman's head, any woman's head for that matter, so like most males with any sense, her gave her space.

After some time, she said, "I guess I'm destined to be and old maid."

"Why is that?" Draper said confused, "You are a beautiful young woman. Give it some time and Dean will have to lock up all the young men in the county."

"I'll want him to be like you."

"No, you don't. Believe me. My ex-lady friend will tell you, I'm no prize."

"Why?"

"Because she's in law enforcement and she can't wrap her head around what I do."

"Maybe I should talk to her."

"Don't think it would help," Draper said.

Draper sat in the Sheriff's office days later pestering Mario Lopez whose temporary job as Acting Sheriff, now faced almost impossible odds. His two remaining Deputies covered twenty-five hundred square miles each, one north and the other south of town. That left Lopez with the office, the town of Highmore and much of the surrounding county a hundred miles or so in any direction. When the stress began to show, Draper suggested he find somebody to hire on a temporary basis.

"And who might that be?" Lopez said acting grumpy as usual and irritated by Draper's presence. "Are you volunteering?"

"Might help you train someone," Draper offered.

"Yeah, and who's going to train you? Law enforcement is different from running around shooting people and acting like some sort of masked avenger. Dean would fire my ass for even considering it."

"How about I ride along in case you need backup, couldn't hurt."

"Shit, I got enough trouble already. Some detective from Billings PD called and asked about you, just the other day; said he was following up on a case."

"What did you tell him?"

"I didn't tell him squat. What I should have told him was you are an annoying son of a bitch who sits around in my office all day pestering me."

"Come on, Mario, you know you love me."

"Like I love a boil on my ass," Mario said, "now what is it you want? I know you're going to ask so do it."

"I want you to dump a cell phone for me. Names and locations of everyone Darchin Kazarian called in the last two weeks. If that doesn't produce anything maybe the last month would."

"Jesus, what do you think I am your personal crime lab?"

"Who else could I ask?"

It took a week. Lopez Fed Ex'd the memory card to the Lewistown forensics lab and Draper paced all seven days. During that time, he took Maricella to Lewistown to pick up Mindy Sterling, who was released from the hospital and to visit Dean Sterling who was not. The Sheriff was improving but not ready yet for home care.

On her first full day home, Mindy Sterling came into the Sheriff's office where Draper was manning the phone while Mario went about the usual Sheriff's business. He sat at Mindy Sterling's desk.

"You look like you fit there. Do I need to be worried about my job?" she said.

"Not in the least," Draper said, "you are way more competent and a hell of a lot better looking."

"Nice of you to say so; even though I know it is bullshit."

"It's the truth."

"I don't believe it but nevertheless I want to ask you about Maricella."

"Ask away," Draper said, "though I will tell you there is one very strong young lady."

"I know, but so far she won't tell me anything."

"Give her time, she will."

"Was she...?"

"Yes," Draper said before she could finish. "Listen, Mindy, she was held for several days, an eternity if you are a captive. She may never tell you about it, but you have to let her pick the time and place if she ever does. You only have to let her know she can."

"I know," Mindy Sterling said.

The crime lab in Lewistown faxed a list of phone numbers and names two days later. Lopez tossed the list at Draper across his Sheriff's desk. Draper picked it up and read it over. One number stood out. The others were Draper's phone and a couple others he knew to be locals. He concentrated on the single outlier, a number with a Connecticut prefix. The name attached was Jafar Abbasi and a billing address in the same locale. Draper left Lopez in a frenzy of law enforcement activity and felt confident the man would not miss him.

Outside Draper dialed a number he knew by heart. The voice that answered said, "Code," in a monotone voice and nothing else. Draper rattled off a fifteen-digit number that did not require previous thought.

"What do you need?" the voice said.

"Anything on Jafar Abbasi, living in Connecticut."

"Call back in an hour."

Draper waited an hour and five minutes. He spent the time pacing back and forth in front of the Sheriff's Office and sitting on a public bench stewing. He watched small town activities, while counting seventeen grain trucks, half loaded and half returning empty from the local elevator. He could see the top of the local grain elevator with its tall concrete tubes higher that most of the surrounding buildings. Draper could not see them but knew the part he could see stood surrounded by a dozen or more shiny round metal storage tanks bursting with local grain. It amazed him that the line of waiting railroad cars changed daily. When the time was up, he dialed.

"The man you asked about is on the terrorist watch list. The committee wants to know if you would accept an assignment."

"How much?" Draper said. He did not care since he already decided. Payment would only sweeten the deal.

"Half-million, deposited in your account."

"Consider it done," Draper said.

"We'll need confirmation."

"You'll get a picture."

"Good. As a side note, if you run into a Darchin Kazarian, he's on the list also."

"You can forget about him, did him for free."

"Do you have confirmation?"

"No," Draper said. "But you can take my word for it, scratch him off."

The phone went dead. "I guess this is goodbye. Probably afraid I'd ask for more money," Draper said to the empty bench and punched the end.

Draper checked out of the motel an hour later after repacking the Lincoln. Finished, he drove to Dean and Mindy's house. The two women sat on the front porch looking through the two big cottonwoods that anchored the front lawn and drinking iced tea. When he walked up to them, they both guessed. "You're leaving," Mindy Sterling said, as a statement of fact.

"Yes," Draper said. "Things are pretty much done here. Dean will return shortly good as new. All the bad guys are either in jail or dead; nothing more to do."

"We are going to go up and get him tomorrow. You could ride along."

"Can't, new assignment; I wanted to say goodbye."

Maricella Abeja stepped off the porch and walked up to Draper. She rolled up on tiptoes and kissed Draper's cheek before saying, "*Gracias, Charlie Draper.*"

"*No es nada,*" Draper said.

"That goes for me also," Mindy Sterling said, standing stoic on the porch.

Chapter Twenty-One

Near Interstate 95 in Connecticut

Jafar Abbasi sat in a comfortable, his easy chair rocking while he stared out at Long Island Sound. The water calm for a change, it allowed a heavy traffic of pleasure boats to mingle with bigger commerce vessels. A large man, not in height but in girth, Abbasi's middle expanded in the years he had lived in the United States. His age somewhere around seventy, Abbasi wore a turban always, quoted the Koran with every order, and interpreted its meaning to suit whatever was the current objective. He held a long-term hatred of women in general, except as a tool of pleasure, and Americans in particular. He killed whenever it was necessary, although his advanced age usually required having someone else handle the actual act for him. His current harem included four young women whose ages ranged from fifteen to nineteen, all of whom were devout followers of Islam, or pretended to be. All were smuggled into the US through its porous borders with relative ease. They were virtual slaves and never allowed outside the house.

Born in Iran and raised under the last Shah of Iran, Mohammad Rezā Shāh Pahlavī Abbasi lived his formative years in a number of Middle Eastern countries all of whom were Islamic led. His radicalization began in Syria as a teenager and continued during his young adult years. Along the way, he learned to kill and developed a

301

hidden hatred for anything Western. He had come to the United States under the Carter Administration on a diplomatic mission and never left after developing a taste for liquor, women, and power, though not necessarily in that order. His native language was Farsi, but he'd become fluent in English, as well.

"والام قام شخص," his second in command said, disturbing his study of the morning paper.

"What is it, man? Speak English. We must integrate ourselves into the infidel society if we are to succeed. What could be so important as to interrupt my morning?" Abbasi said.

"It is Darchin Kazarian, we cannot reach him. He hasn't answered his phone for several days. He said at that time he was expecting the American to come after the young woman he'd captured and the infidel quickly eliminated."

"So... it appears he was not successful."

"It does."

Do we know where the American is now?" Abbasi said.

"We do not."

"Well, find him. Use every resource we have. I want to know where that bastard is as soon as possible."

***

Draper's 182 Cessna had a listed range of a thousand miles, although calculating in an additional safety margin considering head winds, altitude and other variables, he usually felt more comfortable in the nine hundred numbers or fewer. His flight east from Billings, Montana demanded two fuel stops and somewhere along the route, a quick overnight stay. He loaded all his armament into the plane and turned in the Lincoln rental before settling his parking fees on the 182. His flight plan listed an overnight stop in Sioux City, Iowa the

302

first night, a second overnight and fueling stop in Canton, Ohio and then a final leg to Bridgeport, Connecticut.

Leaving Billings, Draper climbed through nine thousand feet and leveled off at nine thousand five hundred to avoid having to use oxygen. Draper decided to take his time, flying under six hours each day in order to be fresh and rested when he arrived. The man he was after would not be an easy target and he figured on several days minimum of hard recon. He wanted to study the man's movements, his habits, and any companions before acting. Concurrent, there would be a study the man's bodyguards. Draper expected well-trained security and considerable risk. He would look for a period of weakness or a bodyguard with careless habits.

In Bridgeport, he rented another Lincoln, transferred his equipment to its trunk, and drove down Interstate 95 until he identified the man's living space. A mansion in every sense of the word, tall security walls surrounded the grounds, an armed guard stood at a gated entrance, and a fit-for-a-king sized manor with thick stucco walls overlooking the Long Island Sound. Getting a floor plan of the structure wasn't hard and took less than an hour at the Department of Public Records. Draper drove into a nearby park, selected a parking area overlooking the mansion, and studied it. Through a pair of binoculars, he could see the top of the wall covered with razor wire, broken glass and looking about three feet thick. Breaching the wall looked risky, if not impossible. Over the next hour, he concentrated on the front guard who looked heavily armed, seemed competent, and never left his post. He decided the man had to have iron lined kidneys or a piss bag.

Draper watched for five days and nothing happened. The daily routine varied, almost as if planned. It was subtle, but since

Draper was keeping close tabs on the activity, he noticed a difference. The same guard held the front and every other movement was identical to the first day. The guard change happened at exactly 8:00 am in the morning and again at 8:00 pm at night. On the next day, a change occurred at eight-fifteen and on the next eight-thirty. On the fifth day, it repeated day number one. The nighttime change occurred right at dark if he waited until the fourth day. He decided on that day right at the shift change. It would require waiting until the guard change occurred and the new guard was alone, but he decided that was his best chance. What he did not know was if there was some sort of 'dead man alarm' that would sound if it were not silenced by a given time. He guessed by the level of security that he had seen there probably was one. That meant he would have fifteen minutes or possibly less to get in, accomplish his task, and get out. He did not like it but there it was. His choice became 'do it' or 'don't do it.' He wasted a week already so his choice clinked into the 'do it' column almost automatically. He watched the cycle one more time and on the fourth night, he moved.

Taking out the guard was not difficult. Like most people whose job is repetitive and bordering on fatal mind numbing, the guards had slipped into inattention mode from many months of inactivity. Draper counted on them fighting the tedium by day dreaming of the last woman they had slept with or fanaticizing about the next. They had to have some mechanism to keep from going crazy. Draper could remember the hours, sometimes days perched in a moss covered tree unable to move enough to keep his bones from aching, waiting for a clear shot, sometimes for hours, even days. They taught him patience, ignoring the pain, and sleeping with your eyes open.

The guard failed to see him and when Draper sapped him, he dropped like a stone. His quarry zip tied and gagged, Draper searched for a dead man switch, finding it hidden under the counter in the guard shack. He pushed the button and looked at his watch. He figured he had a half-hour max and more likely fifteen minutes. He used the guard's keys to enter the compound and dashed across the dark lawn to the main house. The front door locked, it took a couple tries to get it open. Inside he scanned the room to find the stairway he knew from the plans led to upstairs sleeping quarters. At the top of the stairs, he turned left, ran down a wide hallway, and stopped in front of a set of oak double doors; also locked. He resisted the temptation to check the time and tried three keys before it opened. The door swung on greased hinges and did not make a sound. The room was empty. A king-sized bed with an intricately carved walnut headboard sat at one end of the room, still made up. Draper swept the room with the barrel of his M4 and found nothing to shoot. Then voices, muffled, reached his ears and he stepped forward trying to locate the source. On the wall to his right, he could see a partially open door. He crossed the room and stood with his back to the wall ready. The voices were louder, angry. Draper stepped into the room and faced a large man behind a custom desk ornate desk that looked long enough to land small planes on. The man looked startled and pointed a finger at him. Draper recognized his quarry and touched the trigger on the M4 set to a three round burst.

The next few seconds slowed in Draper's mind as if watching an old black and white film. The actor's movements turned jerky, not real, as if suddenly he had stepped into a fantasy. The target fell backwards onto the floor and at almost the same instant a freight train hit Draper's chest. The bullet buried itself deep in his Kevlar vest. In Draper's mind, his fall to the floor took a long time, slow, as if time had stopped a moment, waiting for him to do something. He saw the second man somewhere between the pain in his chest and the second bullet plowing inches below the vest and deep into his guts. He had only a vague memory of triggering the M4 in the general direction of the shooter before his lights went out.

"Please, please wake up," the voice said. It was soft and melodic but sounding desperate, wanting him to do something he did not want to do. He felt cold and wondered in a misty fog why the voice kept talking when all he wanted to do was sleep. Hands shook his arm and pain raced through his chest.

"Let go of me!" he growled. It seemed as if a truck ran over his chest stopping with one wheel on his breastbone. Breathing hurt like the sins of Jacob and pain radiated from his left side, low down.

"Please, Mister, we have to get out of here!" the voice said.

A woman, Draper thought, though putting more than two thoughts together at one time required energy he did not have. She sounded scared and insistent. It took a moment of concentration to remember where he was. Floating far above his head, the black and white movie rolled on with Chaplin-like characters, choppy movements, and comedic action.

Draper opened his eyes. She had long dark hair, no makeup, and clothes that looked like St Vincent de Paul castoffs. In Draper's eyes, she looked about twelve. He did not recognize her and wondered where she came from. Slow as spilled molasses reality returned. He knew his life depended on getting up, but his body resisted. The young woman gripped his arm and tried to pull him up.

"Let go," he said. "I'm okay."

"Come, Mister, they will be here soon, they will kill us if they find us."

"Not unless I kill them first," Draper said, his bravado laced with adrenalin and little practicality. With the girl's help he did get up, though she had to hand him the M4 because his head spun like a top at first and he had to hold on to her to stay upright. Slow as snails, they made it to the stairwell and descended to the first floor. Outside, the girl said, "Give me the gun, you are in no shape to defend us."

Draper did not argue. It did not take a Mensa intellect to ascertain that his fighting ability was limited to those eighty and above and children under five. It felt strange to know his life depended on a young woman of indeterminate age that looked like she had not entered puberty yet. "Is it set on full auto?" she said and surprised him even more.

"No, three-shot burst, you should have a nearly full magazine and there's more in my pants pockets," Draper mumbled, trying to clear his head with only partial success.

At the wall, there were two armed guards inspecting the body of the one Draper had killed. She saw them as they exited the doorway, and the M4 came up in an instant spraying both with two perfectly timed bursts. "Do you have an automobile somewhere?" she said, as if she had just bought groceries instead of killing two armed men.

"Yes, in the park about two blocks away." Draper said.

"You going to be able to make it?" she said and Draper realized for the first time she had large dark eyes, like pools of molten metal in a blast furnace, though she still looked twelve. He could not get past those eyes and wondered what her story could be.

"Going to have to," Draper said, though not with any enthusiasm.

By the time they reached the Lincoln, Draper was certain he could not take another step. In his mind, the options were limited. He could not drive, they could only call for help and hope the bad guys did not find them before the marines arrived. The trip to the park exhausted him and deep down he felt prepared to die. There was not strength left to go on. He looked at his angel and said, "Can you get my phone out of my pocket? I need to call in the rescue squad."

"Give me the goddamn keys," she said, "we can't stay here. Anytime now they'll be swarming all over us. You don't know the depth of their organization."

"Can you drive?" Draper said.

She looked at Draper as if he had lost his senses. "Of course I can drive," she said.

"Where we going," she said at the turn out onto Interstate, "you need a hospital."

"Head for Bridgeport, turn left."

Draper fumbled for his phone. By his calculation, it had been about a half hour since the shooting and he could feel the dampness on the left side below his vest. It seemed to be getting larger. He was light-headed and had trouble concentrating. It had taken three attempts at dialing before he got it right. The voice that answered said, "Yes?"

"The mission is complete, but I've been shot. Need help and medical care."

There was a thirty-second hesitation before the voice said, "We have you on Interstate 95 heading toward Bridgeport, Connecticut. Is that correct?"

"Yes," Draper said.

"We have someone within a mile of you. What are you driving?"

"A black four-door Lincoln Town Car," Draper said, "with a woman driving."

"Who is the woman?"

"Don't know, but she helped me get out."

"Okay, our people are coming up behind you. They will pull in front of you and follow them to the hospital."

Draper mumbled the instructions to the girl and added. "Think you best hurry, I don't feel so good."

"Hang in there, it isn't far now," she said.

"I don't know your name," Draper said. He had trouble concentrating and had to think a moment why he was in a car with a woman he did not know. His head felt disconnected from his body and he was looking down at himself.

"My name is Shira," she said.

Draper heard the name and thought it strange; it sounded familiar, but he hadn't heard it for many years. He was trying to put sense to it when his world went black.

***

Gabriella Riis unlocked the door to her apartment just as two men in dark blue suits, white dress shirts, and narrow ties walked up behind her. Startled, she held her purse close and dipped her hand inside and gripped her Glock nine.

"My name is John Walker. I'm with the National Security Agency. Are you Miss Gabriella Riis?" the younger one said.

"Yes," Gabriella said, her stomach tightening.

"May we come in? We need to speak to you."

"Not unless I see some identification. Bring it out slow and careful because there's a Glock in my purse aimed at your guts," Gabriella said.

"They told us you'd be feisty," the older man said. "I'm going to reach for my ID so please don't go getting trigger-happy, young lady."

"Not as long as you don't do anything stupid," Gabriella said, "believe me; I know how to use a weapon."

"We know that, our records indicate you are a pretty good shot, too. Please don't shoot until after we talk to you," the older man said.

They both handed her ID's. Gabriella took them with her left hand like Draper taught her and not moving her right hand off the Glock.

They seemed to be whom they said they were, so she said, "Talk, I'm listening." She held onto the ID's.

"Can we go inside?" the younger one said.

"No," Gabriella said, "If I have to shoot you I don't want to mess up my apartment."

"I'd hate that also, especially if you shot me. Now, my partner here, not so much," the younger one said, but he smiled when he said it.

Gabriella thought a moment and saw Brad Gutierrez step out of the elevator. He stopped short when he saw the two suits confronting her. She switched gears immediately and said, "The young gentleman behind you is an Ajo County Deputy Sheriff with a bigger weapon than I have. He favors a .45 ACP, which you probably know is a formable weapon capable of blowing a hole in your ass big enough to drive a Mack truck through. He's also my boy friend and he hates guys that pester me."

"What's going on, Gabriella?" Gutierrez said. Gutierrez did not draw his weapon, but he had his hand inside his sport jacket.

"These gentlemen claim to be Feds and here's their ID." Gabriella handed Gutierrez the two IDs. The Deputy looked at them and nodded at her.

"So what is it you gentlemen want?" Gabriella said.

"It's about one of our retired agents, Charles Draper; he listed you as his next of kin," the younger suit said.

"Yes, what about him?" Gabriella had a sinking feeling in her gut that rose into her throat like acid. She reached out and grabbed Gutierrez' hand and held it tight. She knew what was coming and did not want to hear it. She felt his arm surround her and the words the younger suit said seemed far away, as if they were happening to someone else. However, they were not.

"I'm sorry to be the bearer of bad news, Miss Riis. Mr. Draper was killed during a mission back east in Connecticut."

Gabriella's world began to spin and all the things that had happened over the last four years since her adopted father rescued her from Mexican banditos deep in the Sonoran Desert raced through her mind. She did not cry; that would come later.

Instead, she looked at the young agent and said, "How?"

"He was on a mission, I can't tell you the details, except that he completed it and like always he served his country and gave his life for it. We are very sorry for your loss. His wishes were that we ship his remains to you for burial. It'll be a closed casket, I'm afraid."

The agent did not elaborate on the reason for the closed casket and Gabriella did not ask. Later with Gutierrez's arms around her in bed, she cried, long and hard. After it subsided, he continued to hold her until finally she slept.

The funeral came two weeks later. Gabriella, with Gutierrez at her side, made all the arrangements. Burial would be in the Ayo County Cemetery. Gabriella watched the casket lowering and then turned to Gutierrez. "Take me home," she said.

A young women walked up before they could move and said, "Miss Riis?"

"Yes," Gabriella said, wondering who this person was, as she had never seen her before.

"Miss Riis, my name is Shira Seldis. I was with your father in the end. I know he loved you very much. I also owe my life to him."

"Can you tell me about it?" Tears flowed as Gabriella talked. "Dammit," she said. "I'm sorry; I thought I was finished with the weeping."

"That's all right, I understand. I just wanted you to know he saved my life at the expense of his own. I was working undercover also."

"Are you with the NSA also?" Gabriella asked dabbing at her eyes with a Kleenex.

"No, I'm Israeli, we just happened to be working on the same criminals."

"You look so young," Gabriella said.

The woman laughed, "Part of my cover. I was born with good genes. I'm actually almost twenty-one."

On the drive back to the house, Gabriella sat silent. The long driveway passed under the car and Dog, Charlie's long ago acquired pet, waited on the porch. He had stayed with Gutierrez of late and was glad to be back in familiar territory. Gutierrez shut off the car and looked at Gabriella. "What are your plans?"

"I don't know," she said, "I graduate from nursing school in three months, I'll probably start looking for a job in Ajo. Unless Charlie had some other children I don't know about, I guess this place is mine."

"Would you be interested in a husband?"

Gabriella looked startled, "You mean it?

"I wouldn't have asked if I didn't."

Chapter Twenty-Two

Near Ajo, Arizona

The sun beat hard on the Sonoran Desert sand in mid-October driving sane individuals into air-conditioned space and forcing critters of all sizes to seek shade. The geckos and sidewinders sought cool places and the hundred degree daytime temperatures sucked moisture from every crevice. The last semblances of the summer monsoon season kept daytime humidity high and dew points in the stratosphere. Even the slightest effort sapped the strength of even the natives and afternoons left the streets deserted and quiet. A gray Lincoln MKZ hybrid four-door sat on a side street of Ajo, Arizona with the engine running in a nearly impossible effort to keep the car cool. The man inside was tall and slim, his weight down nearly thirty pounds in recent months. His gaunt face aged him and a full beard streaked with grey enhanced the effect. He reached under his suit coat and retrieved a Glock 37 in .45 ACP caliber. The full frame Glock held heavier than he liked, but he'd spent hours at the range practicing with the new weapon and began to like it. He checked it for the third time, making sure it was ready. After a few moments, he pulled out onto the street and headed north to the highway. On the Interstate, he took the eastbound exit and gained speed. Ten miles later, he exited and took a gravel road south.

After five miles, he could see his destination. There were a number of cars parked around the house, he guessed about twenty or so and the crowd had gathered in front. Most moved inside to escape the heat by the time he arrived. He planned his arrival with care, wanting to walk in within minutes of the start. He only needed a short time to scan the small group and make sure. If everything were secure, he would back out and no one would ever know he was there.

The bride stood gorgeous in a knee-length satin lace wedding dress with sashes and beadwork held up by dainty spaghetti straps. The groom stood beside her in a cowboy-cut suit in light cotton tweed. The man looked at them a moment seeming to study their faces before beginning a scan of the audience. It took only a few seconds to spot the one he wanted. He took six short steps until he was very close. Checking the field of fire, he could see there was no one between his target and the outside wall. Plenty of backstop there, he thought, especially after passing through the body. The quarry was looking away and didn't feel threatened until the man whispered, "I have a .45 aimed at your heart. One wrong move and I will kill you where you stand. Let's walk outside very quiet and have a discussion."

Instead, the assassin went for his weapon and the stranger shot him twice, making sure he didn't get up. Several women screamed and the man held up a belt badge and yelled, "Federal Agent, everyone stay calm, Federal Agent!"

"That badge better be authentic, Mister, because if it isn't you'll be the next one on the floor." The groom pointed a Glock 23 at him, which the stranger assumed to be .40 caliber, a law enforcement favorite.

"Relax, Deputy, just a slight delay while we drag the body outside, then the ceremony can continue," the stranger said.

"Hand over your weapon and badge and we'll see," the groom said. "I'm the local law around here."

"And I'm his boss, Sheriff of this county, so I suggest you do as the Deputy says."

The stranger took a quick look behind and saw a woman holding a chrome-plated long barrel .357 pointed at his back. "Ease up folks, everybody stay calm and we'll sort this all out and the wedding can continue." He noticed that the bride looked as if her life had crashed around her and she did not know exactly whom to hit first. He handed his credentials to the Deputy who looked them over, stepped behind him, and handed them to the Sheriff.

"Can I put my hands down now?" the stranger said.

"Let's be a little formal just between our friends. I'm going to ask for your weapon, real nice, with two fingers, but you should know how to do it," the deputy said.

The stranger opened his suit coat slow with his left hand exposing a quality leather shoulder rigging with a quick draw holster. He lifted the weapon out with two fingers on his right and held it up for the Deputy to take.

"Anybody know the guy on the floor?" the Deputy asked the crowd and everyone shook their heads.

"Tell you what, Deputy, if it's all right with your boss there, what say you help me drag this clown outside where he'll keep for a while and we get you two officially married and we can deal with him later. After we get you newlyweds off, I'll answer any questions the Sheriff might have, fair enough?"

"We can't move him, it's a crime scene," the Deputy said.

"True enough," the stranger said, "but, it's a Federal crime scene and I'm claiming jurisdiction. Let's move the body outside and have a wedding."

Two of the younger guests volunteered to do the heavy lifting and once outside they covered the dead man with a tarp. Meanwhile, the Sheriff called the wagon while two older women retrieved a pan of soapy water and cleaned up the spilled blood.

"All right," the stranger said, "let's have a wedding."

"No," Gabriella said, pointing at the stranger, "not until I talk to you; in the kitchen, now."

The man started to follow her to the kitchen, when the groom said, "Am I invited?"

Gabriella turned and said, "Yes, of course you are, Brad, you too, Mom."

The trio followed Gabriella into the kitchen where she slammed the door shut. "Who the hell are you?" she said to the stranger, with fire in her eyes.

"John Smythe, like it says on my badge ID."

"Bullshit," Gabriella said, that name's as big a crock as confederate money." She starred at Smythe for a long time. "Why do you look so familiar; as if I've seen you somewhere before?

"He looks familiar to me also," the Sheriff said.

"Those eyes!" Gabriella said, looking close, "Dad?"

"I'm sorry, Babe," he said.

"It is you, isn't it? You called me, Babe, no one else ever did." Gabriella said, tears flowing down her cheeks. "Why? For four months, I thought you were dead. Goddamn you!"

"Had to be that way, Babe, it's a long story and I'll tell you later, but know I love you and I want this to be the best day of your

318

life. Suffice it to say too many bad people knew my name and it was too dangerous too contact you any sooner. When we had intel that someone was going to try to interrupt the wedding, I had to come.

"God, I missed you, but you look so different."

"Miracle of plastic surgery and the beard; but I'm officially retired now so I'll be around when you kids get back from wherever you're going."

"San Diego for a week, then we both have to be back to work."

"Then we better get on with the wedding," John Smythe said.

After the bride and groom were off and the guests all vacated, they sat on the porch and watched the meat wagon leave rolling desert dust into clouds. He took a sip from his beer and said, "You look good, Molly."

"You look terrible, you've lost weight, and I hate the beard," she said. "So, do I call you John or Charlie?"

"Master of disguise helps, but I think it's safe to call me Charlie now."

"Are you going to tell me about it?" Molly said.

"It's a long story, might take a while."

"That's okay, I've got all night."

###

Books by Dave Folsom

Charlie Draper Series:

Big Sky Dead

Sonoran Justice

Finding Jennifer

Others:

The Dynameos Conspiracy

Scaling Tall Timber

The Zeitgeist Project

Running with Moose

www.ingramcontent.com/pod-product-compliance
Lightning Source LLC
Chambersburg PA
CBHW070736180626
46818CB00007B/2872